BATTLE STATIONS

US Navy Thriller Series
Book One

Irving A Greenfield
writing as
Roger Jewett

SAPERE
BOOKS

BATTLE
STATIONS

Published by Sapere Books.

20 Windermere Drive, Leeds, England, LS17 7UZ,
United Kingdom

saperebooks.com

ISBN: 978-1-913518-63-9

This book is respectfully dedicated to the men of the United States Navy and to the two individuals, Rear Admiral Roger W. Mehle, USN (Ret.) and Captain Clark Gammell, USN (Ret.), whose technical assistance made it possible for the book to be written.

This book is also dedicated to the characters Andrew and Warren Troost, Jacob Miller, Tony Trapasso, and Glen Lescomb, whose exploits are fictionalized versions of real incidents, and I have a special word of thanks to the character Kate, with whom I fell in love while writing this book.

CHAPTER 1

Captain Andrew Troost, United States Navy, was on the bridge of HMS *Broadwater*, a British destroyer under the command of Commander William Blakely, Royal Navy. With his hands clasped behind his back, Troost stood between the starboard window and the ship's captain. Destroyers were not new to him. He'd been the gunnery officer aboard a "tin can," as they were affectionately called by those who had served on them during the First World War; and even after that war, he had on several tours enjoyed destroyer command. And later he had been chief of staff of an American destroyer squadron.

Only Troost's cap device and sleeve insignia distinguished him from the British officers on the bridge. He was a chunky man with a square chin, light gray eyes, and thinning brown hair. Chosen by Admiral Ernest J. King, commander-in-chief of the Atlantic Fleet, to be the liaison officer between the British and American naval units when the *Broadwater* rendezvoused with the eastbound convoy which they were approaching. He was aboard the *Broadwater* to insure that the mid-ocean point (dubbed *MOMP* by the men of both commands) transfer of the slow convoy SC-48 from the American escort force to the British would take place as smoothly as possible.

The convoy was made up of 50 merchant ships sailing in nine columns at seven knots and protected by four destroyers. According to the latest position reports, 11 merchant ships were straggling as the result of increasingly bad weather and heavy seas the second day out of port.

The *Broadwater*'s bridge was dimly lit. Even the binnacle's light was shielded. The men spoke in low tones and only when necessary. Captain Blakely ran a tight ship, even though more than half the men and officers aboard were newly assigned to her, and Troost admired him for it.

Because this was Troost's third voyage aboard the *Broadwater*, he was thoroughly familiar with routine convoy operations, and unless something extraordinary happened, the *Broadwater*, the *Columbia*, the *Levis* and the Free French corvette *Lobelia* would take up the positions vacated at *MOMP* by the escorting American destroyers without having to receive any instructions from him.

Turning slightly to his right, Blakely said, "Captain, our ETA at the *MOMP* is at 0330." He spoke with a heavy Scottish burr, made more difficult to understand by the cigar almost always present in his mouth. As soon as the rendezvous was completed, Blakely would assume overall command of the convoy.

Troost checked his watch: it was 0115; then he gave an acknowledging nod. *MOMP* could be as far east as 22° west longitude, but was always above 58° north latitude. For this trip it was at 24° west longitude and 59° north latitude.

"Another trip or two and the *Broadwater* will be able to find her way here without any help from us," Troost remarked.

Blakely laughed. "She can just about do it now," he answered, adding, "The glass has been falling for the past two hours and the sea has been building, but we should reach *MOMP* before we have any real severe weather." Then he resumed his former position and said something to his operations officer, who was manning the bridge with him.

Troost looked out of the window. Though there was a gibbous moon, there was only enough light to show that the sky was heavily patched over with dark scudding clouds and little moonlight leaked through to touch the already wind-riled sea. Because of the building sea and the German submarine threat, the ship was already buttoned up and all hands were at general quarters.

Suddenly, the *Broadwater* reacted to a strong gust of wind and rolled heavily to her port side.

"Good Christ!" Blakely swore, moving to the rear of the bridge to check the weather instruments. "Where the hell did this come from?" He tapped the glass to steady the needle. "She's gone down five-tenths of an inch within the hour," he said.

Troost suddenly realized that Blakely estimated the storm's center to lie ahead to the southwest. Clearly, now it was coming out of the northeast.

The wind was veering steadily around to the northeast with building velocity and very heavy seas, and the *Broadwater* began to claw her way up to the crest of a wave.

Troost steadied himself against the side of the bridge.

The *Broadwater* crested the wave and plunged into a trough. The next wave smashed down on her stern. The sea poured over the bow, forcing it down. The stern came out of the water. Her single screw flailed in open air. Shuddering, the *Broadwater* again slammed down into the water.

Troost lost his footing and fell against the side of the bridge.

"OPS, put all ship's communication over the ship's broadcast system," Blakely ordered.

"Aye, aye, Captain," the operations officer answered.

The wind backed farther around to the north-northeast.

"Helmsman, left full rudder, come to course 015 degrees," Blakely ordered.

"Aye, aye, sir," the helmsman answered. "Rudder is left full, coming to course 015 degrees."

Troost scrambled to his feet.

Another wave crashed down on the *Broadwater*.

"Helm slow to answer," the helmsman reported.

The *Broadwater*'s stern lifted out of the water again, further reducing the rudder's effectiveness.

"Get your bloody ass down," Blakely shouted above the wail of the wind. "Get it down."

The *Broadwater* shuddered, taking the brunt of the seas on her port side. Her plates began to scream. Then her stern fell back into the sea. The shock passed through the ship's steel hull.

Suddenly, the executive officer at his damage control station in HQ-2 reported to the bridge, "Captain, we're taking on water in the shaft alley."

"Roger that," Blakely responded, and speaking to his exec over the ships' broadcasting system, he said, "Number one, insure that HQ-3 takes all possible steps to control the flooding. We must keep propulsion and steering control."

"Helm not answering," the helmsman reported.

"Keep trying," Blakely answered.

"Aye, aye, Captain," the helmsman said.

The *Broadwater* rolled to the starboard. Another wave slammed into her port. Before she could come out from under the torrent of water, her port motor whaleboat was ripped away from the davits and several life rafts were torn away from their skids. Another wave hammered down on her, smashing the bridge windows and sending a rush of water onto the bridge.

The lights went out.

"Number one, emergency lighting," Blakely yelled into the ship's broadcast mike.

"I can do it," Troost shouted and made his way to the rear panel. A moment later dim lighting was restored to the bridge instruments.

"Captain," the communications officer reported, "we have a report that the convoy was forced to scatter."

"The Jerry fuckers will be at her as soon as this storm stops," Blakely answered.

The *Broadwater* took another wave.

"Helm now answering," the helmsman called out.

"Steady on course 015 degrees," Blakely said.

"Aye, aye, Captain — coming to course 015 degrees."

The *Broadwater* slowly swung around, plunging and rolling.

Troost was close enough to the weather instruments to look at them. The barometer was at 29.1 inches and the wind was blowing at 55 knots and gusting to 70.

"Captain, we have a mayday from the *Sally Blue*," the communications officer reported. "She's foundering."

Blakely went to the chart table. "Position?" he asked, switching on the table lamp.

Troost came to the table. "I can do this," he said. "You have enough to do."

Blakely nodded.

Troost asked for the *Sally Blue*'s position.

"As of 0100 she was 23 and a half degrees west, 57 north," the communications officer answered.

"Roger that," Troost said, using a pencil to mark the *Sally Blue*'s position on the chart with a small x. The *Broadwater*'s last known position had already been placed on the chart. Using a parallel ruler, Troost drew a line between the two positions and measured it. Converting the inches to miles, he said, "Captain, as of our last known position, we are 45 nautical miles northeast of the *Sally Blue*."

The *Broadwater* crested another wave and dropped into the trough behind it. She couldn't make her way out of it before the wave crashed over her.

Another torrent of water gushed onto the bridge, hurtling Blakely and his first officer backwards.

Troost held on to the chart table.

The executive officer in HQ-3 contacted the bridge. "Engineering reports main drive shaft bearing beginning to overheat. Recommend reducing speed to one-third if feasible."

Blakely pulled himself up to a standing position. "Reduce speed to one-third ahead," he ordered the engine order telegraph operator; then he rang the communications officer. "Any more from the *Sally Blue*?" he asked.

"Nothing," Blakely said, repeating what he was told. "Roger that." He put the phone down and said, "We would have never reached her in time."

Almost as dramatically as it had developed, the storm passed and the seas began to abate, and by 0600, Troost noted, the wind had dropped to 10 knots and the barometer stood at 28.94 inches.

"Captain Troost, would you prefer tea or coffee?" Blakely asked, with traditional British aplomb, as he stepped out of the way of a repair crew working to replace the smashed bridge windows.

"Coffee would be fine," Troost answered, admiring Blakely's poise.

Suddenly, over the ship's broadcast system, the sonar officer shouted, "Target bearing —"

The first torpedo exploded amidship on the port side with a huge geyser of water cascading over the ship.

Troost was thrown against the side of the bridge.

Moments later there was a second internal explosion forward of the bridge. Fire burst across the forecastle and the *Broadwater* listed heavily to port.

"Submarine, surfacing four points off port bow," the lookout yelled.

"They're going to finish us off with gunfire," Blakely said. "But we'll give them a run for their money." He ordered all operational guns to "fire at will."

"Mounts one and two out of action," the gunnery officer reported.

"Roger that," Blakely answered.

"Captain we've lost fire-room boiler pressure," the executive officer reported. "The ship is taking more water than the fire and bilge pumps can handle."

"Stand by to abandon ship. All hands, topside," Blakely ordered.

Two bracketing rounds come from the submarine.

The *Broadwater*'s remaining mount, number three, continued to fire. But all rounds fell yards short of the target.

The submarine fired again. This time with fatal effect.

Number three mount dissolved into flame. An instant later an explosion tore away the ship's stern.

"All hands, launch all available life rafts," Blakely ordered over the ship's broadcast system. "All hands... All hands... Abandon ship... Abandon ship." He looked at Troost, and with quiet resignation, said, "Good luck, sailor... Now go."

"I'll stay," Troost offered.

"She's my ship," Blakely answered.

"Good luck, sailor," Troost said, saluting him. Moments after he left the bridge a shell slammed into it. The explosion sent him crashing down in to a smoky blackness. Troost felt himself being dragged along the deck; then he was in the water.

CHAPTER 2

Buoyed by his life jacket, Troost looked back at the *Broadwater*. The stern section had already sunk and what was left of her was burning.

"This way," a man shouted from behind Troost. "This way, man!"

He turned in the water and saw the raft. There were three men on it.

"C'mon, swim," a man on the plunging raft urged, motioning to him.

Suddenly aware of how cold the water was, Troost began to swim. He raised his head to look at the raft. It was bobbing up and down and it seemed to have moved away from him. He propelled himself toward it. Suddenly, for no reason at all, Troost remembered it was his birthday: he was 52 years old.

"52," he told himself, "and not much chance of making 53."

"Keep coming!" the man on the raft shouted.

Troost felt cold and lethargic. The sensation grew, spreading its tendrils into his arms and legs. He was losing strength.

"Don't stop," a man with a cockney accent shouted. "Don't let those sons-of-bitches see a Yank die!"

Troost didn't know what the man was talking about. Who was watching him? To stop for even a few moments would give him the rest he needed...

"Swim ... swim — for the love of Christ, swim!" someone shouted. "You're almost here — a few more strokes."

Troost raised his head. The raft was a blur.

"Don't stop," the Limey cried.

Troost started to raise his right arm. "I can't," he shouted. "I can't." He dropped his arm. "I can't," he said in a low voice and closed his eyes.

"Captain, one more stroke — one more, Captain."

Troost opened his eyes.

"He'll go belly up if he doesn't make it this time," a man said. "He's takin' on water!"

Troost forced his right arm up. Belly up, shit! He pulled himself toward the raft.

"I got him!" a man shouted.

Troost felt several pairs of hands grab hold of him; then he was out of the water, looking up at three oil-stained faces and the gray sky behind them. "Belly up, shit!" he said.

The three faces fractured into grins.

Troost grinned back; then he closed his eyes…

Troost felt the raft's movement before he opened his eyes. He would have decided that he was dreaming if it hadn't been so cold. Then he heard a man say, "Looks like 'e's comin' round." The possibility of being involved in a dream vanished and, opening his eyes, he saw an intense blue sky and then the three oil-stained faces he had seen before. Two were on his right, the third on his left.

"Welcome aboard, Cap'n," the man on the left said.

Troost started to pull himself up into a sitting position.

One of the men on his right offered to help.

"Thank you," Troost said, "but I can manage myself." He looked back over his shoulder.

"We're all that's left," the other man on his right said. "Those that didn't go down with the ship never made it to a raft."

Troost nodded. They were the only survivors out of a complement 225 men.

"Able-Bodied Seaman Raymond Forest, but everyone calls me Ray," the man on his left said.

Troost moved his eyes to the right.

"Machinist second-class John Forster," the man who offered to help said.

"Chief Harry Walker, ship's cook, sir," the other man reported.

"Gentlemen," Troost said, "thank you for —" He smiled. "For having me as your guest."

The men grinned. The three of them, like himself, were shivering.

"Or to say it differently," Troost told them, "thank you for saving my life." And he shook each of their hands, beginning with the man on the left. Then he said, "With some luck I'll stand each of you a good dinner and a pint or two in a few days."

"Captain, how do you make our chances?" Forster asked. He was the gauntest of the three, but even the cook was thin.

Troost looked up at the sky. Grayish white clouds were beginning to scud across it. They were apparently in the eye of the storm, and in a relatively short time they could be in the storm again.

"Maybe 10 percent," he said, looking straight at Forster, then at each of the two other men. "But we have to fight for that 10 percent with everything we have."

"Not much of anytin' is wot we 'ave," Ray said. He was a slight, wiry man with red hair and a freckled face.

Troost judged him to be about 20. He was the youngest of the three survivors.

"He's right, Captain," Forster agreed, shaking his head. "Not even a good line for fishin'."

"Just what do we have?" Troost asked.

None of the men answered.

"Water?" Troost questioned.

"No," the cook said. "I looked in the supply kit. It's empty. It's supposed to have —"

"Don't matter wot it's supposed ta 'ave," Ray exclaimed. "It don't well 'ave bloody anytin'!"

"All right," Troost said. "All right. We're going to need every bit of strength we have." He looked up. The sky was already considerably darker and the clouds were now rushing across it. "The most important thing we can do is keep warm and the best way to do that is to huddle together. We'll take turns being the inside man. Every twenty minutes we'll change, moving from right to left. The first man on the inside will be…" He paused to examine each before he said, "Ray, you're inside. Forster, you're right side. Harry, left side."

"What about you, Captain?" Forster said.

"Nothing about me," Troost answered. "I'll take the first watch. We must keep a sharp lookout."

"Either all of us has a crack at the center," Harry said, "or none of us."

"Cook's bloody well right," Ray commented.

"He's right," Forster said.

"That will come later," Troost snapped, forcing his voice to go hard. "Starting now. Ray, get between your shipmates. Move it!"

Ray hesitated.

Troost leaned toward him. "Let's go my boy! It's important to keep our strength."

Ray stretched out in the center of the raft.

"Okay — Harry, Forster, sandwich him!" Troost barked.

The two men took their positions.

Troost sat down again. The wind had veered around to the southwest and was becoming stronger with each passing minute.

"How the bloody hell are we going to live through this?" Forster shouted.

Troost didn't answer. He'd already asked himself the same question.

The raft began to bob with the building sea; it climbed to the top of a wave and dropped below the rush of water.

Troost grabbed the edge of the raft.

"I can't hold," Harry suddenly screamed, desperately clutching at anyone within reach. "I'm going over!"

Troost saw Harry slide over the raft's shallow edge and then, as the raft came up, Harry was tossed back against its side. Troost reached out, took hold of him with both hands, and almost had him in the raft when another wall of black water crashed down, tearing Harry from his grasp. Troost quickly took Harry's place next to Ray. For what seemed like hours, mountains of water crashed down on the raft.

Troost could hear the men shouting, but not their words. His vision was blurred and his hands were raw and bleeding. Several times he wanted to let go and slide away in a rush of water that would end his suffering. But he couldn't let go: the raft and the men on it were his responsibility. Could this be his final command?

"John is gone! John is gone!" Ray shouted.

"Can you hold?" Troost yelled back, though they were within inches of each other.

"'E just let go."

Troost shouted the question again.

"Till my fuckin' arms are ripped out!" Ray yelled back.

Another flood of water stopped Troost from answering. He buried his face into the bottom of the raft until it came free of the sea's surge.

Several minutes passed and Troost was beginning to feel a difference in the raft's movement. It was edging over the crest of each wave. The wind was dropping; the sea was easing. He raised his head and looked up at the sky. There were several star-sprinkled openings. He pulled himself up into a sitting position. "It's over," he said quietly. "The storm has passed."

Ray sat up. "Gawd, it's a bloody miracle!" he exclaimed.

Troost looked at his watch. "I make it to be 0700."

"You mean, Cap'n, we've been out 'ere for a full 24?"

Troost nodded.

"Now wot do we do, Cap'n?" Ray asked.

"Wait," Troost answered. "We wait and hope to God a search for survivors has been launched."

Ray turned away from him and, looking at the suddenly flat sea, he said, "Somehow it never looked this good before."

"I know what you mean," Troost answered.

"I was the pointer for number one mount," Ray said. "John was a steamie in the boiler room. I didn't really know 'im, but everyone knew ol' 'Arry. That old bastard had a special way of ruinin' the best food."

"Some cooks have that talent," Troost responded.

Ray faced him. Tears skidded down his cheeks. "T'ere were some good blokes aboard the *Broadwater*," he said in a choked voice.

Unable to find the right words, Troost nodded.

Ray moved his knees up, put his arms on them, and cradled his head. Troost reached out and squeezed Ray's shoulder. Ray raised his head, managed a smile, and asked, "If you 'ad a choice right now between a woman an' a plate of fish an' chips, wot would you choose?"

"Fish and chips," Troost answered, suddenly feeling the gnawing hunger in his stomach.

Ray nodded. "Me too. The bird can come later. Me dad runs a fish-and-chip stand in East Central London, down by the Mission School — makes a proper penny from it too."

"Are you going to go into the business after the war?" Troost asked.

"Naw, I'm thinkin' of openin' a proper restaurant, wit' tables an' chairs — you know, a proper place. But t'at's a long ways off. It's goin' to be a long war," Ray said, and he put his head down again.

To ease the cramp in his legs, Troost shifted his position. He looked up at the sky. Large patches of blue were everywhere and through them, especially in the east, yellow columns of sunlight seemed to rest on the surface of the sea.

"Try to sleep," Troost said.

"Aren't you tired?" Ray asked, raising his head.

Troost lied. "Only a little." Then he added, "I'll take the first watch — two hours on, two off. One of us must be awake."

Ray nodded. "You're all navy, aren't you, sir?"

"All the way," Troost answered, knowing exactly what Ray meant and reflecting quietly on his family's past. His father was an admiral and his father before him. There was a Joseph Troost aboard the *Constitution* during the War of 1812, and there was even a Lieutenant Mark Troost, from the southern side of the family, aboard the Confederate raider *Shenandoah* when she destroyed the Union whaling fleet in the Arctic. But there was also a Commander Robert Troost aboard the Union warship *Kearsarge*.

In his reverie suddenly Troost realized that Ray was smiling at him.

"Me dad and 'is dad before 'im was in fish and chips," Ray explained. "But me granddad..." He shook his head. "Your guess is as good as me own."

Feeling paternal, Troost said, "If we make it, I'll have to try some of your dad's fish and chips."

"On the 'ouse," Ray answered, extending his hand.

They shook hands and Troost said, "I'll take you up on that."

"Me word is me bond," Ray told him.

"Try to sleep now," Troost said.

"Aye, aye, Cap'n," Ray answered and cradled his head.

Troost moved again and thought about his son Warren who, according to the last disappointing letter he'd received from him, had failed flight training at Pensacola and been assigned to the *Dee*, *AKO-96*, a small, one-of-a-kind supply ship on the East Coast. That kind of assignment for an Annapolis graduate, who had served two years in the fleet and was already lieutenant (JG), could have resulted only from something Warren did, or did not do. Reading between the lines of Warren's letter, Troost sensed with regret that his son was giving serious thought to resigning his commission and that, when the country was so very close to a shooting war, would be, in his opinion, calamitous.

Suddenly Troost heard the distant drone of an engine. He touched Ray's shoulder. "Listen," he said.

Ray's head came up.

The two of them looked at each other, then searched the horizon around them.

"Could be a U-boat runnin' on the surface," Ray said.

Troost crossed his lips with his finger. "Listen," he whispered.

Ray frowned, tilted his head up, and the next instant was on his feet, shouting, and pointing upward. "T'ere — t'ere up ahead of us!"

Troost scrambled to his feet.

It was a Royal Air Force Coastal Patrol Sunderland.

"'Ere we are. 'Ere we are. Wot's wrong wit' you blokes? Can't you bloody well see us?" Ray shouted excitedly. He started to jump up and down.

Troost grabbed him. "Easy ... easy. The raft will go over," he cautioned.

"'E's *got* to see us!" Ray shouted, twisting free.

The huge seaplane dropped lower; then suddenly it turned toward the raft and, as it roared over them, rolled from side to side.

"He saw us," Troost said, uttering a sigh of relief.

"Gawd, he's coming down," Ray exclaimed. "Oh wot a lovely sight! The bloody blighter is goin' to land." He turned to Troost and threw his arms around him. "I love you, Cap'n — I love you!"

Laughing, Troost returned the embrace and said, "I love you too, son."

The plane touched down, flinging a curtain of white spray on either side of it, turned, and taxied toward the raft.

CHAPTER 3

Ten days after Troost was rescued, he was seated at the head of the Sunday dinner table in the dining room of the small, gray, two-story house, navy-provided quarters, located in one of the few tree-lined streets in the Brooklyn Navy Yard.

Troost moved his eyes to the left, where Lillian, his daughter, sat. Six months ago she'd reached her 20th birthday. She was looking forward to graduating from New York University, where she majored in theater. She hoped to become an actress. Lillian was, even in his admittedly prejudiced view, a beautiful woman, with soft gray eyes, high cheekbones, a figure that even her mother envied, and a voice that caressed when she spoke. He smiled at her and looked at Warren, who was on his right. He was home on a 72-hour shore leave from Norfolk, where his ship, a one-of-a-kind auxiliary oiler and supply ship, the *Dee*, was being fitted with two five-inch deck guns and prepared for its next assignment. Warren resembled his father more than he did his mother, though he did have her sensuous lip line.

Then Troost looked across the table at his wife. Gloria was a few months younger than he and still a good-looking woman.

"Well, Andrew, do I ring for Carrie to begin serving, or do we all silently sit here waiting for you to finish your inspection?" Gloria asked.

"Sorry," Troost said, "I was just trying to remember when was the last time all of us sat down to Sunday dinner like this."

"A long time ago, sir," Warren answered.

Troost nodded and said, "You may ring for Carrie." He really wanted to tell them he'd been selected for flag rank and given new orders that would take him to Pearl Harbor, but he decided to wait for a more propitious moment.

Gloria picked up the silver dinner bell and shook it twice; then she said, "Lillian, will you please pass the white wine."

Troost stiffened. "I'd prefer —"

Gloria smiled. "I know what you'd prefer. But I'd prefer a drink of white wine. Now Lillian, will you please pass the decanter. Thank you."

"Well I can see," Warren said, "the more things change, the more they remain the same."

Troost caught the withering look that flew across the table from Lillian to her brother. He would have been willing to bet she also kicked him.

"Your father makes such a fuss about this tiny bit of wine," Gloria said, holding up the glass to show that she'd taken a small amount, "but says nothing about the smell that comes from the brewery just a short distance from here. Take several deep breaths when the wind is right and you're in pink-elephant land."

"Dad," Lillian said, before Troost could answer, "I may get a chance to act in summer stock theater on Cape Cod."

Troost checked himself, then forced himself to nod and smile. "That's wonderful."

"Any idea what part?" Warren asked.

Lillian shook her head, making her blonde hair swing from side to side. "Rich —"

"Rich?" Warren questioned. "The last man's name I heard was Steve, and that was the last time I was home."

"Professor Richard Gordon. He's assistant chairman of the theater department — a darling man. A few years younger than you, Dad, and he has the most wonderful contacts. He's been giving me private coaching lessons."

"At the college?" Warren asked.

"Mostly in his apartment in the Village," she answered. "He's divorced."

This time Troost and his son exchanged a quick, knowing glance.

Carrie came into the dining room from the kitchen. She was a big, black woman who cooked and cleaned for the Troosts. "I hope everyone here is hungry," she said, putting a sliced grapefruit topped with a maraschino cherry in front of Troost.

"Starved," Warren answered.

"Anyway," Lillian continued, "Rich says he's going to speak to some of his friends about me."

"I bet," Warren mumbled.

"And what was that supposed to mean?" Lillian challenged.

"We're very pleased for you," Troost said. He already had decided to pay Rich a visit before leaving for Pearl.

The dinner moved along at a leisurely pace. Carrie had prepared two main courses — a roast turkey with sausage stuffing and a rib roast.

Troost complimented her on every dish she served. When she brought dessert, it was her own version of baked Alaska.

"Sir, aren't you going to tell us what happened to you?" Warren asked, stirring sugar into his coffee.

"The newspaper made quite a fuss over him when the plane landed at the naval air station at Floyd Bennett," Gloria said, filling her glass with wine. "The base admiral even sent his car for him."

"His picture was on the front pages of every newspaper in the city," Lillian said.

Troost hesitated for several moments; then he said, "I don't have any more to add to what you already have read in the newspapers."

"According to the newspapers you saved that British sailor's life," Lillian said. "At least, tell how you did it."

Troost leaned back into the chair. "I didn't save anyone's life," he said quietly. "The three men on that raft pulled me out of the water."

"But —" Lillian began.

"Two of the men were washed overboard during the storm," Troost explained, looking down at his coffee. "One was torn out of my grasp; the other didn't have the strength to hold on and let go. If it hadn't been for the fact that the U-boat commander reported the spot where he torpedoed and sank the *Broadwater*, the British Coastal Command Search Aircraft wouldn't have known her last position. It was just luck that young Ray Forest and I were found."

"So much for your father, the hero," Gloria said, raising her wine glass toward Troost.

"Sorry to disappoint you," he responded. "But I saved no one."

"The important thing," Lillian said, taking hold of her father's hand, "is that you're alive."

Troost smiled. "I'd have to admit that's very important to me."

"To all of us," Lillian told him.

"Now, if I may, I'd like to propose a toast," Troost said.

"Excellent idea!" Gloria exclaimed.

Troost filled his glass with red wine. Lillian chose white, Warren red, and Gloria refilled her glass with white.

"To the men of the *Broadwater*," Troost said, raising his glass.

Lillian and Warren echoed their father's words, then drank.

"I have a toast to make too," Gloria announced.

"By all means, make it," Troost said, though he really wanted to stop her.

"To all the lovely women who are married to all the handsome naval officers. To all the women who grow old and dry up waiting —"

"Mother!" Lillian exclaimed.

"Let her finish," Troost said tightly. "Let the woman finish!"

"To all those women," Gloria said, her speech now slurred, "I salute you... We salute you." She raised her glass to her lips and gulped the wine; then she put the glass down on the table and accidentally knocked it over. "I want to go to my room," she told them.

"Lillian, help your mother," Troost ordered; then in a softer voice, he said, "Please."

Troost waited until Lillian had managed to guide Gloria out of the room before he said, "That's the way she is."

Warren watched his mother and sister. "How often?"

"This is the third time since I'm home," Troost said.

"Has she seen a doctor?" Warren asked, facing his father.

"She won't admit to having a problem," Troost said. "By tomorrow, she'll have forgotten what happened at the table."

Warren pursed his lips; then he said, "I haven't seen her this bad for a long time."

Troost shrugged. "During the time I was away I almost forgot what she's like when she's drunk."

"Mind if I smoke?" Warren asked.

Troost shook his head. "I'll have one too," he said.

Warren thumbed the cigarette lighter and held it for his father; then he lit his own cigarette. "Scuttlebutt says we're heading for Pearl, or maybe to the Philippines."

Troost let smoke out of his nose. "Are you going to stay in the navy?" he asked directly.

"I'm not sure," Warren answered. "The ship is an old bucket and its skipper, Lieutenant Commander Hacker, is an asshole.

He's a mustang and doesn't think much of anyone who is an Annapolis graduate, especially me."

"How come you wound up aboard her in the first place?" Troost asked.

"It's a long story," Warren said.

"I'd like to hear it."

Warren shook his head. "I don't want to tell it," he said.

"Naval aviation is where the future is," Troost commented.

"Sir, I don't want to discuss it."

"That's your privilege," Troost said. "But it's also my privilege and my duty, as your father, to say that, after having flunked out of flight training, don't make leaving the navy your second blunder."

"I'll remember that, sir," Warren answered.

Troost knew his son well enough to know that anything else he'd say on the subject would be superfluous. Warren's stubbornness easily matched his, when it came to meeting him eyeball to eyeball.

"She's asleep," Lillian announced, as she re-entered the dining room and sat down at the table again.

Troost stubbed out his cigarette. "In a few days," he said, "I'll be leaving for Pearl and —"

"But you just came home," Lillian exclaimed.

"Orders," Troost answered, knowing she probably understood the meaning of that word more than she understood anything else. "I'm assigned to Admiral Kirst's staff at Pearl."

"Staff," Warren repeated.

Troost nodded. "King called me late Friday afternoon," he said. "I'll have the written orders early tomorrow morning."

Warren grinned. "You got your stars, didn't you?"

"Dad, you're an admiral!" Lillian exclaimed.

Troost smiled. "Yes, I'm a rear admiral."

Lillian launched herself out of the chair and, throwing her arms around her father, she kissed him on the top of his head. "I'm so happy for you."

Warren offered his hand. "Congratulations, Dad," he said, vigorously shaking his father's hand. "I know how important this is to you."

"Mother will be so proud," Lillian said, sitting down again. "I just know she will."

"She will," Warren agreed.

"Yes, I think so too," Troost said for the benefit of his children, though he was sure Gloria would resent it, as much as, perhaps even more, vehemently than she resented other assignments in the past that advanced his career.

"This calls for a celebration," Lillian said.

Troost waved his hand.

"At least a toast!" she offered.

"I'll settle for that," Troost told her.

"You make it, Warren," Lillian said, after their glasses were filled with wine.

The three of them stood up.

Warren extended his glass to his father and said, "To you Dad... I — I mean, we love you."

"To the newest and best admiral in the navy!" Lillian exclaimed.

Troost touched each of his children's glasses with his own and said, "May each of you have happiness and success in life." Then he drank.

"When will I be able to join you?" Gloria asked.

"I don't know," Troost answered. He had waited until after dinner the following evening to tell her about his promotion and orders. They were alone. Earlier in the afternoon, Warren had hopped a flight from the naval air station at Floyd Bennett to Norfolk, and Lillian had phoned and said she'd be out for the evening.

Gloria chipped at a piece of piecrust with her fork; then looking at him, she said, "I'm happy for you."

"I knew you would be," he murmured.

She smiled at him. "All day I felt as if something was going to happen," she said. "I just felt it."

"I suppose January would be reasonable for you to join me," Troost said.

"And when was the navy ever reasonable?" she challenged, dropping the fork on the plate.

Backing away from a confrontation, Troost said, "I'll find a nice house in Honolulu for us — maybe one of those new, tropical ranch types."

She uttered a snort of disdain. "I surely don't want you to pick out a house without me."

"I might come across —"

"I don't ever want to live in an old barn like this again," she said, looking around. "I hate this place."

Troost placed his elbows on the table. He liked the old quarters house. It had *character*.

"Well, at least I'll be an admiral's wife," she said. "I know there has to be something in that, though, for the moment, I can't for the life of me think of what it might be."

Troost wanted to escape. He knew exactly what was coming.

"But admirals' wives seldom, if ever, get the credit for what they have done to help their husbands to become admirals." She smiled at him. "You're the one who wears the stars, but I'm the one who put them there. I made it possible for you to become what you are and now with a war coming, your star is rising and mine — mine never had a chance to climb..."

Troost ran his hand over his face.

"I'm going to be left here alone to pack everything up and —"

"Lillian will help you," Troost said.

"She's worse than useless," Gloria shot back. "All she's interested in is her acting and someone named Rich. Good God, when I was her age, I already had the responsibility of caring for a dying father and —"

Finally exasperated, Troost said, "Gloria, I've heard that more times than I want to remember. It has nothing to do with our situation. I can't delay my going to Pearl."

"You could if you wanted to!"

"I —"

"You're an admiral," she shouted. "You can do anything you want — anything — but you can't get away from here fast enough. You just can't wait, can you?"

Troost stood up.

"Where are you going?" Gloria yelled.

"Out," Troost answered. "I'm going out."

"Where? Where are you going?"

"I don't know," Troost answered. "I don't know." And he went to the closet for his coat and hat.

"If you go out that door, Andrew, don't think you're going to make it up in bed with me," she screamed, following him out to the door.

Troost whirled around. "Don't ever threaten me with that," he growled fiercely.

"I give you —"

"Nothing," Troost said flatly, "or damn near nothing."

"Oh!" Gloria cried, her hand flying to her mouth.

The moment he spoke, Troost was sorry. He shook his head, turned, and closing the door behind him, left the house.

Troost made arrangements to fly out of New York early Thursday morning to San Francisco aboard an Army Air Corps transport (with a stopover in St. Louis), and then from San Francisco to Pearl by a Navy transport plane. If there were no delays, he'd reach his destination late Sunday.

But now it was 1500 Wednesday afternoon. A drizzling rain was falling and Troost's driver, scanning the numbers of the houses on Horatio street, exclaimed, "It's across the street, Admiral."

"I'll be back in a few minutes," Troost said.

"Aye, aye, sir," the man answered, bringing the car to a stop at the curb. A moment later, he left the car, went around to the right rear side, and opened the door.

Troost left the car, returned the driver's salute, and walked toward the entrance of number 26. The previous day, he had asked Lieutenant Commander Joseph Collins, a shore patrol officer he knew, to use his connections with the New York City Police Department to find out where Professor Richard Gordon lived.

Troost entered the building's vestibule and looked at the names below the brass mailboxes and above the black bell buttons. There were four apartments on each floor. Gordon's apartment was on the fifth floor, apartment B. Troost had no intention of revealing his presence or his identity until he was standing face-to-face with Gordon.

Arbitrarily, Troost chose a bell to ring. Within moments, he was buzzed into the house.

A door opened and a woman called, "Who is it?"

"Sorry, wrong apartment," Troost answered.

The door slammed.

Troost began to climb the narrow, steep staircase. Each of the landings was illuminated by a single electric bulb. There was a skylight on the roof and the hallway, though clean, was filled with the heavy scents of fried fish and something that was seasoned with garlic, and what smelled like cabbage or cauliflower being cooked.

When he reached the fifth floor, Troost paused, looked at the letters on each of the doors, and discovered that B was a front apartment. He started toward it, then suddenly realized his heart was beating very fast. Maybe he had no right to do what he was going to do. There was still time for him to turn around.

He squared his shoulders. He wasn't about to stand by and let someone take advantage of his daughter. Troost went up to Gordon's door and rapped three times on it.

No one answered.

Troost rapped again, using more force.

"All right, I heard you the first time," a man called out from behind the door.

"Then why the hell didn't you answer," Troost mumbled under his breath and knocked again.

"For Christ's sake, hold your horses," the man said, working the lock.

The door swung open.

Troost found himself looking at a thin man with a balding head, who smelled of cologne, wearing a red silk bathrobe over his otherwise naked body.

"Oh my God!" Gordon exclaimed, looking at Troost.

"Who is it, Rich?" a woman called from the bedroom.

Troost glared at Gordon.

"It's not —"

"I know she's not my daughter," Troost growled. "But she's some other man's, isn't she?" And without waiting for an answer, he shoved Gordon aside and went straight into the bedroom.

Naked, the young woman was sprawled out on the bed. She took one look at Troost and screamed.

Gordon rushed into the bedroom.

"Get your clothes on, young lady," Troost ordered.

"Who is he?" she cried, looking at Gordon.

"Tell her," Troost said, driving his forefinger into Gordon's chest. "Tell her who I am."

"Admiral Troost —"

"Lillian's father?" the young woman asked.

Troost nodded. "Now tell me who you are?"

"Iris Freely," the young woman answered.

"Tell her what you promised to do for Lillian."

Gordon hesitated.

"Goddamn you, I said tell her," Troost growled, backhanding him.

Gordon staggered. Blood leaked out of the right corner of his mouth.

"What are you doing?" Iris shouted, covering her body with a sheet.

Troost looked at her. "He promised to put my daughter in summer stock."

Iris's eyes went wide, her jaw dropped, and her lips began to tremble.

"Isn't that so, Rich?" Troost said. "Didn't you promise Lillian that? Weren't you giving her coaching lessons the same way you are coaching Miss Freely?"

"Rich —" Iris started to say; then suddenly she began to weep.

34

"I'll wait for you in the other room," Troost said, dragging Gordon after him.

"Let go of me!" Gordon complained.

Troost pushed him down on the couch.

"You're crazy," Gordon said, pointing a finger at Troost. "You're one of those crazy, power-happy —"

"Shut the fuck up and listen to me," Troost ordered. Pushing his face very close to Gordon's, he said, "If I ever hear you're coaching my daughter again, I'll kill you."

"She wasn't a virgin —"

Troost grabbed him by the neck and shook him. "Listen to me!" he shouted.

"You're choking me!" Gordon screamed, fighting to free himself.

Troost released him and stepped back. "Stay away from her," he said, breathing hard. "Stay away!"

"I'm ready," Iris said, coming out of the bedroom.

Troost pointed his finger at Gordon. "Don't let there be a second meeting between us," he said.

"There won't be," Gordon answered.

"Come, Miss Freely," Troost said, beckoning to her. "My car is downstairs."

Without looking at Gordon, the young woman crossed the room, opened the door, and left the apartment.

Troost followed her out.

Troost stood against the door inside Lillian's room. "I paid a visit to Professor Gordon this afternoon," he said, wondering how long it had been since he'd been inside the room — years probably.

Lillian dropped the *Cosmopolitan* magazine she'd been reading.

"We had a very meaningful talk," Troost said.

Lillian shook her head. "You didn't…"

Troost nodded.

"Oh my God," she wailed. "Oh my God!" And threw herself down on the bed, burying her face under her arms.

"There was another young woman being coached," Troost said.

Lillian sat up. "I'm ruined," she cried. "You've finished my career even before it started. Rich was going to give me my big chance!"

"And what were you giving him in return?"

"That's the way it's done," she wept. "Don't you understand — that's the way it's done. It doesn't mean all that much, it really doesn't."

"What's going on here?" Gloria asked, suddenly pushing her way into the room.

"He paid a visit to Rich," Lillian shouted. "He's destroyed my life."

"He's very good at doing that," Gloria said.

Troost glared at the two of them, did a precise about-face and stomped out of the room. Tomorrow he'd be in the air and on his way to something new and exciting. He heaved a ragged sigh and, going into his den, settled down in the easy chair next to the fire.

CHAPTER 4

On Saturday, November 22, at the beginning of the Second Dog Watch, Warren and the chief quartermaster, Frank Berk, went to the *Dee*'s bridge to take a sextant sighting of several evening stars to obtain a fix on the ship's latitude and longitude. This would be Warren's sixth try in the last three days to "shoot the stars" to accurately fix the position of the ship. His lack of experience in practical navigation was catching up with him. This failure made it necessary for the ship's mustang captain, Lieutenant Commander Dwight Hacker, to radio only estimated positions at the prescribed reporting times to the Service Force Commander at Pac Fleet Headquarters at Pearl Harbor. His inability to obtain a good fix provided Hacker with a reason for voicing his displeasure at having an Annapolis graduate, a "ring knocker," and, what was even worse, the son of an admiral, as an officer aboard his ship. Warren was standing on the bridge looking toward the horizon, where a mass of red and orange clouds rested on the silver edge of the sea. Five days before, as the ship transited and cleared the Panama Canal, Hacker had called him to his quarters. "You're finished with your *make you learn*. All of you Annapolis graduates are better than the rest of us — better in everything, even navigation. Right?"

Warren remained silent.

"Well, we'll see. As of now, you're the ship's navigator," Hacker said. "You better damn well be on the fucking mark, or even if you're an admiral's son, I'll make you wish you weren't on my ship. That's all."

The first two days out of the canal were a breeze. His morning and evening "Stars" resulted in fixes that seemed accurate. He plotted the Great Circle course the ship would sail from the Pacific end of the canal for the first 5000-mile leg to Pearl and the second leg of 5000 miles from Pearl to the Cavite Naval Station in the Philippines. He actually began to enjoy being the ship's navigator.

On the morning of the third day, his problems began. Neither that day or the next could he get his lines of position to intersect at a point so that he could report the ship's position to Hacker. The lines maddeningly persisted, morning and evening, in intersecting only in an area the size of a quarter. That was the beginning.

Warren shook his head. The *Dee* was carrying a load of navy standard fuel and diesel for yard craft at Cavite and Subic Bay. After it reached its destination, it was his guess the ship — nicknamed the Sick Bitch by the crew, because her number-two boiler was down for maintenance more than it was on the line — would be used as milch cow for various small ships and shore stations in the Philippines. If he and the rest of the crew, with the exception of Hacker, had their way, she'd be scrapped.

"Let's see if we can't do it this time," Warren said, looking at Berk and moving out to the port wing of the flying bridge.

"Just give me the numbers," the chief answered. He was a thin, raw-boned man with hash marks that added up to 20 years.

Warren lifted the sextant to his eye, sighted the first star, checked the scale, brought the star down to the horizon, and said, "Mark." Then he gave the reading to the chief, who recorded it along with the exact time the mark was given. He shot a second and a third star. Afraid to trust his initial readings, Warren was just about to take another set of sightings before the horizon faded into darkness when he suddenly saw a white flash of light in the twilight.

"Did you see that, chief?" Warren asked.

"What?"

"A flash of light out there abaft the port beam," he said, looking at Berk.

"I didn't see anything, Mister Troost," Berk answered.

"I'm sure it was a flare, could be a distress signal."

Berk shook his head; then he asked, "Don't you want to get that second set of readings?"

Warren nodded, started to lift the sextant again, and, changing his mind, said, "We'll use the first, Chief. You start working the sights out. I'm going to call Hacker to the bridge."

"First, let's make sure we've got a good fix before you call the captain," Berk said.

"Use what you have. Let's see what you come up with," Warren said.

"Aye, aye, sir," Berk answered.

Warren moved inside and reported what he had just seen to Lieutenant Edward Rawlins, the watch officer. "I believe we should notify the captain," Warren said.

"Did the chief see it also?" Rawlins asked. He was a small wiry man with 10 years' service.

"No, but —"

"Are you sure it was a flare?" Rawlins asked.

"Positive."

Rawlins took a deep breath and, after he slowly exhaled, he said in a low voice, "He's riding you hard now. Don't give him something else to hold over you."

"It was a flare," Warren said steadfastly.

Rawlins nodded. "All right, call him," he said.

Warren went over to the bank of intercom phones and, picking up the one that linked the bridge directly with Hacker's cabin, pushed the call button and waited until he heard Hacker's voice before he said, "Sir, this is Lieutenant Troost."

"Have you finally got an accurate fix?" Hacker asked.

Warren felt the heat creep into his cheeks. "Sir," he said, "I spotted a distress signal."

"What?" Hacker shouted.

"A white flare," Warren answered.

"I'm coming to the bridge," Hacker said.

"Yes, sir," Warren answered and, putting down the phone, he looked at Rawlins. "He's coming."

"I hope you know what you're doing," Rawlins said. "You still have the chance to tell him you made a mistake."

"But I didn't," Warren said, stepping into the chart house at the rear of the bridge where Berk was working on the sights just taken and preparing to plot the lines to fix the ship's position. "Any better, Chief?"

"Shit, sir, we're still out of the money," Berk said, bending away from the table, after he penciled in the lines.

Warren looked down at the chart. Three crossed. They described an area of ocean as large as a half dollar. "Christ," he muttered, "it's even worse than the last one."

"We — you were lucky the first couple of days," Berk said. "Now I don't know what the hell is going wrong. Maybe you're not reading the sextant right… You'll get better."

"Tell that to Hacker," Warren answered.

"Tell what to Hacker?" Hacker asked.

Warren looked toward the door. Hacker was framed in it. He was big, broad-shouldered man, with blond hair graying at the temples, and a deceptively boyish face.

In three strides, Hacker went from the door to the chart table, looked at the position lines, and pointing his finger at them, said in a loud voice, "Most people get better, but you, Mister Troost, are not most people, are you?"

Warren remained silent.

"Maybe by the time we get to Cavite, you'll be able to tell me exactly where the fuck this ship is," Hacker said.

"Yes, sir," Warren answered, coming to attention.

"All right, now tell me about the flare you saw," Hacker said.

"Abaft the port beam, maybe one point — ten degrees or so above the horizon."

"Flare, eh!" Hacker exclaimed. "You would have done the ship a better service to get a good fix than to look at your so-called flare."

"Sir —"

"On the port side," Hacker said, turning and walking out onto the wing of the bridge.

Warren followed him.

After a few moments, Hacker said, "There's nothing out there."

"Sir, I saw it," Warren answered. "I'm sure there's a ship out there, back there." He pointed in the general direction where he saw the light.

"Did you take a bearing? No! I'd expect a more professional reaction from an Annapolis graduate. Certainly there's a ship out there, and no doubt one to our stern, port, and starboard sides, and goddamn it, all of them, I'd be willing to bet, have a navigator who produces fixes and doesn't go around seeing spooks, which is more than this ship has."

"It was a flare," Warren said tightly, trying hard to suppress his anger, but knowing the tone of his voice and the look on his face betrayed his feelings.

Hacker smiled.

"Mister Rawlins," Hacker called.

"Yes, sir," Rawlins said, coming to the opening between the bridge and the flying bridge. "No doubt Mister Troost has told you about the flare he saw."

"Yes, sir, he did."

"What is your considered opinion on the nature of our navigator's sighting?" Hacker asked.

Rawlins looked at Warren. "It is easy to confuse a sudden falling star at sea for a flare," he said gently.

Obviously enjoying himself, Hacker turned to Warren. "You still think you saw a flare, Mister Troost."

Before Warren could answer, one of the telephones on the bridge rang.

All conversation ceased while the duty quartermaster answered it, listened a moment, and then said, "Mister Rawlins, it's the radio shack. They're picking up an SOS from the Australian ship *Chessy.*"

Rawlins immediately went to the phone. "Have you got her position?"

Warren and Hacker moved to the chart table.

"She's 08 north latitude," Rawlins said, repeating what the radio officer was telling him. "The rest is garbled. There's a great deal of interference." Then he asked the RO, "Can she receive?"

"I don't know."

"Try to raise her. Tell her, if she can give us her exact longitude, we'll be on our way to assist."

"Belay that last statement," Hacker ordered.

"Belay my last," Rawlins said and put down the phone.

"All right, Mister Troost," Hacker began, "where do you put that ship with respect to us?"

Warren bent over the chart. If he didn't know exactly where the *Dee* and the *Chessy* were, how could he tell Hacker how far they were from the distressed ship? The *Dee's* last known position was marked in pencil on the chart. Given her subsequent speed and headings, Warren walked the dividers to where he guessed it should now be and marked it with a small x; from there he walked the dividers to where the *Chessy* might be. "Not more than 20 miles from us," he said with bravado; then looking up at Hacker, he added, "Of course it could be more."

"Maybe an hour from here if we go to flank," Rawlins said.

The phone rang again.

Rawlins went to it. "Mister Rawlins here." Then looking toward Warren and Hacker, he said, "The RO can't raise her and she's stopped sending." He put the phone down.

"That doesn't mean she sank," Warren said. "Even if she has, there might be survivors." His father's recent experience aboard the *Broadwater* suddenly became more meaningful.

Hacker looked down at the chart. "We don't know where the hell she is and we don't know where the hell we are," he growled.

"She has to be relatively close," Warren said. "All we have to do is go —"

"We're staying on our course, such as it is," Hacker said. "We still have 3000 miles to go before we reach Pearl. I have to be there at a specific time and I'm not going to backtrack and go on any wild-goose chase."

"I wouldn't exactly say this is a wild-goose chase," Warren challenged.

Hacker glared at him.

"I told you I saw a distress flare —"

"Mister Troost," Hacker said, "you can hardly blame me for doubting what you say you saw, given your lack of ability to perform the task assigned you."

Warren ignored the gibe. "As I see it, the customs of the sea require us to try to help," he answered.

"My duty is to this ship," Hacker shot back, his face now flushed. "There are other ships in the area who are close and who will go to her aid."

"Are you refusing —"

Rawlins came to Warren's side and took hold of his arm. "Easy, Warren — easy," he whispered.

"This ship remains on its course," Hacker said.

"You really don't care about those people out there," Warren responded.

"I care about this ship and her crew," Hacker said.

Warren was about to tell Hacker that when they reached Pearl, he intended to bring the entire matter before the proper authorities, when the phone from the radio room rang for a third time.

Rawlins answered it. "The RO picked up a message from CinPac Fleet," he said, "Australian freighter *Chessy* was torpedoed by a German submarine. And the *Bristol* has been sent into the area to assist."

"That's what I've been saying... Hold our present course, Mister Rawlins," Hacker said.

"Aye, aye, sir," Rawlins answered.

"Mister Troost, in the morning you'd better give me an accurate fix for this ship," Hacker said.

"Aye, aye, sir," Warren answered.

CHAPTER 5

Rear Admiral Andrew Troost, chief of staff to Admiral Donald Sprat, Commander Cruisers and Destroyers, Pacific Fleet, was junior to the other admirals at the conference table. The two principals were Admiral Harry E. Kirst, Commander and Chief of the Pacific Fleet, and Vice Admiral William (Bull) Gower, Commander Aircraft, Battle force.

Kirst sat at the head of the table. Gower was on his right and Troost on his left. Kirst, a tall, dignified man in his dress whites, looked the part of a naval officer. But even in his whites, Gower didn't. He was an elfin man, with crinkled skin and mischievous blue eyes.

"Well, Andy," Gower asked, before Kirst spoke, "have you settled in yet?"

"Getting there, sir," Troost answered.

"When you say, you're 'getting there,'" Gower said, with a twinkle in his eye, "means one of two things: either you're so fouled up, you'll never get there, or we're so fouled up, you wonder how we managed to get there, wherever there is... Which is it, Andy?"

Troost laughed. "Not much of a choice there," he said.

"Not much," Gower answered.

Kirst cleared his throat.

Gower gestured with a thumb toward the head of the table. "That was meant for us."

Troost looked toward Kirst, who nodded and said, "Bill, it's very close to zero hour. The Commander-in-Chief says it could come any time. We know the Japanese fleet is already on the move."

Gower helped himself to a cigarette and, as he lit it, he asked, "How much time do the boys in Washington figure we have?"

"They won't crystal-ball it," Kirst answered. "But as things stand now, it's absolutely imperative to get more fighting aircraft to the marines on Wake."

"I'm listening," Gower said, suddenly becoming more serious.

"We're almost sure the Japanese are going to attack somewhere," Kirst said. "Everything points to it. Wake would be a high-priority target for them."

"Pearl would be a more likely target," Troost offered, instantly realizing he'd said the wrong thing.

Kirst snapped his eyes to Troost. His brow furrowed. "Wake is where the planes are needed now," he said curtly. "They'd be crazy to attack Pearl, or Singapore, or even our bases in the Philippines. They'll go for an easier mark."

Troost nodded. He understood that Pearl, as far as Kirst was concerned, was not a likely target. Besides, Kirst's temper was legendary. He was not above throwing whatever was handy at the person who angered him.

"Let's get back to you, Bill," Kirst said.

"You want to use one or more of my carriers to make the delivery, is that it?" Gower asked, blowing smoke off to his left.

"One Carrier Task Group, and I want you to take overall command," Kirst said.

"When?"

"The day after tomorrow, on the 27th," Kirst answered; then he looked at Troost. "You and Bill work out how many destroyers and maybe a cruiser or two will be needed to provide escort and screen. We know the Japanese have deployed several submarines in the area around Wake."

Troost nodded.

"This is a secret mission," Kirst said. "I don't want the marine fighter squadron to be aboard the carrier when it sorties. Its own air group can be, if you like. But take the marine aircraft on board when you're out of sight of land."

"It'll be a tight fit, but we've done it before," Gower responded.

"Radio silence must be maintained going and coming," Kirst said; then he asked, "Do you want to take a battleship with you?"

"Hell, no," Gower answered. "If I have to run I don't want anything to interfere with my running." Then he asked, "Do I have complete operational authority?"

Kirst nodded.

"How far do I go?"

"Goddamn it, use your common sense!"

Troost was aware of the significance of the silent exchange between the two men. Kirst implicitly had given Gower authority to fight a shooting battle if it became necessary.

Gower nodded, and turning his attention to Troost, he asked, as if joking, "Andy, do you think your ships can keep up with my carrier?"

"They won't have much choice, will they?"

"None," Gower said. "Not if you or their skippers want to run with me."

"Better start the wheels turning, Bill," Kirst said. "I want that marine fighter squadron on Wake Island as soon as possible."

Gower made a few notations on the yellow pad of paper in front of him; then he said, "If we're not to come in empty, we'll have to refuel on December fourth."

"There'll be an oiler at sea wherever and whenever you say," Kirst responded.

"We'll refuel on the way back… Troost, work it out with my staff so the operation order provides for replenishment."

Troost nodded.

"I figure we should be back in Pearl no later than noon on Sunday, the seventh," Gower said.

"I don't see any problem with that," Kirst answered. Then he said, "Just to make it look like an ordinary exercise, take a couple of battleships with you."

"Not all the way," Gower responded.

"What you do with them once you're over the horizon is your business," Kirst said, and standing up, he looked at Troost. "It will take time, but you'll get used to Bill."

"I don't think he'll give me any other choice," Troost said with a straight face.

Gower exploded into laughter. "Son-of-a-bitch," he swore, pointing his finger at Troost, "he has me tagged."

CHAPTER 6

At 0800 on the 22nd of November, Troost was on the flag bridge of the heavy cruiser *Albany*. The morning was bright with sunshine, and on the way out of the harbor, they passed Battleship Row, where *Arizona*, *West Virginia*, and *California* were tied up; and beyond them, to the port side, several destroyers were nested alongside a destroyer tender.

Troost paid close attention to the activity of his staff on the bridge. They were involved in making sure that the screening destroyers and supporting cruisers took their proper stations around the carrier *Endeavor* and responded promptly to all course and speed changes coming from Admiral Gower in the carrier.

As soon as they had lost sight of land, Gower signaled the force to divide according to a prearranged plan that created Task Group Eight, consisting of the *Endeavor*, two heavy cruisers, and six destroyers, and Task Force Two, under the tactical command of Rear Admiral Drewel, which was made up of two battleships and several destroyers.

Task Group Eight began to assemble and swung toward Wake, while Task Force Two continued to steam to the designated exercise area.

On the *Albany*'s flag bridge, Troost raised the glasses to survey the formation. Suddenly the phone connecting Troost to the signal bridge rang. "Troost here," he answered.

"Sir, message coming in from Admiral Gower to you," the signal officer said.

"Standing by," Troost said. "Give it to my orderly when you have it copied." But he could read Morse code too and trained his glasses on the *Endeavor*'s signal bridge.

"Aye, aye, sir," the SO answered.

Troost could plainly see the carrier. A light directed at the *Albany* began to flash Morse code. "Battle Order Number One… Task Group Eight is now operating under full wartime conditions. Install active warheads in all destroyer torpedoes. Bring service ammunition to all gun mounts and turrets. Regard any submarine sighted as hostile until positive identification is made. Arm all aircraft with full loads of ammunition and bombs. Destroy any Japanese surface ship or aircraft encountered. Observe strict radio silence."

"The message is on its way to your bridge, sir," the SO said.

"Roger, I too have copied. Acknowledge receipt and relay the same message to all ships under my command," Troost said, suddenly remembering the silent exchange between Kirst and Gower.

"Aye, aye, sir," the SO responded.

Troost put the phone down, called down to the ship's captain, Captain Peter Hasse, on the intercom, and said, "Admiral Gower has just signaled a number one readiness."

"Goddamn," Hasse exclaimed in his western drawl, "that sure as hell means he's about to start a shooting war!"

Troost nodded. "That it does," he said. "That it does."

CHAPTER 7

Dressed in civvies, Lieutenant (JG) Jacob Miller was at the table with his family for the traditional Friday night dinner in their fourth-floor apartment on Chester Street in Brooklyn. Newly winged, after successfully completing flight training at the Pensacola Naval Air Station, Jacob was on a 30-day leave before proceeding to the West Coast for assignment to a carrier fighter group. He'd arrived home, two days before, on Wednesday, December third.

Jacob's father, Sam, sat at one end of the kitchen table; his mother, Hanna, at the other. He was to his father's right and his sister, Miriam, to the left. A year had passed since he'd last seen them. His father, a dealer in the diamond exchange on the Bowery, was perceptibly older looking. There were more wrinkles at the corners of his eyes than Jacob remembered, and a weariness on his face that was new. But his sister, who had turned 18 the previous month, was a blonde, green-eyed beauty resembling their mother, who had been, from what the photographs in the family album showed, a beautiful woman when she was younger. Even today, with her finely wrought features and long gray hair, gathered into a huge bun on the back of her head, she was beautiful. But Jacob, taller than his father by a full head, didn't resemble him at all, nor did he possess any of the features of his mother. He was broader, with a square jaw, steel gray eyes, and a swarthy complexion.

Like his father, Jacob wore a yarmulke, and at his father's request, he recited the berakhah over the bread before cutting it. His mother set the table with her best dishes — the set she used only for holidays and other special occasions. And the

Shabbos candles were in the brass holders her grandmother had carried all the way from Kiev, some 75 years before. Not only was there a large roasted chicken on the table, but his mother also had made a chicken soup with matzoh balls and noodle pudding laced with raisins, and she'd baked a honey cake, topped with bits of dried fruit.

"I can't get over the way you look," his mother said, finally sitting down, after seeing that everything needed on the table was there. "You're tan like you spent all of your time in the sun."

"A good deal of it was outside," Jacob said. "But much of it was inside in ground-school classrooms learning about the aircraft and —"

"Ah," his mother exclaimed. "I forgot all about it! A letter came for you this afternoon." She left the table, went to the counter under the cupboard, picked up an envelope, and looking at it, said, "It's from Lieutenant (J.G.) Warren Troost."

"He's a friend of mine," Jacob said, taking the letter from his mother.

"And I thought it was from a girl," Miriam teased.

Jacob shook his head. "I'm not ready for that yet," he said and started to pocket the letter.

"Go on, read it," his mother said.

"It can wait."

"I know you want to read it, so read it," his mother said.

Jacob looked questioningly at his father.

"Get it over with," the old man said.

Jacob used his knife to open it, took out the sheet of paper, and unfolding it, began to read:

Hi friend —

From the logo you can see what kind of an assignment I pulled after busting out. The AKO-96 is a spit-kit if there ever was one. In Norfolk she was refitted with 5" deck guns for duty in the North Atlantic, but we're on our way to the Pacific. Scuttlebutt says we'll wind up in the Philippines.

Despite what happened to me in flight training, I have decided to remain in the navy. There's a war coming and I think I can still make a good officer... I know you will be a very good one and so does everyone else who was in our class.

Good luck and always come out of the sun.

Sincerely,

Warren Troost

P.S. My father finally got his stars.

Jacob smiled, refolded the letter, and put it back in the envelope. "He's on an *AKO* — a kind of special ship — probably on the way to the Philippines."

"Jake, do you know where you'll be sent?" Miriam asked.

He shook his head. "To a carrier in the Pacific. I qualified for training as a fighter pilot."

"Better you should have qualified as a rabbi," his father growled.

Jacob flashed his mother a look.

"I have tickets to the Bell Telephone Hour on Sunday, the seventh — Gladys Swarthout is one of my favorite singers."

"Is Miriam going with us?" Jake asked.

His mother nodded. "Sure."

"Good, I'll treat the two of you to late lunch," Jake said.

"You got money to throwaway now that you're a bigtime—"

"Papa, I was paid before I left Pensacola," Jacob said, looking at his father, a stocky man of 64 with snow white hair and pale gray eyes.

After a long pause, his father exclaimed, "Blood money!"

Jacob nodded and said in a very quiet voice, "You won't leave it alone, will you?"

"Leave it alone, is that what you want me to do — leave it alone, eh? I raise a son. I want my son to be a rabbi and my son becomes a killer."

Jacob took several deep breaths.

"Sam, you shouldn't say that," Mrs. Miller said. "You can't make a man into something he doesn't want to be."

"Ach, what does he know!" he answered. "My father was a rabbi and his father before him." He pointed a finger at Jacob. "He could have been one, but because I wanted it, he didn't."

"Papa, that's not true," Jacob said. "There was nothing that drew me to it."

"The Almighty would have," his father answered. "But you never gave Him a chance — never gave yourself a chance."

Jacob ran his hand over his chin, then over his hair. "Papa, I couldn't become a rabbi just because you wanted me to. There's a terrible war raging, and sooner or later we're going to be in it."

"So you want to kill!"

"Papa, there isn't any other way. Praying to God to stop what Hitler's doing to the Jews won't stop it. It won't stop the Japanese from killing tens of thousands of innocent people in China."

"You're going to stop it?" his father challenged.

"I'm going to help stop it," Jacob answered.

"Those who live by the sword will die by the sword!"

Jacob remained silent. He was foolish to think that his father wouldn't renew the antagonism that had existed between them for some years.

"You wanted to go to Brooklyn College," his father said, "I let you; then you wanted to go to that goyisher place, Annapolis, and I prayed you wouldn't be accepted —"

"You would still have me working in Macy's selling toys at Christmas to people who can't afford them. Listen, Papa, I couldn't be a rabbi, but I'm still a Jew —"

"A Jew doesn't fight!" his father shouted. "A Jew doesn't spill another person's blood. A Jew puts his faith in God."

Jacob slowly stood up.

"Where are you going?" his mother asked.

"I don't want to say anything I'll regret," Jacob answered, shaking his head.

"Please, Jacob, sit down," his mother said softly. "Please, do it for me."

Jacob looked questioningly at his father.

"All right, I said what I wanted to say. Sit down, Jacob, and have coffee and cake."

Jacob nodded and sat down.

CHAPTER 8

Tony Trapasso sat at the bar in Luigi's, a grill on the northeast corner of Hudson Avenue and Grove Street in Newark, New Jersey. His greatcoat was draped over the back of the stool. Now and then he sipped a beer. It was early Sunday afternoon, and except for four punks at the side table, none of the guys he knew was there.

"Your uncle Mike tol' me you wuz in," Luigi said. "You jus' finish some school —"

"Submarine school," Tony said.

"Yeah, that's it... Yeah, I know you went to college," Luigi said. "You're a navy officer, right?"

"Right," Tony answered.

"Hey, anythin' you want is on the house," Luigi said with a smile. He was a tall, gaunt man with deep-set eyes. Now and then he worked for Tony's father. "I'm goin' ta set up the free-lunch table. It's still the best in South Newark."

"I don't doubt it," Tony said.

"You want anudder brew?"

Tony put his hand over the top of the glass. "I'm fine," Tony answered.

Luigi nodded and walked away.

Tony looked at himself in the mirror behind the bar. This dimly lit, sour-smelling place had been one of the centers of his world; the other had been the Italian-American Social Club on Third Street. His eyes moved to the reflection of the street kids at the side table. A few years back and he could have traded places with any one of them. He shook his head, picked up his beer, and drank.

Suddenly Tony became aware of the scraping sound made by chairs being moved on a wooden floor. He looked up into the mirror. The four were coming toward the bar. He put his beer down. "Hey, you a sailor boy?" the tallest one asked. The others giggled.

Tony eased himself around. He was of middling height, compactly built, with unmistakably Latin features.

"Hey, he's even wearin' a white silk scarf," another one of the men said. "Maybe he's a fuckin' queer!"

Luigi started to move from the free-lunch counter back toward the bar.

"It's okay," Tony called out. "I can handle it."

"Hey, this guy says he can handle it," the tallest one said. "Maybe what he means is that he'd like to handle this." And he grabbed his own genitals.

The others laughed.

"Sailor boy, is that what you meant?"

"Why don't all of you go back to the table before you get hurt?" Tony said calmly.

"How much money you got, sailor boy?" one of the others asked.

Tony smiled. "More money than all of you have put together. Now go away before I get angry."

"Hey, you make me shake, I'm so afraid," the tall one said, reaching for the scarf.

"Mistake!" Tony said, backhanding him across the face.

The blow staggered him; blood poured from his nose.

"I told you to go back to the table and sit down," Tony said.

"Get the bastard!" the tall one shouted.

Tony leapt to his feet, grabbed the one nearest to him, and twisted him around until he had his head on the bar. "Any one of you so much as breathes too hard, I'll break his fucking neck." He applied pressure to the back of the punk's neck.

"Do what he says!" the kid cried out. "He's killin' me."

None of the other three moved.

"We wuz only foolin' wid ya," the tallest one said.

"Now I'm only foolin'," Tony responded.

Luigi was behind his bar again. "Like the ol' days, eh, Tony," he said. "I ain't seen nobody move as fast as you, since you —"

"Luigi, tell these thugs who I am."

"He's Tony Trapasso," Luigi said.

"Hey, Mr. Trapasso," the tall one said, "we do odd jobs for your father."

"Not anymore," Tony responded in a flat, low voice. "If you ever see me again, walk the other way — because if you don't, you're dead. Do you understand that?"

They didn't answer.

"Do you understand what I just said?" Tony roared.

"Yes," one of the three standing said.

"What about you?" Tony asked, looking at the tallest one.

He nodded.

"And you?" Tony questioned, moving his eyes to another one.

"I understand" he answered.

Tony relaxed his hold on the one he was holding. "I don't have to ask you if you understand, do I?" he said.

The guy shook his head.

Tony let go of him. "Now, the four of you get the hell out of here," he said.

They turned and ran out the door.

Tony suddenly felt drained. He faced Luigi. "Give me a double scotch neat."

"Sure, Tony," Luigi said, reaching for the bottle. "Your papa an' uncle shoulda been here. I swear by the Virgin," he said, crossing himself, "I ain't seen no one move like that." He poured the scotch and put the glass and the bottle in front of Tony. "Drink as much as you want. That tall one is Vinny Luna. He's head of the Red Devils."

"Shit," Tony answered; then lifting his drink, he said, "Salute!"

Luigi grinned. "Salute, Tony!"

CHAPTER 9

The sky was leaden, and a strong wind coming out of the northwest pushed against the *Albany* and all the other ships in the task group, causing them to roll and plunge.

"Admiral, from the looks of them, those two aren't having an easy time of it," Captain Hasse commented, referring to the fleet oiler *Neuse* and the supply ship *Iroquois* that were three points off the starboard bow, with a thousand yards between them.

Troost, visiting Hasse on the navigation bridge, raised his glasses, and looked at the *Neuse* first, then at the *Iroquois*. "In this sea, it won't be easy to come alongside them," he said, suddenly thinking about Warren. Before he left Pearl, he'd heard that the *AKO-96* was due on the ninth.

"The waves are running about 12 feet."

Troost stepped backwards, turned, and went to the rear of the bridge where the weather instruments were located. "The wind is up to 40 knots, with higher gusts. The barometer is off by three hundredths." He returned to the front of the bridge and said, "This is going to blow for a while."

"Old Bull Gower is just damn lucky it's happening now, on the way back to Pearl, and not on the way out when he had the marine fighter planes on the flight deck," Hasse said. "He'd have lost some of them for sure."

"Before the old bastard would let that happen," Troost answered, "he'd have had the whole damn ship's crew, including himself, on deck holding them down."

Suddenly the *Albany*'s bow went under and a wall of water crashed down over her foredeck.

Troost steadied himself and looked at the nearest destroyer.

"We can make Pearl with the bunker we have, sir," Hasse said. "But we'll be down to about 10 percent when we get there."

"Everyone's getting down. That was the reason for this refueling," Troost said. "We don't want to come in low on fuel and supplies. CinPac Fleet wants us to be able to get underway again in a hurry if we have to."

Hasse nodded. "The radio officer says there's a lot of heavy traffic out of Tokyo and most of it is coded."

"Nothing going in?"

"Not nearly as much as is going out."

"When and where, that's the million-dollar question," Troost said, just as one of the bridge phones rang.

A junior officer answered it. "Admiral, the signal bridge has a message for you coming in from the *Endeavor.*"

Troost took the phone. "Troost standing by," he said, looking at the *Endeavor,* which was two miles astern. Big as she was, she was also doing some significant pitching. He could see the signal light begin to flash, but didn't try to read it.

"For Troost: Can your ships commence replenishment. Gower," the SO said.

For the last few minutes, Troost had been mulling over refueling under the present conditions. "I'll answer it," he said.

"Aye, aye, sir," the SO responded. "Copying."

"For Admiral Gower. Highly recommend postponing replenishment until seas moderate. Consider risk to men and ships too great to begin evolution at this time. Also suggest reducing speed to minimum required to hold steerageway. Troost. Read it back." Troost listened; then he said, "Send it." Suddenly he realized that Hasse and the other officers on the bridge were looking at him as if he'd suddenly turned green, or worse, changed into a Japanese officer before their very eyes. Gower didn't brook any questioning of his orders.

Troost shrugged. He didn't have any doubt that Gower's elfin face would turn red when he read the answer, and neither did he have any doubt that Gower, an old sea dog, would see things his way.

The phone from the SO rang again.

Troost answered it.

"From Admiral Gower to you," the SO said.

"Read it."

"Ship's company and I furious at you for keeping us at sea Saturday night. Gower."

"Thank you," Troost smiled, allowing himself the luxury of a soft sigh of relief before he said to Hasse, "That means wait until the weather moderates before refueling and that we won't be back in Pearl until Sunday morning."

"Aye, aye, sir," Hasse grinned.

Troost returned to his own bridge, where he was told that Gower had just ordered a speed reduction for the entire group. Troost realized that he had been tested by Gower and come through, as the expression went, with flying colors.

CHAPTER 10

In the radio studio, Jacob sat between his mother and his sister. Shortly before noon, the musicians, all of them wearing tuxedos, filed onto the stage through a small door to the left. It was Sunday, December seventh.

"I'm so happy we're here," his mother said, "I wish Papa was with us."

"You know him," Miriam said. "This is his busy season. Between Thanksgiving and Christmas he could make as much as he makes all year."

Suddenly a door on the right side of the stage opened and Miss Swarthout walked out. She wore a bright red, body-hugging, long-sleeved gown.

Instantly the audience erupted into applause.

She blew them kisses.

"Red is her favorite color," Mrs. Miller said.

"How do you know that?" Jacob asked, looking at his watch. It was 12:01.

"She said so," his mother answered.

The door on the right opened again and the conductor, wearing tails, started out; then suddenly he stopped, turned, and walked back to the open door. Another man, dressed in an ordinary business suit, appeared in the doorway and said something to the conductor, who nodded and took his place on the podium.

Jacob looked at the ON THE AIR/OFF THE AIR indicators. The OFF THE AIR was on, and the studio clock above them read 12:03.

"They're late getting started," Miriam commented.

"Maybe someone is sick," her mother said.

A brief exchange took place between Miss Swarthout and the conductor; then she stepped up to the edge of the stage and said, "We are truly sorry for the delay and —"

The door on the right opened.

Miss Swarthout looked toward it.

The man said something.

An instant later the green OFF THE AIR indicator was replaced by the red ON THE AIR warning.

The orchestra played the theme music and Miss Swarthout began to sing, "If I should lose you…"

The hour passed quickly. Miss Swarthout sang several Lehar songs, the "Habanera" from *Carmen*, and "Mon coeur s'ouvre à ta voix" from *Samson and Delilah*. And the orchestra played the overture to Rossini's *Thieving Magpie*, the Carmen phantasy, and finished with Sousa's "Stars and Stripes Forever."

Even as the audience gave Miss Swarthout and the orchestra a standing ovation, the red ON THE AIR sign went off and the green one came on.

Suddenly the announcer said, "Ladies and gentlemen, please remain in your seats."

The applause died and Mrs. Miller looked questioningly at her son.

"Maybe there's been an accident," Miriam offered, as she sat down again.

Again the announcer spoke, "Ladies and gentlemen, we have been advised that, approximately one hour ago, Japanese aircraft attacked and bombed Pearl Harbor and —"

"Oh my God," a woman screamed, "my son is there — my boy is there."

"Please," the announcer said, "please listen to me. All military personnel must report to the nearest army or navy installation."

Mrs. Miller grabbed hold of Jacob's hand and held it tightly.

"Where is Pearl Harbor?" a voice called out.

"Any word about casualties?" a man called, two rows down from where Jacob was sitting.

"Only that there are casualties," the announcer answered; then he said, "Outside of the studio and on Broadway thousands of people have gathered. Please, be careful when you leave." Then he turned to Miss Swarthout, who stepped forward and said, "Ladies and gentlemen, would you please join me in singing our National Anthem."

The entire audience stood up and began to sing.

When it was over, the doors in the rear of the studio were opened and people began to leave.

"Jake, are you going to go right away?" Miriam asked, as they moved into the aisle.

"Pretty soon. First we're going to have that late lunch, then —" He stopped. A woman in front of them suddenly began to sob. He looked at his mother; she was biting her lower lip. There was nothing he could say to assuage her fear, and he certainly couldn't reveal his own. In some strange way he could accept the possibility that he might be killed more easily than he could the possibility that he might be maimed, which in his mind was worse.

The street was crowded with people. Men and women cried openly. There wasn't enough room on the sidewalk for all of them.

Newsboys hawked their Extras and mounted policemen patroled the streets.

Holding on to his mother and sister, Jacob walked toward the moving headline sign around the middle of the Times Building at the foot of Times Square.

Tony and his father were at a table in Toots Shor's. His father was a tall, muscular man with thinning black hair, coal black eyes, and a hard-featured face. There was no mistaking the relationship between the two.

His father picked up the bottle of champagne from the nearby ice bucket, and filled Tony's glass and then his own before he said, "Now we talk; later we'll eat."

Tony smiled. "I knew there had to be a reason why you didn't want to have Sunday lunch home," he said.

"Too much noise with your sisters and their kids," he answered; then with a broad smile, he added, "Makes me feel 200 years old. Here I have the best food, friends if I want them, and beautiful women to look at."

"Just to look at?" Tony teased, aware since he was a boy of 12, when he saw him humping the butcher's young wife on the couch in the back room of the club, that his father played around.

His father waved his hand dismissively at him, but he didn't answer.

"Okay, okay," Tony said, "have it your way. Let's talk."

"Tell me what happens to you now?" his father asked, lifting the glass of champagne and slowly sipping it.

"I'll be assigned to a submarine."

"And then what?"

Tony said, "Tell me what you want to tell me and cut the rest of the crap out."

His father put down the glass. "I can arrange things for you. You can put in the time you have to in Washington and then, when you're finished being a sailor, you come in with me and your uncle Mike."

Tony looked hard at his father. He had expected him to say what he did and now he had to answer. "I don't want you to fix anything. Nothing."

"But —"

"I don't want any part of the family," Tony said, in a low tight voice. "I thought you knew that."

"If it wasn't for you, who did I build the organization for?"

"Papa, after —"

"I know, after you and Frank pulled the freight yard job and you almost got tagged because Frank set you up, you didn't want anything more to do with..." At a loss for the word, he motioned with his left hand until he said, "I let you go your own way. You went to college in New Haven and joined the reserves and became a navy officer. I'm proud of you, Tony — very proud. But I built something out of nothing and it can be yours. There's a war coming and we're going to make a lot of money when it does come."

"That's not the kind of money I want," Tony said shaking his head.

"What do you want?" his father asked.

"I'm not —"

"The Japs bombed Pearl Harbor!" a man yelled, running into the restaurant. "It's on the radio. The bastards bombed us!"

The people at the tables started to yell. Several ran into the street and one came back shouting, "It's true, it's true. We're at war."

"Let's get out of here," Tony said, rising to his feet. "If it's true, I'm sure I'm going to have to report right away."

His father looked confused. "We haven't eaten."

Tony stood up. "I don't want to eat now."

"But you're home for 30 days," his father said, dropping a 50-dollar bill on the table and standing.

"Not anymore," Tony answered, heading for the coatroom. "This changes everything. It's a different ball game now."

They had to wait a few minutes before they could get their coats, and when they were finally out on the street, they moved with the crowd toward Times Square.

"For Christ's sake, will you look at all these people!" his father said, as they finally came onto Broadway, where everyone was looking up at the latest news reports as they moved around the Times Building.

"Now will you let me do something for you?" his father asked, almost shouting to make himself heard.

"No," Tony said. "No."

"I don't want you to risk your life —"

"It's my life and my risk," Tony answered. "Stay out of it. And I mean stay out of it." He was looking at his father and suddenly crashed headlong into a woman. He wheeled around and grabbed her. "I'm sorry. I —" He found himself looking at another ensign.

"Are you all right, Mom?" Jacob asked.

Mrs. Miller nodded.

"I didn't see her," Tony said. "I'm sorry." His eyes moved from the officer, to the young woman next to him, then back to the officer. "I'm Tony Trapasso. This is my father, Dom." He offered his hand.

"Jacob Miller," Jacob said, shaking it. "My mother and my sister Miriam."

The two men looked at each other for a moment and smiled, then Jacob said, "I'm home on leave."

"Me too," Tony said. "I just finished submarine school in New London."

"Flight training in Pensacola," Jacob said.

"Any details?" Tony asked, looking toward the *Times*'s sign.

"Manila has been bombed too," Jacob responded.

Tony shook his head. "I didn't figure it would come this way, did you?" he asked.

"No," Jacob answered, "not this way."

Suddenly a loud speaker blared: "All military personnel must report to an army or navy base immediately. Army and navy personnel on pass immediately report back to your units. Army and navy personnel on extended leave must report to either Governor's Island or Fort Hamilton in Brooklyn. All navy personnel report to the Brooklyn Navy Yard."

"I guess we go to the navy yard," Tony said to Jacob, but looking at Miriam.

She smiled, then cast her eyes down.

Suddenly speaking Italian, Tony's father said, "She's like a ripe peach — ready for the plucking."

Tony forced a smile and answered in Italian, "You have a dirty mind." Then Tony said, still looking at Miriam, but speaking to Jacob, "My father just said he'd drive to the navy yard."

"Are you joking?" Jacob asked.

Tony shook his head. "Am I joking?" he asked his father.

Mr. Trapasso shook his head. "The car is in a garage a few blocks from here — near Toots Shor's."

"I was going to take my mother and sister to Lindy's," Jacob said.

"I lost my appetite. I couldn't eat anything now," Mrs. Miller said.

"Are you sure, Mom?"

"I'm sure."

"Miriam?" Jacob questioned.

She shook her head. "I couldn't eat anything either."

"We'll take your mother and sister home first," Tony said, "then we'll go to the navy yard."

"Thanks," Jacob said. "Thanks Mr, Trapasso. I really do appreciate this."

"Hey, aren't all of us in this war together?" Tony asked.

"Yes, we're in it together," Jacob answered.

"Now all we have to do is get through the crowds," the older Trapasso said.

CHAPTER 11

"Admiral," the flag bridge watch officer said, "*Endeavor* is preparing to launch the morning search ahead."

"Thank you," Troost answered.

"A signal is flying to put her into the wind on course 034 true."

"Have the screening ships acknowledged?" Troost asked.

"Aye, aye, sir."

Putting the phone down, Troost went to look at the unfolding horizon. First light was still minutes away and by 1300 they'd be back in Pearl. The delay in fueling had cost them a full day in their planned return. He had already shaved and showered, and his steward brought him juice and coffee. Ordinarily, he'd wait until the scouting aircraft from the *Endeavor* returned safely before he left the bridge to have breakfast. But because this morning the scouts searching ahead of the group were directed to land at Ford Island at Pearl, Troost retired to the flag mess, where he had a slice of dry toast, one poached egg, and two more cups of coffee.

After breakfast, Troost decided to visit the navigation bridge, rather than return to his own. The ship's navigator and chief quartermaster were busy at the chart table, fixing the ship's position, and the task group was turning, with the *Endeavor* at the center as the guide.

For several minutes, Troost watched the maneuver through a pair of high-powered binoculars; then he went to the telephone bank and, picking up the signal bridge phone, said, "Admiral here. Signal the destroyer *Cresip* that she turned too slowly."

"Aye, aye, sir," the SO answered.

"Over and out." Troost put the phone down and walked to the forward part of the bridge. "Overall," he commented to Hasse, "not bad at all."

"That's what I was thinking," Hasse said. "I'd be willing to bet Admiral Gower's thinking the same thing."

"The admiral appreciates good seamanship and smart ship-handling," Troost responded.

For several minutes, neither man spoke; then Hasse said, "Admiral, if you don't have plans for this evening, why don't you join Kate and me for dinner at the house?"

"Are you sure Kate wouldn't mind?" Troost asked, aware of how much he always enjoyed Kate's company.

Hasse shook his head. "It won't be anything elaborate, but it will be adequate and the bar is good."

Troost grinned. "You have a guest," he said, waiting until he saw the *Endeavor* turn, before he put the glasses up to his eyes and focused them on the *Cresip*. "Better," he commented and lowered his glasses. "Much better."

"Do you think Admiral Gower will go to a readiness condition three before we make Pearl?" Hasse asked.

"Not likely," Troost replied. "He'll want to be safely at anchor before he does. That reminds me, when we left Pearl, I was surprised to see some of battleships tied up at Ford Island the way they were. It struck me that they were very vulnerable to an air attack."

"Admiral Kirst says it gives the local public confidence to see the array of warships that guard them."

"It doesn't do that for me," Troost said, remembering Kirst's reaction when he'd suggested that Pearl might be a priority target for the Japanese.

Hasse shrugged. "It takes a lot of guts to tell a four-star admiral what to do, doesn't it?" he asked, with a twinkle in his eyes.

"I'm going to pretend I didn't hear the question," Troost said.

Just as some of the men for the afternoon watch came to the bridge, a phone rang.

The relief helmsman answered it; then he said, "Skipper, you better take this."

Hasse immediately went to the phone.

Troost turned. The sailor stood stiffly by, but not at attention. Worry or pain — possibly both — marked his face.

"Pearl is being bombed," Hasse said in a quietly strained voice. "The RO is monitoring Pearl now... AIR RAID PEARL HARBOR X THIS IS NO DRILL."

Troost's eyes went to the ship's clock. It was 0700 local time.

Another phone rang. Hasse answered it. "Signal flags going up on *Endeavor*'s yardarm. Signal reads: PREPARE FOR BATTLE."

Earlier, Warren had obtained a perfect fix, and was now relaxing in the new gun tub below the bridge. In another two days the *Dee* would be in Pearl and he'd have at least 48 hours to himself. He'd go straight to the Royal Hawaiian and —

"Mr. Troost," the chief in charge of the radio shack called down to him, "would you please come up here?"

"Coming," Warren answered. Leaving the railing and his daydreams about what he'd do in Pearl, he hurried up the ladder. "What's up, Chief?" he asked, entering the radio shack.

"Smitty here," he said, putting his huge hand on the radio operator's shoulder, "says he's gettin' a lot of gobbledegook out of Pearl. I'd called the XO, but I seen you takin' the mornin' sun and I figured you wouldn't mind bein' distoibed."

"I'll remember that when I see you resting that gorilla-like body of yours," Warren answered.

The three of them laughed; then Warren asked, "When did it start?"

Smitty looked up at the clock. "Make it 0650."

"10 minutes ago?"

"Something is coming now," Smitty said, beginning to copy. "Jesus, Pearl is being bombed." He handed Warren the message: AIR RAID PEARL HARBOR X THIS IS NO DRILL.

"You sure you got this straight?" Warren asked.

"I sure as hell did," Smitty answered.

Warren reached for the phone and called the bridge. "Is the captain there?" he asked, after identifying himself.

"He went down to the wardroom for breakfast," Rawlins said. "Anything up?"

"Radio message from Pearl says they're being bombed," Warren answered.

"Better get it to Hacker on the double."

"I'm on my way," Warren said, hanging up the phone. "I'm going to the captain." He left the radio shack and ran along a short passageway and down two ladders, made a right turn, and entered the wardroom.

Hacker looked at him. He was about to bite into a slice of toast.

"Message from Pearl," Warren said, holding the yellow copy paper in front of him.

"Why didn't the chief —"

"I think you better read this now, Captain," Warren said.

Hacker glared at him, took the paper, and leaping to his feet, rushed out of the wardroom and up to the radio shack.

Warren followed him.

"Have you checked this?" Hacker shouted, entering the room and waving the paper in front of him.

"Smitty just copied this," the chief said, handing another piece of paper to him.

Hacker read the message aloud. "Alert X Japanese planes attacking Ford Island, ships in Pearl Harbor, and army airfields on Oahu."

Hacker punched the 1MC button to the bridge. "Bridge, this is the Captain... Put the exec on the pipe... Rawlins, go to general quarters."

Within moments the Klaxon brayed.

"Mister, Troost, come with me," Hacker said, leaving the radio shack. "From now on, we will observe radio silence unless I say otherwise. You'll take over coding and decoding all radio traffic. And you are now the gunnery officer as well."

"Aye, aye, sir," Warren answered.

When they reached the bridge, Hacker went directly to the 1MC and, depressing the buttons for all the circuits, he said, "Now hear this... All hands, now hear this... This is the Captain speaking... The Japanese have bombed Pearl Harbor... We are in condition one and can expect an air strike at any time... We are at war..."

CHAPTER 12

Glen Lascomb and Lucy Porter were lying on a large mound of hay in the back of the barn, where the yellow light from a single lantern hung from a beam halfway to the door did not reach them. Glen was a recent graduate of the Iowa State University Agricultural School, where he had played football and completed the Naval Reserve Training Program. He was a tall, broad-shouldered man with blond curly hair and blue eyes.

Glen's hand was inside Lucy's bra. Her nipple pushed gently into the palm of his hand. "Lucy, I want you so badly," he said huskily.

Lucy squirmed against him and ran her hand over his fly. "Fit to burst," she giggled.

"You're just teasing me," Glen said, gently squeezing her breast and at the same time trying to get his other hand up her dress.

She started to move away.

"C'mon Lucy. A man needs to be treated like a man," Glen said.

"I'll do you like I always do you and that's all I'll do," Lucy answered. "If you want more, you can go to those girls in Mason City. For two dollars, I hear, you can ride them —"

The barn door suddenly sprang open. "Glen?"

"It's Peter," Glen whispered, identifying his younger brother. "Christ, what a time for him to start yelling for me."

"Take your hand off me," Lucy said, tugging at her breast. Though her head came up only to the top of Glen's shoulder, she was surprisingly strong.

"Glen, I know you're back there… Glen, the Japs bombed Pearl Harbor."

"Holy shit!" Glen exclaimed, scrambling to his feet.

"It came over the radio. Mom was listening to the radio," Peter exclaimed.

"I'll be right in," Glen said.

"Mom and Dad are real worried about Hank. The guy on the radio said there were a lot of men killed."

"C'mon Lucy, get yourself together," Glen said, looking down at the girl. "My brother Hank is a CPO aboard the battleship *Arizona*. I bet this means I'll be called."

"You comin', Glen?" Peter called.

Lucy lifted her head toward Glen. "Pull me up," she said.

Glen brought Lucy to her feet.

She pressed against him. "Now if we were to be engaged, Glen, it would be a whole different matter. It would be silly not to give what I'd give you anyway."

"Glen, are you comin'?" Peter shouted. "There's a damn war on."

"You mean what you just said?" Glen asked, holding her to him. He could smell the scent of the hay in her hair.

"Glen Lascomb, that's not something I'd say if I didn't mean it," Lucy answered. "But the only way you'll really know is by doing it with a ring to make it proper an' all."

"I'm going back to the house without you," Peter shouted.

Glen took hold of Lucy's hand. "I'll think about it," he said; then he called to his brother. "Hold your damn horses! We're coming." And a moment later he and Lucy stepped around the haystack.

"By the time you two are finished, the war will be over," Peter said, as the three of them left the barn and walked across the snow-covered Iowa cornfield toward the house. Their breath steamed in the cold air.

"You really will think about it?" Lucy asked.

"I said I would," Glen answered.

"The only thing to think about is the war," Peter said. "If I was old enough I'd go down to town and enlist tomorrow."

"Farmers won't have to go," Lucy responded. "Glen is an Aggie graduate from the state university. He's needed here on the farm."

"Where did you hear that?" Peter challenged.

"I read it in a magazine."

"He won't have much choice, if they call him. He's in the Navy Reserve. He's almost an officer."

Glen didn't pay much attention to what either Peter or Lucy said. Come Monday morning, he'd volunteer for active duty and he'd be sent to a 90-day officer's course. He wasn't about to let the war pass him by. The farm would be waiting for him when he got back.

"You haven't said two words," Lucy commented, as they went up the three steps to the porch.

"Nothing much to say," Glen answered, "what's happened says it all."

"And what does that mean?" she asked.

Peter opened the front door.

"You go on in," Glen told his brother. "Lucy and I will be in in a minute."

"You're going to go, aren't you?" Lucy questioned.

Glen nodded. "I want to."

"I thought you wanted me," she said in a choked voice.

"I do."

She shook her head.

"I'll give you a ring and when I come home on my first leave, we'll get married."

"You really mean that?" she asked, throwing her arms around him. "You wouldn't be telling me this just to —"

"I mean it," he said, gathering her up into his arms and kissing her.

Lucy opened her mouth and pressed his mittened hand against her breast. "You going to tell your folks we're engaged?"

Glen hesitated.

"If we are, you tell them now and when I go home, I'll tell mine."

"All right, I'll tell them," Glen said.

"Oh I do love you!" Lucy exclaimed.

"I love you too," Glen said, opening the door.

CHAPTER 13

Warren was in his bunk. The only light in the small room came from the desk lamp. It was 2330. He couldn't sleep. Earlier CinPac Fleet sent a coded message to Hacker ordering the *AKO-96* to bypass Honolulu and proceed at maximum speed directly to Cavite, which also had been attacked by the Japanese. Warren had hoped to see his father in Pearl and now, for the first time in his adult life he was worried about him. Despite the differences between them, he had a profound respect for the man and — he was even going to admit that he loved him, when suddenly a sustained blast from the Klaxon signaled *general quarters.*

Warren grabbed his life vest and steel helmet and was out of the door before word came over the 1MC: "General Quarters... General Quarters... All hands man your battle stations."

Warren raced to the bridge and picked up the phone. "Mount number one?" he asked.

"Mount number one manned and ready," came the answer.

"Roger," Warren answered. "Stand by."

"Aye, aye, sir."

He repeated the same sequence with the after gun mount; then he reported to Hacker, "Mounts one and two ready, sir."

Hacker acknowledged the report with a nod; then he said, "Helmsman, keep her steady."

"Steady on course 0284," the helmsman answered.

Warren stepped up to Rawlins, who was OOD whenever the ship went to general quarters. "What the hell is going on?" he whispered.

"We've got a blip on the radar. It could be a sub," Rawlins answered.

"Where?"

"Two points forward of the port beam."

"Maybe, if it is a sub and if we're lucky," Hacker said, peering at the hooded display tube, "she won't see us."

Warren went to the window and looked up. The sky was patched with clouds and the moonlight, when it did show through, came from a quarter moon.

Hacker moved to the phones, picked one up, and asked, "Lookout, do you see anything?" He listened for a few moments and, putting the phone down, said, "He doesn't yet."

"How far?" Warren asked.

Hacker looked at him. "Range on the scope shows it to be 4000 yards."

"He could be coming in for a surface shot," Rawlins suggested, "or maybe its skipper is going to try to get us with deck guns?"

Hacker frowned.

Warren and everyone else aboard the *Dee* knew that one well-placed round could turn her into an inferno.

"We can't outrun her if she's on the surface," Hacker said, "and if she dives she just might be able to put a fish into us. But she'll be slower, a hell of a lot slower. Down to 10 knots at the most." He ran his hand over his chin, then said, "Helmsman, come left to 262."

"Coming left to 262," the helmsman said. "Mr. Rawlins, all ahead flank speed," Hacker said.

"All ahead flank speed," Rawlins answered, ringing the order up on engine room telegraph.

"Mister Troost, order number one mount to load service ammunition and two to load star shells and stand by," Hacker said.

"Aye, aye, sir," Warren responded, realizing, as he relayed the orders to the gun captains, that Hacker was showing more guts than he'd given him credit for having. He was going to try to force the sub to dive and then run like hell.

The *Dee* was heeling slightly to the starboard as she came to the new course.

The phone from the crow's nest rang.

Warren picked it up.

"Bridge, I make out a surfaced submarine dead ahead. We're closing fast," the lookout reported.

"Roger," Warren answered; then he said, "Skipper, lookout reports a sub dead ahead. We're closing fast."

"Stand by on mount one," Hacker said.

Warren repeated the order.

"Helmsman," Hacker said, "stand by."

"Aye, aye, standing by," the helmsman answered.

Hacker looked at his watch; then he said, "Helmsman, right, full rudder."

"Right, full rudder," the helmsman responded.

"Mount number one —"

"Blinker signal coming from sub!" Rawlins exclaimed.

"It's a standard recognition signal," Warren said. "It's one of ours."

"Reduce speed to ahead full, come back to course 284," Hacker ordered, with an audible sigh of relief.

Rawlins rang up the change of speed and ordered the course change.

"Mr. Troost, have the signalman tell the sub we recognize her," Hacker said.

"Aye, aye, skipper," Troost answered, motioning the signalman to follow him out onto the flying bridge.

A quick exchange of flashing light signals passed between the two vessels.

"She says she surfaced to recharge her batteries," the signalman said.

Warren passed the information to Hacker.

"Does she need help?" Hacker asked.

The signalman flashed the question to the sub and, after a minute or two, he said, "Negative, Mister Troost."

Warren went back inside the bridge.

"Exec," Hacker said, "secure from General Quarters."

"Aye, aye, skipper," Rawlins answered.

Hacker smiled and looking at Warren, he said, "Seems like I suddenly have a new name around here."

"Seems that way, skipper," Warren answered.

CHAPTER 14

Task Group Eight returned to Pearl at sunset on the eighth. The Big E's planes had searched for the Japanese force for 30 hours, but failed to locate it, and now with the western sky a mixture of reds, yellows, and purples, the ships of Task Group Eight moved slowly past the still smoldering battleships.

From the *Albany*'s navigation bridge, Troost saw the extent of the destruction. On Hospital Point, the battleship *Nevada* was aground and listing heavily to the port. At Ford Island the battleship *Utah* was ripped open. Only the toppled superstructure of the *Arizona* showed above the surface of the water. Smoke was coming from a dozen other ships.

"They did a job," Hasse said in a low voice.

Troost nodded. "It's a damn miracle the destroyers and cruisers that rendezvoused with us yesterday were able to fight their way out of here."

"What the hell would have happened if we had found the Japs, or if they had found us?" Hasse asked.

"That's a nightmare I'm sure some of us will have," Troost answered. "But what you see," he said, gesturing toward the ships in the task group, "is what we have left right now — and it's not a hell of a lot."

The *Albany* continued slowly up the channel and approached her assigned berth in the southeast lock. Hasse and Troost had already received their orders. Hasse was going to be there only overnight to refuel. In the morning she'd sortie with the Big E again and Troost would be back in ComCruDesPac Headquarters.

"All engines stop," Hasse ordered, as the ship was alongside the pier and the lines were started out.

"All engines stop," the engine signalman said, ringing the engine room.

"All lines secured," the OOD shortly reported, "and fuel barges request permission to come alongside and begin refueling."

Hasse nodded. "Permission granted," he responded; then turning to Troost, he said, "I'm sorry you won't be with us tomorrow when we go out again."

"I'm sorry too," Troost answered. "I'd rather be at sea than behind a desk. But my boss says I'm needed here for a while." He extended his hand. "I guess I'll have to take a rain check on dinner."

They shook hands.

"Good luck," Troost said.

"Good luck to you, sir," Hasse answered, stepped back, and saluted.

Admiral Troost returned the courtesy and left the bridge.

CHAPTER 15

"Papa, I'm going to meet Tony at the Information Booth," Jacob said, as the taxi stopped for a red light at Third Avenue and Forty-Second Street. All the way from Brooklyn his father had said nothing, and when his mother and sister spoke to each other, or to him, it was muted.

"Grand Central is a big place," his father said. "Maybe there's more than one information booth."

"The main one," Jacob answered. His father was a lot more nervous than he thought he'd be. "Don't worry, Papa, I'll find him. If I don't, I'll have to stand all the way to San Francisco. He has the tickets."

"They wouldn't make you do that, would they?" his mother asked.

"I was only joking," Jacob said.

"Don't make jokes at a time like this," his father said.

Jacob was going to say, *it's not the end of the world*. But then he realized that it could very well seem like it to them. It certainly was so important to his father that, even though it was a Thursday, he took the morning off to go to the station with him. "All of you listen," he said, "I'll be all right. Mom, Papa, Miriam — I'll be all right, I really will."

"Admiral, is it okay if I stop in front of the entrance on Forty-Second Street?" the cabbie asked.

"That'll be fine," Jacob answered.

"The Japs are tryin' to take Wake," the cabbie said, and he held up the *Daily News* to show its headline. "Yeah, if I was younger, I'd go myself. But they need young guys. The younger the better."

The cabbie's brief monologue silenced all of them.

A few minutes later the cab pulled up in front of the station. Jacob started to pay the cabbie, but his father said, "This time I pay."

"All right," Jacob said, "this time you pay."

"Knock 'em dead, Admiral," the cabbie said, looking back at them.

Jacob suddenly felt embarrassed and managed a nod.

The four of them piled out of the cab. Jacob picked up his valise and for a few moments stood on the sidewalk in front of the entrance to the station. The morning was gray with a raw December cold that made people walk quickly, with their heads down, as if they were butting against an invisible wall.

A young sailor passed and saluted.

Jacob snapped his hand up to the peak of his cap.

"What time does the train leave?" Miriam asked, as the four of them entered the station.

"Noon," Jacob answered, looking at his watch. "It's only 10:30 now."

"There are thousands of soldiers and sailors here!" his mother exclaimed. "Thousands."

"How are you going to find your friend?" his father asked, looking even more worried than he had in the cab.

"He'll be at the booth," Jacob said, leading the way toward the center of the main entrance. There were Christmas decorations everywhere and against one wall, on the Lexington Avenue side, there was a huge Christmas tree, around which were strung hundreds of winking colored lights, crowned by a glistening silver star.

Even before they reached the information booth, Tony was shouting, "Jacob! Jacob, I'm over here."

Jacob grinned. "I told you it would be easy, Papa."

"I was hoping you'd get here early so we'd have time to have some coffee," Tony said, coming up to Jacob and shaking his hand.

"You already met my mother and sister," Jacob responded. Not only had Tony met them on December seventh, but he'd driven out to Brooklyn twice to visit them. Each time he took Jacob and Miriam for a ride. Once, though it was snowing lightly, the three of them went to Nathan's in Coney Island for hot dogs. The second time he brought them to Torre's, an Italian restaurant on Bay Parkway. It was the first time Miriam had tasted Italian food and she loved it. On both occasions his father wasn't home.

"Yes," Tony said and greeted each of them with a kiss on the cheek.

"My father — Papa, Tony."

Tony shook Mr. Miller's hand. "It's a pleasure to finally meet you, sir," he said; then glancing over his shoulder, he motioned to two men who were standing behind him. "My father and my uncle Mike. Ensign Miller, Mr. and Mrs. Miller, and their daughter Miriam."

After another round of handshaking, Tony said, "I really need a cup of Java."

"There's a Child's restaurant inside the station," Mr. Trapasso said. "They bake their own cakes and pies."

"Coffee, Papa?" Jacob asked, realizing Child's wasn't kosher.

"Coffee. Why not coffee, at a time like this, Mr. Trapasso," Mr. Miller answered.

Tony's father nodded. "But please don't call me Mr. Trapasso," he said. "All my friends call me Dom — short for Dominic."

Jacob noticed that Tony fell in alongside Miriam; his mother and father walked with Mr. Trapasso, and he was left with

Tony's uncle Mike, a tall, broad-shouldered, silent man with fierce hawk-like eyes and a face to match.

In the restaurant, a gray-haired hostess, holding a half dozen menus, seated them at a large round table close to a wall decorated with a holly wreath. Off in one corner of the room was a sad-looking Christmas tree.

Soon a waitress wearing a black dress and a small white apron took their orders. Only Tony's uncle Mike asked for a open-faced roast beef sandwich in addition to the coffee and pie.

The two fathers exchanged comments about the weather, but neither mentioned the war, or the kind of business they were in. For Jacob, it was a totally new experience. Right before his eyes, his father was doing something he would have never thought him capable of doing: he was verbally dancing and dancing very well.

"What time does your train leave?" Jacob's mother asked.

"Noon," Jacob answered. "Don't worry, Mom, I won't miss it," he assured her.

Then Tony said, "Mr. Miller, is it all right if I write to your daughter? What I mean is, will you please let her answer my letters?"

From the astonished look on his father's face, Jacob knew the question took him by surprise. Even Miriam looked surprised. And everyone else seemed to be holding his breath.

"You wouldn't be Jacob's friend," his father answered, "if you weren't a good man, and if you're a good man, there's no reason for you not to write to my daughter."

Tony grinned.

"Thank you, Papa," Miriam said in soft but strong voice.

Mr. Trapasso asked for the check and insisted on paying it before they left the restaurant.

A few minutes later they were at the train gate.

"I guess this is it," Jacob said.

His mother began to sniffle.

He hugged her to him and kissed her forehead. "I'll be all right," he whispered.

"Don't do anything foolish, promise me."

"I promise."

She kissed him on the forehead, then on his lips.

He let go of her and turned his attention to Miriam. "Take care of them and take care of yourself," he said.

She nodded. There were tears in her eyes.

He put his arms around her.

"You're the best brother a girl could have," she told him.

"Now that I'm going away you tell me that," he said, trying to bring a smile to her face.

"Come home safe," she said.

"I'll do my best," Jacob answered; then he turned to his father. "Papa —" he faltered. There were tears in father's eyes. "Papa —" he began again, but couldn't continue. Suddenly he found himself in his father's arms.

"I love you," his father said in Yiddish.

"And I love you, Papa," Jacob answered in the same language.

"Take good care of yourself."

"I will."

"Come home safely. Do what you must do to survive. But don't do anything that you would be ashamed to tell your son, God willing, you should father one."

Jacob nodded.

"Then go with my blessing," his father said, patting him gently on the back.

Jacob separated from his father and took a few moments to shake hands with Mr. Trapasso and Mike, while Tony did the same thing with his mother and father. But when he came to Miriam, Tony put his arms around her and, gently kissing her on the lips, he said, "I'll write as often as I can."

"I'll answer," she said.

"Keep well."

"I will," Miriam answered.

He kissed her again, let go of her, turned, and said, "Okay, fly-boy, if I stand around here any longer, I'll be the one to cry."

"Ready," Jacob said, picking up his valise.

Tony lifted his.

They nodded at each other, turned, and walked through the gate and onto the station platform.

Jacob had to clear the knot in his stomach before he could say, "You took my father by surprise."

"I took me by surprise too," Tony said.

"That's what I thought," Jacob responded.

CHAPTER 16

The Klaxon on the *AKO-96* screamed.

"General Quarters... General Quarters," Rawlins said on 1MC. "All hands... All hands man your battle stations."

Warren was already on the bridge when the RO reported that radar at Cavite and Subic Bay picked up enemy planes in the area.

Hacker rushed onto the bridge.

"Enemy planes coming in from the northwest," Rawlins said.

Warren checked the status of the ship's two guns. "Mounts one and two ready, skipper," he reported.

"How far are we from port?" Hacker asked.

"Approximately 20 miles, at the very most," Warren answered.

Hacker picked up the mike, switched on the 1MC and said, "All hands now hear this... Now hear this... This is the Captain... Enemy aircraft are in our area and are approaching. Mount number one, cover the starboard side. Mount number two, the port side. Fire at will... Repeat, fire at will..." He switched off the 1MC and commented, "A few 50s and 20s would come in handy now."

Suddenly the lookout on the bow shouted, "Bridge, sky forward, plane two points on our port bow, elevation zero six zero, moving right."

Warren clicked on the telephone. "Mount number two, target approaching port bow."

"See him," the other end answered.

Dull claps of thunder rolled out of the northeast, and within moments huge plumes of smoke appeared in the direction of the Cavite naval station.

A phone rang. "Troost here."

The RO reported. "Cavite is under attack," he said.

"Roger," Warren answered and relayed the information to Hacker.

Another lookout picked up a second plane coming in on the portside.

Mount number two started to fire.

The planes bored in.

Mount number two opened up.

The plumes of black smoke over Cavite spread black smudges across the intensely blue sky.

"Helmsman, right full rudder," Hacker said, maneuvering his ship to enable both mounts to bear on the plane.

"Right full rudder," the helmsman answered.

With its machine guns firing, the first enemy plane on the port side dropped lower.

Gun mounts continued to fire and their bursts began to surround the approaching planes.

The plane suddenly veered to the right. The next instant it turned into a ball of fire that continued to move, then slowed and arced into the water not far off the port side.

Dropping four bombs from its wing racks, the second plane roared over turning the ship. Three exploded harmlessly in the water. But the fourth detonated very close to the stern. The explosion sent a shudder through the ship.

Mount number one swung around and continued to fire at the departing aircraft.

"Get a damage control report," Hacker said.

Warren picked up the phone. "The skipper wants to know what the situation is down there," he said, speaking to a repair party talker on the fantail.

"Damage topside, but nothing too serious."

"Roger," Warren answered and gave the information to Hacker.

Suddenly the bridge came under machine-gun fire from a third aircraft making a low-level strafing attack from the port side.

"Hit the deck!" Hacker shouted.

The helmsman screamed and, letting go of the wheel, slumped to the floor.

The helm was spinning.

Warren crawled to the helm, rolled the dead man away, and stopped the wheel.

The strafing aircraft passed overhead with a roar.

Hacker, Rawlins, and the rest of the bridge watch pulled themselves upright.

"What course, skipper?" Warren asked.

"Make it zero four five," Hacker answered.

"Course zero four five," Warren said, turning the helm over.

A final attacking plane coming in over the stern raked the ship again with machine-gun fire and then disappeared toward Cavite.

"Skipper, we have rudder control," Warren reported, suddenly realizing his shirt was soaked with sweat.

Hacker acknowledged the report with a grateful nod.

Hacker went to the phone bank, picked up, and said, "Report damage." He listened for a few moments; then putting the phone down, he said, "We're okay down below." Then he picked up the phone connected to the gun mount positions and asked for a status report. "Two men hit on number one and one on two… They say they can still fight," he said to no one in particular.

"Aye, aye, skipper," Warren answered.

Hacker walked over to where the helmsman lay, looked at him for several seconds, then said in a quiet voice, "Mister Rawlins, get a detail to remove the body."

"Aye, aye, skipper," Rawlins answered.

"Port-side gyro repeater is out," Hacker said. Then looking toward Cavite, he commented, "What they don't need right now is an *AKO* tied up anywhere near those fires."

He went to the ship's phone bank and called the signal officer, "If you can raise Cavite, tell them we'll lay off the coast until they're ready to take us. Tell them that we came under attack and knocked down one of the Jap fuckers." He put the phone down and walked to the forward part of the bridge. "Exec, get rid of the empty shell cases down there and get the repeater fixed," he said to Rawlins; then he added, "You and your men gave a good account of yourselves."

"I'll tell them that, sir," Rawlins answered.

Admiral Troost read the daily report that came out of the Headquarters of the Commander and Chief of the Asiatic Fleet. Almost at the end of the report, there was a brief account of the attack on the *AKO-96*. It was bombed and strafed on its way into Cavite, and Warren was mentioned in the report for taking the ship's helm after the helmsman had been killed and while the bridge was still taking machine-gun fire from an enemy plane…

Immensely pleased by Warren's actions, Troost decided to go out for dinner and drink a toast to his son. Usually he worked until 20- or 2100, then dined alone or with some other staff members in the headquarters mess, or in the officers' club. And a few times, when Hasse was ashore, he was invited to have dinner with him and his wife Kate.

Troost rested against the back of the swivel chair and, opening the side drawer of the desk, he took out Gloria's last letter to him. It had arrived two days before and, though he read it as soon as it came, he hadn't as yet answered it. The letter was full of complaints and a demand that he pull the necessary strings to get her and Lillian out to Pearl. "If you don't take any action," she wrote, "I will use what influence I have…"

Troost returned the letter to the drawer and shut it. Suddenly, he found himself thinking about Kate. There was something about the woman that made him very aware of her whenever she was close. Two days ago they had accidentally met on the street. She was on her way to the commissary and he was taking a few minutes for himself away from his desk. She was behind him and called him by his given name. Surprised to hear a woman call him, he turned and was even more surprised to see her. She was wearing a simple dress. White with small red roses on it, he remembered. She was smiling. Her long red hair glistened in the sunlight.

"I'm on my way back from the university," she said, "and I decided to stop and pick up a few things in case Peter comes back for the weekend."

"I needed some fresh air," Troost said, as they started to walk together. He knew that Peter wouldn't be back for at least 10 days. Task Group Eight was scheduled to be refueled and resupplied at sea. To avoid having to answer any questions about Peter, he asked, "And what are you doing at the university?"

"Finishing my education," she answered proudly. "I have another 15 credits and I'm done: I'll have my degree."

"In what?"

"English literature," she answered. "Modern American and English literature is my field."

"Wonderful!" he exclaimed, as they stopped in front of the commissary.

She smiled. "Do you really think so?"

"I wouldn't say so if I didn't," he answered.

For several moments, she stared straight at him. "No, you wouldn't," she said.

There was a strange, almost conspiratorial, expression on her face, as if she'd just shared a secret with him. There was also something in her blue eyes that made him look straight into them.

"If I asked you to have dinner with me would you go?" He spoke even as he thought over each word. For an instant, he felt himself to be in limbo. He was ready to apologize. Ready to accept her rejection with as much dignity as he'd be able to muster.

"Yes," she said quietly. "I'd like that."

Troost nodded.

She looked over her shoulder at the commissary and then at him. "Thank you for the lovely walk," she said.

"The pleasure was all mine," he answered, saluting; then he said, "I'll call."

She smiled. "Please do," she said.

As he watched her walk into the building, he realized how much he wanted her.

Troost picked up the phone, asked the operator for an outside line, and dialed the Hasse's number. He was certain she'd find some excuse to avoid going to dinner with him. The phone rang several times and she didn't answer it. Suddenly he was caught between not wanting her to answer and being disappointed that she wasn't home, even wondering where she could be.

"I'll let it ring two more times before I hang up," he said, as if he were offering a challenge to some unseen being.

After the next ring, Kate said, "Captain Hasse's residence."

Troost panicked. He couldn't find his voice.

"I know someone is there," she said.

Troost cleared his throat. "It's Andrew," he responded.

"I was beginning to wonder if you would ever call," she said.

"Are you free for dinner tonight?" Troost asked.

"Yes," Kate answered. "Yes, I'm free."

"Good," Troost said. "Very good. I'll pick you up in a half hour."

"That will be fine."

"See you," Troost said, and smiling to himself, he put the phone down. He felt boyishly happy.

CHAPTER 17

Jacob and Tony were at the bar in the club car. It was almost midnight and the barkeeper was getting ready to close down.

Tony looked around. There were two soldiers at the far end of the car, a marine second lieutenant and a bleached blonde woman were seated opposite each other at a small round table, and a man, about their own age, dressed in civvies, occupied a club chair close to the bar.

"When did we leave St. Louis?" Tony asked.

"At 2000," Jacob answered.

Tony shook his head. "Slow," he commented. "Slow … slow."

"The train will be 14 hours late when we reach San Diego, that's if there aren't any more delays," Jacob said.

Tony smiled. "10 bucks says we'll cut it to 12," he said.

"You're on," Jacob answered.

Tony leaned close to Jacob. "That guy there in the club chair has been looking at us for the past 10 or 15 minutes."

Jacob looked over his shoulder. "He's getting up. He's coming —"

"I can see what he's doing," Tony responded. "Christ, I'm only half-crocked."

"Excuse me," the man said, "but I'd like to buy you gents a drink before the bar closes." He spoke with midwestern twang.

"He wants to buy us a drink," Tony commented.

"Why?" Jacob asked.

"I —"

"My momma told me to beware of strange men who offer to buy me drinks on the train," Tony said.

The man's face turned red. "I'm an officer — I mean I will be an officer as soon as I finish my time in San Diego."

"NROTC?" Jacob asked.

"Yes. Iowa State."

Tony started to laugh. "I thought —"

"I guess if I were you, I would have thought the same thing."

"What the hell is your name?" Tony asked.

"Glen Lascomb."

"Glad to have you aboard, Mister Lascomb," Tony said, highballing him.

"Glad to be aboard," Glen answered, responding with a salute.

"Let's celebrate Glen coming aboard," Tony suggested.

"I'm buying," Jacob said.

"No, that pleasure is mine," Tony insisted.

"Gents," Glen told them, with exaggerated dignity, "the first round is mine. After that, it's up to your individual conscience and sense of honor."

"Hey, I like this corn grower," Tony said, slapping Glen in the back.

"An officer and a gentleman," Jacob commented, making room for him at the bar.

CHAPTER 18

Cavite and Subic Bay were reduced to rubble. Manila was abandoned and declared an "open city." General MacArthur's troops were moving toward Bataan.

On December 31, the *AKO-96* was moving south off the east coast of Mindoro. She was on her way to join up with the remnants of the Asiatic Fleet. She still had fuel in her bunkers. Twice in the last two days she'd delivered bunker to other ships, rendezvousing with the destroyer *Perry* at twilight to transfer the fuel under cover of darkness; then she met the submarine tender *Holland* at 0300 and completed the operation before first light.

Warren was plotting a course that would bring them into Javanese waters within four days, if they didn't stop to refuel any more ships. And that was a big if.

"What do you think, Chief?" he asked, leaning away from the chart table and at the same time, using a handkerchief to wipe the sweat off his brow and the back of his neck.

Berk studied it. "Looks good to me," he said.

"The tricky part is going to be when we get close inshore," Warren said. "Our charts just don't have enough detail."

"Maybe we'll get a set of new ones," Berk offered.

"Not likely."

One of the phones rang.

A yeoman answered it, listened, then responded with, "Aye, aye, sir. I'll pass the word." He put the phone down and said, "Mister Troost, the skipper wants to see you in his quarters."

"Another rendezvous?" Berk asked.

Warren shrugged. "Might be," he said, leaving the chart table and checking the gyro repeaters and then the binnacle.

"Anything wrong?" the OOD asked. A raw-faced young man, Ensign Donald Bradly was new to the ship. He'd come aboard the day they arrived in Cavite.

"Nothing, Mister Bradly. You'll hold the present heading for another two hours, then change to the heading indicated on the chart. Be sure to notify the skipper before you make the change."

"Aye, aye, Mister Troost," Bradly answered.

Warren left the bridge and reported to Hacker.

"Sit down," Hacker said, holding out a pack of Luckies to him.

Warren took one, lit it, and blew smoke up toward the ceiling, where a small fan circulated air through the cabin.

Hacker lit up too before he said, "Mister Rawlins will be here momentarily."

Even as he spoke, there was a knock on the door.

"Come in," Hacker said.

Rawlins entered and closed the door behind him.

"Sit down," Hacker told him, pointing to the only empty chair in the cabin. "You may smoke your pipe if you want to." He waited until Rawlins filled and lit his pipe before he said, "The RO copied a coded message that was designated for *my eyes only*. I decoded it and it boils down to this: the *AKO-96* will not continue on its present course. It will remain in the vicinity of Bataan and make itself available for use by the army." He paused to take a long drag on his cigarette before he asked if there were any questions.

"Too many to figure out which one to ask first," Warren said.

"That just about scratches our chances of getting out of here," Rawlins said.

"It certainly minimizes them," Hacker responded.

"Any other ships —?"

"The oceangoing tug AT-sixty, the Bay," Hacker said.

"What do we do with the fuel we're carrying?" Warren asked.

"Pump it into the storage tanks at Corregidor and, if we can't do that, we'll dump it out at sea. But we have enough to keep us going for a long time."

"Skipper, just what are we going to do?" Warren asked. "We're not built to do anything but deliver fuel to other ships."

Hacker shook his head. "I don't know. But my best guess is that we'll probably be used to transport troops between Bataan and Corregidor. The same probably goes for the Bay."

"Christ," Warren exclaimed, "there are hundreds of ships better suited for that than we are!" His voice rose in pitch. "Why us?"

Warren's eyes met Hacker's.

"Maybe we'll get lucky," Warren said, "and be ordered out of here in a few days."

"No we won't," Rawlins said in a choked voice. "No we won't."

"Skipper, we're going to need some more armament if we're going to stay around here. A few 50s would be good to have and maybe a 40- or 37-millimeter gun."

"When we get to Corregidor I'll see what I can scrounge," Hacker said. "But don't expect much. The army is short on everything."

"Whatever we get will be more than we have," Warren responded.

"Now for the good news," Hacker said.

"I didn't think there was any," Rawlins commented, puffing on his pipe.

"Mister Troost, as of January one, you will be a lieutenant. Congratulations," Hacker said, offering his hand.

"Thanks, skipper," Warren answered.

Rawlins congratulated him, but without any enthusiasm.

Hacker stubbed out his cigarette. "If anyone had told me when you first came aboard that I'd be congratulating you for anything," Hacker said, "I'd have told them they were nuts."

Warren nodded. "I would have agreed with you."

"Before we turn this ship around," Hacker said, "there's one more thing. No, two more things I have to talk about. First, we're going to do most of our sailing at night. During the day we'll hide in a cove, and there are enough of them for us to use. That means our course must be laid out from cove to cove."

"I understand," Warren said, "and if I may make a suggestion?"

"Go ahead."

"We should paint the ship a camouflage green to blend in with the jungle. We can even cut palm fronds and cover the deck and the bridge with them."

"See to it," Hacker said, looking at Rawlins.

"Aye, aye, sir," Rawlins responded.

"Any other suggestions?" Hacker asked. "None? All right, the next item." He shook another cigarette out of the pack, lit it, and pushed the pack across the desk to Warren.

Warren declined the offer.

"The crew is going to be upset when I tell them what our new orders are," Hacker said. "I think we need something to lessen the blow and, since in a few hours it will be New Year's Eve, I'd like to give the men a New Year's Eve party. I've already spoken to the chief cook about it and he's going to come up with something. We have a few bottles of whiskey aboard for medicinal purposes that can be used to make everyone feel better."

"I'll find us a nice quiet cove," Warren said. He looked at his watch. "It's 1300 now. Say we'll run until 1800. At 16 knots that will put us about 85 miles north of here. Say 90."

"We'll lay over tonight and move out just after darkness sets in tomorrow night," Hacker said.

"Any news about what's happening in other places?" Warren asked.

Hacker shook his head. "It's as if the rest of the world didn't exist."

"It's we who don't exist," Rawlins said, "only we're too stupid to see it. But we don't exist. We've already been crossed off the books."

CHAPTER 19

Troost excused himself from the table at the officer's club and went directly to a telephone booth, closed the door, deposited a dime, and dialed Kate's number.

She answered.

"I want to be with you," he said.

"Aren't you supposed to be at the club?" she responded.

"I am there," he said, pausing before adding, "Everyone is trying hard to have a good time, and the harder they try the sadder the whole thing becomes."

"Yes, I know that feeling," Kate said.

"Look, you're alone and so am I," he told her.

"I'll meet you somewhere," she said.

"I'll go anywhere —"

"Palm and Anderson," Kate said. "It's five blocks from where I live. Stay on Palm Avenue and you'll come to it."

"About 30 minutes," he answered.

"What will you say to the people at your table?" she asked.

"I'll tell one of the men that I developed a very bad headache. Everyone has been having them lately. See you," he said.

"Yes," Kate responded and hung up.

Troost opened the booth door and returned to the table to give his excuse; in less than 30 minutes he pulled up at the corner of Palm and Anderson.

Because of the blackout, the streets were absolutely dark, and even the headlights and taillights of his car and all the other vehicles on the island were painted over with black paint, except in the center of the lens, where a cross-like pattern was left open.

Troost got out of the car. The trees and blacked-out house were darker shadows in the night. But overhead the sky was filled with diamond glistening stars.

He filled his pipe, lit it, and found himself wondering if she'd really meet him. She was 14 years younger than he, a woman in her prime, while he was verging on middle age. But he was never so alive as when he was near her. Then suddenly he heard the rhythmic clicking of high heels on the sidewalk. He took the pipe out of his mouth, smiled, and started toward her.

"Andrew?" Kate called.

"Yes," he answered, cleaning the pipe's bowl against the palm of his hand. He could see her clearly now. She was wearing a white blouse and dark skirt.

A few moments later, they came together. Troost put his arms around her, kissed her on her lips, and said, "I'm glad you came."

"Didn't you think I would?"

"I was afraid you'd change your mind," he answered truthfully.

She took hold of his hand, squeezed it gently, and softly said, "I wouldn't do that to you."

He kissed the back of her hand and escorting her to the car, he said, "We could go to the Hali Kalani."

"Yes, it's the closest," she answered, settling in the car and moving close to him.

He turned to her, placed his hand on the side of her face, and drawing her toward him, kissed her. "Thank you for coming," he whispered.

"Thank you for asking me," Kate responded.

Troost looked at his watch. "Another hour and it will be curfew time," he said, turning on the ignition and shifting into first.

Kate leaned back. "I was thinking about you earlier in the evening."

"Oh, good thoughts I hope," Troost said, moving into third.

She put her hand on his arm. "Yes, very good thoughts."

He glanced at her. This was the sixth time they were together. They had kissed; he had caressed her breasts and the insides of thighs through her clothing.

"What are you thinking about?" she asked.

"How much I want to make love to you," he said, glancing at her again as he spoke.

She smiled. "I was beginning to get that impression."

"When?"

"The first time you phoned."

"The afternoon we met and —"

"Then?"

"Then," Troost answered. "I sensed something. I don't know what it was, but I felt it."

Kate was silent for a few moments before she said, "I sensed you were a lonely, almost sad man."

Troost uttered a deep sigh. "I don't want pity, Kate." He'd told her about Gloria's drinking.

"If I thought that's what you wanted from me, I'd have gladly given it to you, but I wouldn't be here."

Satisfied, he nodded and put his hand between her thighs.

After a moment of silence, Kate said, "I wouldn't be here, if I didn't want to be, and if I didn't want your hand to be where it is, it wouldn't be there."

"I know that," Troost answered.

She put her hand over his and leaned against him. "Sometimes," she said in almost a whisper, "I think about you out here on a raft with only you and that young sailor and I want to weep."

Surprised and deeply touched, he asked, "How did you know about it?"

"The paper carried the story. There was even a picture of you, and then when were you assigned to destroyer and cruiser operations, Peter told me about it."

Again, he kissed the back of her hand. "We were just two frightened men," he said. "That young sailor saved my life." And he told her the story of how he swam to the raft and then how he was goaded into staying alive.

"If you hadn't survived," she said, pressing his hand under hers, "I would have been the loser."

Troost smiled. "And certainly so would I," he said, turning into the parking area next to the Hali Kalani. "Stay in the car. I'll register —"

"As husband and wife?"

"Would you mind?"

She shook her head. "No," she answered, lifting her head off of his, "I'd rather like that."

Troost leaned over, kissed her, and then left the car. In less than 10 minutes he was back. "There were only two rooms left," he said, sliding behind the wheel again, "and we have one of them."

The room was on the far end of the parking area and Troost stopped the car a few feet away from the door. "The restaurant is very crowded," he said, "and some people in the lobby looked as if they'll never make it to midnight."

They entered the room.

Troost closed the door after them and locked it before he switched on the lights. Dull gray drapes hid the window from view.

"If I turned off the lights," he said, "we could have the curtain open and look out at the water."

"I want to look at you," Kate said, moving close to him.

He took her in his arms and, passionately kissing her, moved his hands over her supple body. "Kate," he whispered, "Kate!"

Opening her mouth, she pressed herself against him.

They undressed one another, and when they were completely naked, Troost knelt down and kissed the warm soft hollow of her stomach.

Arching to him, she gently caressed the top of his head.

Troost stood up and led her to the bed. "You're beautiful," he said, looking at her.

"Love me," she whispered.

CHAPTER 20

"Ten fathoms," Chief Quartermaster Berk called out from his station at the Fathometer.

"Check," Warren answered, looking at the chart. He'd found a cove on the coast of Mindoro. "Skipper, we can ease her in another 1000 yards to the north bank. According to the chart, the depth is eight fathoms 100 yards offshore."

"Helmsman, steady as she goes," Hacker said.

"Nine fathoms," the chief called out.

"Check," Warren answered, taking a bearing on a prominent point on the shore and said, "Now skipper."

"All engines back one third," Hacker ordered.

"All engines back one third," the engine signalman said, at the engine telegraph.

"Stand by to let go port anchor," Hacker said.

A talker relayed Hacker's order to the anchor detail.

"Let go the port anchor... All engines stopped," Hacker said.

An instant later the rattle of the anchor chain broke the stillness of the cove. The ship quickly lost her forward momentum and was brought to a complete stop by the anchor taking hold of the bottom.

"Well done," Hacker exclaimed, "very well done indeed!"

"Skipper, there's still enough light for a party of men to go ashore and get some palm fronds to camouflage the bridge deck and the stack," Warren said.

Hacker nodded. "Mister Bradly, take a half dozen men ashore and collect the necessary palm fronds to do the job. Chief, go with him and make sure all the men are armed."

"Aye, aye, sir," the chief answered.

"How's the camouflaging coming?" Hacker asked, looking at Rawlins.

"We probably won't have enough paint to complete the job," Rawlins answered.

"Maybe we'll be able to pick a few more gallons up at Corregidor," Hacker answered; then he said, "We'll maintain our regular watch schedule and mount an additional one for the port and starboard sides — two hours on, four hours off. Rawlins, make up a guard roster. Have it begin at 1800 tonight."

"Aye, aye, sir," Rawlins answered.

Hacker nodded. "I'll see you gentlemen later this evening," he said and left the bridge.

"Mister Bradly," the chief called, "we better move, if we're going to get those fronds before darkness sets in."

Rawlins turned to Warren. "I'll finish out this watch," he said. "I don't feel much like celebrating."

"I know what you mean," Warren answered.

"How the hell do you know what I mean!" Rawlins exclaimed loud enough to make the other members of the bridge detail look at him.

"I only meant —"

"Don't you ever say 'you know what I mean' to me again," Rawlins said in a tight voice. "Don't you ever say that again."

Warren nodded, took a step backward, turned, and started to leave the bridge.

"Mister Troost," Rawlins called.

Warren stopped and faced him.

"Please convey my respects to the captain and tell him that I will not attend the New Year's Eve celebration," Rawlins said.

Warren approached him. "That's something I think you should tell him yourself."

"I gave you an order, Mister Troost," Rawlins snapped.

"He's going to ask why," Warren said.

Rawlins thought for a moment; then he said, "Because I choose not to — because the very idea of celebrating one's own death is as close to the barbaric as — for Christ's sakes, just tell him I won't be there."

"Aye, aye, sir," Warren responded; he turned and this time left the bridge. A few minutes later, he knocked on the door of Hacker's cabin.

"Come," Hacker called out.

Warren entered the cabin and closed the door.

Hacker was at his desk, where he'd obviously been writing a letter. He was wearing a white cotton bathrobe, and a cigarette hung out of the side of his mouth. "Writing to my son," he said, "just in case we get a chance to mail a few letters."

"Maybe at Corregidor," Warren answered. He hadn't known that Hacker was married.

"Maybe," Hacker agreed.

"Skipper, Rawlins —"

Hacker held up his hand. "He's got a bad case of the jitters. I have too. But it will pass."

"He asked me to convey his respects and tell you that he won't attend the ship's party," Warren said.

Hacker squinted up at him. "Did he say why?"

"He said the idea of celebrating his own death was barbaric."

Hacker stood up, took a deep drag on the cigarette, and stubbing it out in an ashtray made from the back of a five-inch shell casing, he said, "He's not really that wrong, but he's not that right either. I never did see any sense in throwing in the towel. What about you?"

Warren shook his head. "I don't either," he said.

Hacker smiled. "I guess that's something they taught you at Annapolis, isn't it?"

"For those who wanted to learn it," Warren answered. "But I was lucky: my father taught it to me, or maybe some of his grit rubbed off on me."

"Either way, you've come out ahead," Hacker said; then he looked down at the unfinished letter. "He's at Annapolis now. He'll graduate in June. Maybe you'll have a chance to meet him. I also have a daughter, Irene. She's an army nurse."

"If I meet either one, dinner and drinks will be on me," Warren responded, not knowing what else to say.

"Uses his mother's maiden name Branigan, Sean Branigan," Hacker said. "His mother and I were divorced years ago."

For a moment. Warren thought about his own parents. There wasn't any doubt in his mind that each of them would have been much happier without the other.

Then Hacker said, "Rawlins has a wife and four-year-old daughter back in Norfolk."

Warren knew that.

"I don't want to order him to celebrate," Hacker said. "If you see him again, tell him that if he changes his mind, he's welcome."

"I'll tell him, skipper," Warren responded.

"Now get out of here and let me finish my letter," Hacker said.

"Aye, aye, sir," Warren answered, opening the door and leaving. In a few brief moments, he'd learned more about Hacker than he had known since he'd come aboard the ship.

The party was held on the quarterdeck. Because of the blackout, no lights were permitted, and when a man wanted to smoke, he had to go into the mess area to do it. But by 2300 the men got into the spirit of it and were having a good time.

The cooks had prepared roast beef and roast pork and baked apple and cherry pies. One of the men took it upon himself to be the emcee and another of the men was a good harmonica player. Two others played the guitar. And there was even a stand-up comic who could imitate Hacker's growly voice to perfection.

One of the men brought out a windup phonograph, played "Bewitched, Bothered and Bewildered," and had just put "Deep in the Heart of Texas" on the turntable when, suddenly, the IMC system came on and Rawlins said, "Now hear this... All hands now hear this... I have taken command of this ship —"

Hacker and Warren were on their feet.

"All hands to their duty stations," Rawlins said. "All hands to their duty stations... Mister Troost and Mister Bradly to the bridge..."

"You can bet he's armed," Warren said.

Hacker agreed.

"What the hell are we going to do?" Bradly asked.

Hacker looked up at the bridge windows. "He can't see us and we can't see him," he said in a low voice. "Keep the party going," he told the men. "Troost, Bradly, and Berk, come with me."

Warren followed Hacker along the passageway to the arms room, where Hacker paused to issue .45s and a clip of ammunition to him, Bradly and Berk.

"Mister Troost, Mister Bradly," Rawlins called, "come to the bridge immediately..."

Warren raced up the steps after Hacker. "Rawlins," Hacker called out, "you know you can't finish what you started."

A shot exploded on the other side of the door. Warren grabbed hold of Hacker and started to pull, when Hacker uttered a wordless scream and fell across him.

"Berk, get the skipper down to sick bay," Warren ordered.

"Aye, aye," the chief answered, and lifting Hacker up, he said, "He's been hit bad, Mister Troost."

"Get him down to sick bay," Warren said. "Bradly, give him a hand, then the two of you get back here on the double." Then he called out, "Rawlins, you hit the skipper. Put down your gun and come out now."

Rawlins didn't answer.

"I'll give you exactly ten seconds to come out," Warren said, "or I'm coming —"

Another shot exploded behind the door.

Warren was on his feet, kicked the door open, and holding the gun with his two hands, swung it in a wide arc. But he didn't see Rawlins until he looked at the floor near the chart table.

"Rawlins?" he called, moving closer.

The XO didn't answer.

Finally, Warren stood over him. The top of his head wasn't there! The food in Warren's stomach started to come up. He forced himself to swallow. He looked at the wall behind the chart table: it was blotched with blood. So was the ceiling above the table and wall.

Bradly and Berk rushed into the bridge.

"Holy Mother of God!" Berk exclaimed, looking down at Rawlins.

Bradly turned around and vomited.

"How bad is the skipper?" Warren asked.

"You're the skipper now, Mister Troost," Berk answered.

CHAPTER 21

"I'm really sorry about Hank," Lucy said.

Glen swallowed hard. He was sitting on the bed in a motel room a few miles from the San Diego navy base. The day after he'd arrived his father had called and told him that his brother Hank was among the 1200 men who were in the *Arizona* when she went down and rolled over on her side. Every time he thought about Hank, his throat tightened and his eyes became watery.

Lucy came to the bed and sat down alongside him. "You look tired, honey," she said, touching his face. "Are you working hard?"

"Jesus, Lucy, it's New Year's Day. I didn't get back to the barracks until five o'clock in the morning and then the officer of the watch gave me your message. How the hell did you find this place?" he asked, looking around the room. The wallpaper was torn and spotted with dirt; the single window was hidden by a yellowed shade; the rug on the floor was spotted with burn holes.

"I asked a cab driver to take me to a motel that was close to the base," she answered. "I didn't want to stay in the train station all night."

"This is a whore's motel," Glen said.

"Glen Lascomb! Since when did you start using words like that!" she cried, leaving the bed.

"That's what it is," he said sullenly. "You shouldn't have come. You shouldn't be here. I shouldn't be here."

Lucy sat down on the bed again and, linking her arm with his, said softly, "We have to talk, Glen."

"You came here just to talk to me?" he questioned incredulously. "Lucy —"

"Glen Lascomb, I had to come. I just had to. I wouldn't have, if —" She began to sniffle. "Glen, I missed my period. I was supposed to get it on the 10th. I have the date marked on the calendar." Her sniffles turned to sobs. "I just know I'm pregnant."

Pulling away from her, Glen stood up. "How could you be? We only did it once!"

"I thought you'd be happy," Lucy sobbed. "I thought you'd want me to have your — our — baby!"

"Lucy, it's New Year's Day. Give me a chance. I didn't expect you to come here." He lit a cigarette and began to pace.

"I don't care what day it is," she said, taking time between the words to blow her nose. "I came here full of love for you, and you're being hateful."

Glen stopped pacing and faced her. She was pretty, with blonde hair done up in curls and pert breasts jutting against the front of her dress. But there was nothing about her that made her look pregnant.

"Why are you staring at me?" she asked.

Glen shook his head.

"Yes, you were staring. Do you think you can see if I am pregnant?"

He flushed.

"That's what you were trying to do, wasn't it?"

Glen turned to the dresser, found a chipped ashtray, and stubbed out the cigarette in it.

"You know you were the first and the only one," Lucy said. "I never let another boy touch me there."

Glen faced her.

"We planned to get married —" she started to say.

"Maybe that wasn't such a good plan."

Her lips began to tremble.

Glen stepped away from the dresser. "I might —" Thinking about Hank, he paused before he said, "I might get killed out there; then what will happen to you and the baby?"

Lucy shook her head. "My prayers will protect you."

"It doesn't happen that way," Glen said quietly. "My mother prayed for Hank and —"

"Don't you still believe in God?"

He wasn't sure. But whether he believed or disbelieved wasn't the problem. "I just don't think we should get married now."

"I can't go back home," she cried, "unless I'm married. Don't you understand, I'll be carrying your child — your bastard. Everyone will know it's yours."

Glen glanced toward the door. He wanted to run out of the room.

"I'll be a fallen woman!" she cried. "Is that what you want to happen to me?"

Glen lit another cigarette and began to pace again.

"I can't believe you're doing this to me," Lucy sobbed. "You're ruining my life and the life of our child."

He wanted to say, that it wasn't his child, but he knew it was. Lucy was "cherry" when he had her.

"You said you loved me; you said you'd marry me... I'd have never let you do it, if we —"

"Do my folks know?" Glen asked.

"I didn't come straight out and tell them, but they're smart enough to read between the lines," Lucy answered.

"You tell your folks?"

"Told my ma," she said. "My pa'd kill me if he knew. Ma gave me her egg money to buy a train ticket, and I had some saved."

Glen knew the Porters. Old man Porter was a hard, God-fearing man who sure as hell would turn Lucy out of the house if he found out she was pregnant.

"Did my folks say anything special?" Glen asked.

"Only that God would guide us," Lucy answered.

"My dad?"

"Nothing."

Glen stubbed out the cigarette. He suddenly felt drained. "I go on duty in four hours and I need to sleep for a while," he said.

She patted the bed. "Sleep here."

His eyes met hers.

"I'm tired too," Lucy said. "I didn't get much sleep last night."

Glen nodded. He knew what would happen as soon as they were in bed and he also knew that he would agree to marry her.

"I'll make it good for you," Lucy said. "I promise I will."

Glen started to unbutton his jacket. Hell, he could have gotten a lot worse. She was really a very pretty woman.

Lucy stood up, pulled back the blue, threadbare bedspread, smiled at Glen, and began to undress.

CHAPTER 22

Tony was OOD. The skipper of the *Tarpon*, Lieutenant Commander Michael Brisson, was with him on the bridge.

Brisson had come topside, as he usually did, just before the *Tarpon* submerged for the day. "We'll take another half hour before we go down," Brisson said, scanning the eastern sky, already sufficiently light enough to see the dark mass of Luzon on the horizon. He spoke with a definite "down east" accent, broadening the A sounds and dropping the R's. "We have only a few hours to get in and out — and the Japs are going to be swarming all over the damn bay."

"Maybe we'll be lucky and they won't notice us," Tony answered, trying to conceal a smile. The first time they submerged, just after they cleared Pearl, Brisson got on the horn and told them that they were going to Corregidor to deliver ammunition and pick up a half dozen pilots and several nurses. Two days later they rendezvoused with the submarine tender *Orion*, loaded 50-caliber rounds, 37mm ammunition, and medical supplies for the "Rock."

Brisson chuckled. "I don't think there's that much luck in the world," he said, putting his face against the night glasses and making a 360° sweep with them. "Looks good. I'm going below. You have the conn?"

Tony nodded and waited until Brisson disappeared into the hatchway, before he stepped forward to the small control console. He liked the skipper and Christopher Bond, the executive officer, whom everyone called "Chris." The *Tarpon* was a new fleet-type boat, and her crew was new to it. Other than taking the boat on its sea trials and sailing her from San

Diego to Pearl, this was their first combat patrol together. But the crew, thanks to the skipper and Chris, was already a smoothly functioning unit and —

"Contact bearing zero two eight," the port-side lookout called from his position behind the periscope shears.

Tony swung his glasses to the bearing. A feather of black smoke was rising out of the sky. Estimating it to be at least sixteen miles away, he watched it for two minutes; then he picked up the phone. "Bridge here, target on the horizon bearing zero two eight three. Range approximately 10,000 yards."

"Skipper is on his way," the Exec answered.

Even as Tony put the phone back on the console, Brisson was scrambling up through the hatch. He nodded to Tony, put his eyes to the glasses, took a long look, then shouted, "Dive… Dive… Dive." He placed his hand on the Klaxon, giving a long continuous blast on it. "Clear the bridge!" Then bending over the open hatchway, he shouted, "Take her down, Chris."

The lookouts leapt from their positions and went down the open hatch. Tony and the captain, pulling down the lanyard to bring the hatch cover into place, followed.

Small spurts of water ran along the side of the hull as the main vents were suddenly opened. The noise made by the diesel exhaust stopped. The air intake valve for the ventilation system and the diesel engines clanked shut. Power was being shifted to the electric motors, and the bow planes were starting to rig out and bite into the water.

The quartermaster spun the locking wheel. "Hatch secured," he reported.

Air began to blow into the boat.

Tony swallowed to equalize the pressure in his ears.

Brisson went to the periscope platform and ordered, "Go to one zero zero feet."

Tony took his place at the torpedo data computer and turned it on. This wasn't a drill. They were in enemy waters. That plume of black smoke could have only come from a Japanese ship. He checked the dials. The boat's course, speed, and depth were indicated. He looked toward Brisson. There was a new kind of tension in the air. Somehow the men knew that they had spotted a Japanese ship.

The boat was down five degrees at the bow.

"Secure the air," Chris ordered in the control room below.

The roaring of the air stopped. The air pressure remained constant.

"Air holding steady, skipper," Chris reported, checking the pressure gage. "Blow negative to the mark," he ordered.

Mayer twisted the blow valve open.

The rush of air into the tank under the pressure hull made a loud hissing noise. Chief Thomas watched the needle move counterclockwise. "Negative blown to the mark," Thomas reported, after a few seconds.

"Shut negative flood valve," Chris said.

Tony heard the valve thump shut. He was able to identify the specific valve in the various systems by the sound it made when it was opened or closed in response to the skipper's or exec's commands.

"Negative flood valve shut," the man answered, taking his hand off the lever.

"Vent negative!"

More air blew into the control room.

"Negative tank vented... Vent shut," was the report.

"All ahead two thirds," Brisson ordered.

"All ahead two thirds answered, sir," the quartermaster replied.

"Negative tank is blown and secured, conn," Chris called out. "Passing through 60 feet... Trim looks good."

Brisson silently monitored the depth gages and the inclinometer; then he said, "Level off at zero one zero zero feet, control... Tell me when you have two thirds speed trim."

"One zero zero feet... Two thirds trim, aye, aye," Chris responded. "Passing zero six five feet, conn."

Visualizing what was happening below, Tony listened carefully to Brisson's commands and the exchange between him and Chris.

"Flood forward trim from the sea, 1000 pounds," Chris ordered. Moments later, he said, "Conn, forward trim flooded 1000 pounds... Stern planes on zero," Chris went on. "Pump from forward trim to after trim 500 pounds." He paused for a few moments; then he added, "Pump 500 pounds from the auxiliary tanks to the sea... Bow planes on zero." Another few moments passed before Chris called up, "Final trim, conn, one zero zero feet."

"Control," Brisson said, "good work... Bring her slowly up to periscope depth."

"Coming to periscope depth," Chris responded.

Tony felt the slight rise in the *Tarpon*'s bow. "Boat's depth zero six five feet," he told the yeoman working with him on TDC.

"Zero six five feet set," the man answered.

"Begin your search at two eight zero, true," Brisson told the sonarman.

Tony watched the sonarman adjust his headphones and twist the various knobs on the control panel. Then he moved his eyes to the target bearing indicator dials. One would show the sonar indication and the other would be set from the periscope's sighting. When the two matched, Tony knew they had an exact bearing.

"Periscope depth, conn," Chris called out.

"Hold her level," Brisson answered, kneeling down to ride the periscope out of its well.

"Target bearing two nine five," the sonarman called out, "Range, 12,000 yards... Speed 20 knots."

Brisson moved the periscope around, then stopped. "Destroyer... Down periscope," he snapped the handles up, closing them. "Helmsman, steer one six five."

"Coming to one six five," the helmsman answered.

"Chris, take her to the bottom," Brisson said. "Pass the word, rig for silent running."

"Aye, aye, sir. Passing one nine zero feet," Chris answered.

"All engines stop," Brisson ordered.

"All engines answer stop, sir," the quartermaster reported.

Brisson smiled at Tony. "We'll sit this one out and, if we're very quiet, that big cat up there won't know that this mouse is down here." Then he added, "That's what luck is all about, isn't it?"

Tony nodded. It would be a long, hot, sweaty wait until nightfall.

CHAPTER 23

Troost and Kate sat at a table in a small restaurant overlooking Waimanalo Bay. It was late Tuesday afternoon. They had driven across the Pali earlier in the day and would soon be driving back to Pearl.

"I've had such a wonderful day," Kate said.

"So have I," Troost responded, reaching across the table for her hand.

"But you're sad, aren't you?" she asked.

He kissed the back of her hand. "Not about us. I'm sad because once we're back in Pearl we have to go our separate ways."

"I understand that," Kate said, nodding, "but there's something else, isn't there?"

"Warren," he said softly.

"What about Warren?" she asked, her eyes opening wide. "He's all right, isn't he?"

"I read the reports coming out of ABDAFLOAT, that's Admiral Hows's command — what's left of our Asiatic fleet and a combination of British and Dutch warships."

"Warren's ship is with them?" Kate asked.

Troost shook his head. "It was ordered to remain in the Philippines."

"But why?" she asked.

He shrugged. "I don't know... She's not going to have much of a chance of making it."

"Can't you at least ask —"

"No. I might consider asking if the ship came under CinPacFlt," he said, "but it doesn't."

Kate looked toward the bay. "I can't even tell you to —" She looked at him. "I wish I could help you."

"I know," he nodded.

"Come with me back to the room before you leave?" Kate asked.

Troost looked out at the bay. Its clear blue water suddenly became a blur. "It would hurt to lose him, Kate."

She reached across the table and with her handkerchief wiped the tears from his eyes.

"I'm sorry," Troost said. "I shouldn't be doing this."

Kate put her hand over his. "Why shouldn't you? We should be able to share more than just our bodies. If you hadn't told me, who would you have told?"

"No one."

She kissed the tips of his fingers.

The *Tarpon* surfaced and ran awash, ready to dive the moment Brisson shouted the order and gave a single sustained blast on the Klaxon.

Tony was in the conning tower with Wally Triman, another junior officer, who had joined the boat in Pearl. Wally was the boat's designated Torpedo Officer. He was a small man with an owl-like face, whose father was the editor-in-chief of Royal Books. Wally's stated ambition was to write novels.

The two of them were waiting to be called to the bridge. Brisson put Tony in charge of the detail and named Wally as his second. They were responsible for off-loading the ammo and medical supplies and then bringing pilots and nurses on board. And Brisson stressed speed. "We've got to get in and out as quickly as possible," he said. "We have to be out of there in a matter of hours." Then he told them to curtain off three bunks to provide the nurses with some small measure of privacy. But the pilots would have to occupy whatever deck space was available.

Tony positioned himself close to the open hatch. With the *Tarpon* underway at 16 knots, there was a good flow of fresh air, some of which reached into the forward and after sections of the hull. But unless all the hatches were open and the blowers working, the air in those areas of the boat would remain hot, moist, and smelly.

"Do you think we'll head back to Pearl?" Wally asked.

"There or Australia," Tony answered.

Suddenly Wally grinned. "Wouldn't it be great if we had to take the nurses and pilots back to the States?" he asked.

"I don't know," Tony answered. "It's going to be more than a little tight in here and —"

"Unloading detail stand by," Chris called through the open hatch.

Tony put on his red goggles. "Better get them on before you go topside," he said to Wally, "or you'll lose some of your vision for a while."

Wally waved the suggestion aside. "For the first few minutes we'll be on deck and, besides, there'll be some light."

Tony shook his head. "Everything will be done in total blackness. No light coming from the open hatches."

"Christ, how the hell are we expected to see anything?"

"Put the goggles on," Tony said.

"With reluctance," Wally answered, donning the goggles.

"All engines back one third," Brisson called.

"All engines back one third, sir," the quartermaster responded.

"Rudder amidships," Brisson said, as the *Tarpon* nudged gently into the pier.

"All engines stop, secure the plant."

"All engines answer stop, sir," the quartermaster called out.

The pounding noise of the diesels abruptly ceased, leaving only the softer sound of the generators.

"Forward and after torpedo rooms, all lights out," Chris ordered.

Tony repeated the command into his sound-powered phones.

"All lights out forward torpedo room," a man responded.

"Lights out, forward and after torpedo rooms," Tony said.

Chris gave the order to open the forward and after hatches; then he called for the deck detail. "Bow line out... Stern line... Midship line."

"Lines secured," the chief called.

"All stations remain at the ready," Brisson ordered.

"Off-loading detail, topside," Chris ordered.

"That's us," Tony said, scrambling up through the open hatch.

Brisson pointed at the pier. "There are a couple of trucks. Get our men working."

"Aye, aye, sir," Tony answered and, turning to Wally, he said, "Get the medical supplies out. I'll take the ammo."

Tony worked the gang on the forward hatch. Heavy wooden boxes with Manila rope handles were hefted through the narrow hatch opening onto the deck.

Tony worked along with the men. In a matter of moments, he was sweating profusely. The night was hot and very humid. But it was worse for the men inside the boat, where the humidity was 100 percent and the temperature at the 90-degree mark.

Whenever Tony sensed a slowing in the tempo of the work, he leaned over the open hatch and shouted, "Keep moving those boxes; we don't have all night."

"How many more to go?" Brisson called down from the bridge.

Tony repeated the question to the men in the torpedo room.

"Half dozen," someone answered.

"Half dozen, skipper," Tony said.

"Let the chief handle the rest of it," Brisson told him. "You pick up our passengers. They should be waiting at the Malinta tunnel entrance, just up the road. I want to get us the hell out of here as soon as I can."

"Aye, aye, sir," Tony answered, and walked across the narrow board that served as a gangplank between the *Tarpon* and the small dock. A half dozen soldiers, stripped to the waist but wearing their "tin helmets," were hefting the ammo crates and medical supply boxes onto a couple of three-quarter-ton trucks. They worked silently.

100 yards, at the most, from the pier, Tony found himself approaching one of the entrances to the tunnel network that had been cut out of the island's rock. Designed to be impregnable, it now housed thousands of men, and its ability to withstand a sustained and concentrated assault by the Japanese was in doubt.

As he moved closer, a sewer-like smell almost made him gag. The entrance was completely dark, but about 100 feet inside there was a small glow of yellow light that washed over the ceiling and down the walls. Then, to his surprise, he realized there were men sprawled out on the floor at the entrance. He stopped. Those that were close he could see. They were as skeletal as men could be and still be alive. And their eyes were wide with fear.

Suddenly a voice to Tony's right asked, "You from the sub?"

"Ensign Trapasso," he said, peering into the darkness.

"Warrant Officer Brooks… Six pilots, three nurses, and six more on stretchers," Brooks said.

"Six on stretchers?" Tony repeated.

"Two officers and four EMs," Brooks explained. "Can't do anything for them here. But if you can get them to a ship, maybe they'll live." He spoke matter-of-factly, almost as if he were talking about something completely unimportant. "The nurses will take care of them."

Tony hesitated. The men on the *Tarpon* would be hard pressed for living- and workspace with just the nurses and pilots aboard. But six stretcher cases would —

"Anything wrong?" Brooks asked.

Tony motioned him closer. "We have to talk." Because of the darkness he still hadn't seen anything more than the man's form, which was tall and thin.

"Follow me," Brooks ordered.

Tony moved deeper into the tunnel, stepping over or walking around hundreds of men. Some were leaning against the black tunnel walls; others were stretched out on the floor. The sewer-like smell became heavier. Finally, they came into the diluted penumbra of the light and stopped.

Brooks faced him. He was a man somewhere in his 40s: a lifer. "Talk," he said. A dirty, bloodstained bandage was wrapped around his head. An unbuttoned shirt revealed that another bandage, bloodstained and as dirty as the one around his head, covered his chest. He wore a .45 low on his right hip and a trench knife on his left. He was gaunt; his wide and staring eyes, ringed with dark circles, burned with fever.

Tony had never seen a face like that and knew, even as he was looking at it, he would remember it for the rest of his life.

"You wanted to talk," Brooks said.

"The stretcher cases —"

"What about them?" Brooks challenged.

Tony took a deep breath and immediately started to cough.

"They're going with you," Brooks snarled, his hand dropping down to the hilt of the trench knife.

Tony stopped coughing. The decision wasn't Brooks's; it was his. The *Tarpon* and its crew were his responsibility. "Only the nurses and pilots," he said quietly.

Brooks grabbed him by the front of his shirt and pinned him against the rock wall. "Listen, Admiral, those stretcher cases are going on your fucking boat, or I'm going to slice you so bad, your own fucking mother wouldn't recognize you."

Tony took a deep breath. He felt the razor-sharp edge against his right cheek. None of the men nearby seemed to be aware of what was happening, or if they were, they either didn't care or lacked the strength to intervene.

"I say they're going," Brooks breathed. "What do you say, Admiral?"

"Put the knife down and step back," Tony ordered, putting authority into his voice.

"Sure, Admiral, as soon as I get the word from —"

Tony jerked his head away and kneed Brooks in the groin.

"Fucking son-of-a-bitch!" Brooks roared, staggering backwards.

Tony jumped away from the wall.

With the knife still in his hand, Brooks pulled himself up.

"Mister, put that knife away," Tony snapped.

Brooks's lips curled into a snarl. He bent into a low crouch. "This ain't settled yet, Admiral," he said, beginning to move toward Tony. "I'm not going anywhere and I have nothing to lose."

Tony backed away. Years before, when he was a runner for his father, he faced a man with knife. It was around

Thanksgiving. He was returning to the club's store with a brown paper bag that had the day's receipts from the neighborhood number operators. As he passed in front of an abandoned store, a punk came out of the entrance and, pulling a knife on him, demanded the paper bag. He dropped the bag and, grabbing the hand that held the knife, twisted it back until he heard the bones snap and saw the punk let go of the weapon.

"Those stretcher cases go, Admiral, or —"

A sudden explosion shook the tunnel. The light dimmed then brightened. Another explosion crashed down — and another.

A siren began to wail.

The men in the tunnel drew themselves up into a sitting position and, resting their arms on their knees, buried their heads in them.

Brooks stopped. His jaw went slack. He looked dazed.

From somewhere on the island, heavy guns were fired.

More rounds crashed against the island.

Tony looked back toward the entrance, wondering if the *Tarpon* was safe.

"For the love of God," Brooks said, with tears streaming down his face, "take those men."

Explosion after explosion shook the tunnel, and each one dimmed the lights.

"The nurses and the pilots," Tony said. "Get them now, or I leave without them."

Brooks turned and staggered deeper into the tunnel.

Tony went after him.

"Here," Brooks said, gesturing to a bay on the right side.

"Where the hell have you been?" one of the pilots asked.

The bay was steeped in darkness.

"Let's move," Tony said.

"Give me a hand with this stretcher," one pilot said to another.

More shells crashed down.

"Only six pilots and three nurses," Tony said. "Now let's move."

"These men —" a nurse started to say.

"I tried," Brooks said with a sob in his voice. "Admiral, didn't I try... Tell them I tried."

"He tried," Tony said, forcing the knot out of his throat. "Now let's get the fuck out of here or there won't be a boat left to take you."

There was some whispering in the bay; then one of the pilots said, "As soon as we're on your ship, I want to speak to your captain."

"That's your right," Tony answered. "Now let's move out." He turned, and without looking back to see if anyone was following him, he walked quickly toward the tunnel entrance.

Outside, Tony took several deep breaths, but the heavy moist air was filled with the stench of burnt powder. The trucks were gone. He turned. There were nine people following him. Because the nurses wore pants and shirts, he couldn't distinguish the men from the women. But each of them had a musette bag slung from their right shoulder.

"Bridge, Ensign Trapasso and nine others coming aboard," Tony called out.

"Come aboard," Brisson called out. "Deck detail, stand by to cast off."

"Standing by," the chief answered.

Tony crossed the gangplank.

"Get those people below as quickly as possible," Brisson ordered.

"Aye, aye, sir," Tony responded.

"Captain, I'm Colonel Henderson and I must speak to you," one of the men called out. He stopped on the deck and looked up toward the bridge. "There are six stretcher cases back there that your officer refused to take. I demand —"

"Get below, Colonel," Brisson said.

"Better do what he says, Colonel," Tony advised.

Henderson looked as if he were about to say something more; then changing his mind, he climbed down the hatch.

"All visiting personnel below," Tony reported.

"Mr. Trapasso, report to the bridge," Chris said.

"Aye, aye, sir," Tony answered.

"Take in all lines," Chris ordered. "Rudder amidships." He waited until the helmsman responded before he ordered, "One third back."

The diesels coughed and began to pound. The *Tarpon* backed slowly away from the pier.

The *AKO-96* was in a cove on the northeast coast of Panay. As soon as it was dark enough for her to get underway, she'd been ordered earlier in the day by ABDAFLOAT to rendezvous with the *Tarpon* five miles offshore and refuel her. Though Bradly had the watch and now, as acting exec, he was an experienced hand at getting the ship underway, Warren came up to the bridge.

"I'd say we have 20 minutes of light left," Bradly commented.

Warren agreed with a silent nod and looked at the nearby bank. It was thick with foliage. Huge cypresses came right to the water's edge and thick liana vines circled around the trunks and branches of the trees. And there seemed to be thousands of white, purple, and pink wild orchids. It reminded him of a movie set for a Tarzan film, or perhaps what he might have imagined the jungle to look like when, as a boy, he read all of the *Bomba the Jungle Boy* books he was able to get his hands on. He even had several of his own that his father had bought him for Christmas. Just beyond the bank, it was already dark and very, very quiet.

Warren looked toward the mouth of the cove. It was clear. On the starboard side was a sand spit and on the port side, the trees came down to the water. Between the two arms was an opening about 50 yards wide.

"Radar on," Bradly ordered.

"Radar on," the radar operator answered.

Bradly walked over to the chart table. "It would be a hell of a lot easier," he commented aloud, "if we could back out."

Warren turned from the jungle to him. "Too tricky without lights. As it is, we have —" A sudden noise came across the patch of water from the jungle and the next instant a flock of birds swished into the air. He glanced over his shoulder; then looking straight at Bradly, he said, "Pass the word, battle stations."

Bradly hesitated for an instant.

"Move!"

Bradly went to the phone bank.

Within minutes the forward and aft gun crews reported they were "ready." And the four .50s Warren had managed to scrounge from one of the makeshift navy bases 200 miles to the south were covering bow, stern, and both sides of the ship.

"Weigh anchor," Warren said, sweat beginning to soak through his shirt.

Bradly relayed the order to the anchor detail at the winch.

The chain rattled in and the ship began to pull up on the anchor.

"Helmsman, rudder amidships," Warren said, in a voice so low that Bradly repeated it.

"Rudder amidships, sir," the yeoman responded.

The instant the anchor broke free of the bottom, the bow began to slide to the starboard, pointing it toward the cove's entrance.

Swallowing to ease the tightness in his throat, Warren ordered, "One third ahead."

"One third ahead," the engine room signalman repeated.

Warren looked at the jungle: it was considerably darker now than it had been. The sky was sufficiently dark for several of the brighter stars to show. "The Japs are in the fucking jungle," he rasped, wondering why they hadn't opened up. "They're there."

Bradly looked at him questioningly. "Maybe they're not... Maybe it was a large animal that scared the birds," he said.

Warren didn't answer. He was concentrating on the movement of the ship toward the entrance. There was just enough light left for him to see the two sides of the opening. "Helmsman, ease to zero two zero," he said.

"Easing to zero two zero," the helmsman answered.

"Steer for the middle of the opening," Warren said.

"Aye, aye, sir," came the response.

The ship's bow was between the two tips of the opening, when the radarman said, "Skipper —"

Two enormous bright lights flashed down on the port bow.

"Back full!" Warren shouted.

"Back full," the man at the engine room telegraph answered.

Within seconds two heavy-caliber rounds slammed into the jungle on the starboard side, and at the same time another round splashed short of the stern.

"Put a couple of rounds from mount two on the bank astern of us," Warren said.

The after gun responded with two rounds close to the bank.

"There's the bastard!" the chief exclaimed, as the Japanese gunboat slid into view at the cove's entrance.

"Forward gun commence firing!" Warren ordered.

An instant later mount one began firing.

"All stop," Warren said.

"All stop," the engine room signalman answered.

Machine-gun fire raked the ship's stern. Several more rounds splashed close to her port side.

Then suddenly there was more cannon fire from the jungle.

A round dropped on the stern. The explosion wrecked the ship's number two mount and tossed the men on the .50s into the air. Two slammed down on the deck and the third went over the side.

"Knock out those floodlights," Warren said.

Bradly relayed the order to the .50-caliber crew on the bow.

One light flashed out, then the other.

Suddenly a Japanese speaking English said over the gunboat's hailing system, "Captain, you can't get out... There are soldiers in the jungle behind you and my ship is here. Surrender now and save the useless loss of life. I'd prefer not to have to sink you or call for an air strike against you at dawn... You have 10 minutes to make your decision."

The ship was dead in the water.

"Give me nine hundred RPMs so we can hold steerageway," Warren said.

The engine room signal man relayed the order by phone; then he answered, "900 RPMs, sir."

The gunboat was reversing course just beyond the cove.

Warren paced the deck. He had already lost three men and, if he tried to fight it out, he'd lose more. But surrendering the ship and the fuel to the Japanese didn't sit well with him either, nor did the idea of sitting in a Japanese prison camp. The few times he'd made supply runs to Bataan and Corregidor, he'd heard what the Japanese did to prisoners. He took several deep breaths, but the hot humid air he forced into his lungs didn't satisfy his need for fresh air. "They want this ship," he said, voicing his thoughts. "If they didn't, that Jap captain would have tried to blow us out of the water."

Just as the gunboat slid past the cove again, the Japanese officer said, "Captain, the war is over for you and your men. I urge you to think about —"

A sudden explosion turned the gunboat into a yellow and red sphere of flames.

Even as the men began to cheer, Warren ordered, "All ahead flank!"

"All ahead flank, sir," the answer came and the *AKO-96* surged out of the cove.

"Look, it's that sub we're supposed to meet!" Bradly exclaimed.

"It sure is," Warren responded. "It has to be the most wonderful, most beautiful sub in the world!"

CHAPTER 24

While the *Tarpon* lay alongside the *AKO-96* having her tanks pumped full of diesel fuel, Warren and Brisson were in the wardroom having coffee and recounting the events of the last few hours.

"The Japs were so busy with you," Brisson said, "they never saw me. I don't think they knew a sub was there until the torpedo hit and then it was too late."

"But what made you come so close inshore?" Warren asked, lighting a cigarette and offering one to Brisson.

"We were running on the surface when the OOD, Ensign Trapasso, was sure he heard gunfire," Brisson said. "We checked the charts and saw that there was a cove and figured that was where you were. The rest you know."

"It was just damn lucky that your OOD was alert," Warren commented.

"And you're damn lucky to have your own command, Lieutenant," Brisson said.

Warren studied his coffee mug for a few moments; then having made his decision, he said, "I got it by default. Commander Hacker was the ship's skipper."

"Hacker?"

"Did you know him?" Warren asked.

Brisson shook his head. "One of the nurses we took off Corregidor is Lieutenant Irene Hacker," he said, lifting a glass of iced tea.

"He mentioned he had a daughter who was a nurse and he has a son who graduates from the Academy this June," Warren said.

"Well, you'll certainly want to tell her where her father is."

"He's dead."

Brisson looked at him questioningly.

"So is Lieutenant Rawlins, the XO," Warren said.

"Both killed in action?"

Warren shook his head. "Rawlins killed Hacker; then he blew his brains out."

Brisson's hand trembled, making the ice clink against the glass. "Did you file a report?"

"Only that both officers were accidentally killed when a —"

Brisson held up his hand. "I don't want to know what you did, but I'm sure you did the right thing."

Warren nodded. "I did what had to be done to protect the reputations and the families of both men."

"Do you want to speak to Irene?" Brisson asked.

Warren thought for a moment. "I'm not a good actor. She'd know I wasn't telling the truth. If it's all the same to you, I'd prefer to pass on that one."

"I understand," Brisson said.

The two of them stood up.

"I've arranged for some of the stores to be transferred from —" he was going to say *my ship*, but instead, he said, "from this ship to your boat."

Brisson thanked him.

"We owe you," Warren said. "That Jap gunboat had us between a rock and hard place. I wasn't about to surrender."

"Didn't think you would have," Brisson responded, as they left the wardroom and went out on deck. "And thank you for allowing all of us to use your showers."

Warren smiled. "It was a lot easier than having to smell you."

"Stated bluntly, but honestly," Brisson responded.

A man from the *Tarpon* approached Brisson. "Skipper, we should be finished taking on fuel in about 15 minutes. The EO wants to top the tanks."

Brisson nodded. "Ensign Tony Trapasso, Lieutenant Warren Troost, skipper of this ship."

Tony flashed a smile. He was sweaty and stained with oil. He started to salute and said, "It gets kind of dirty from time to time."

"A handshake will do," Warren said, extending his hand. "Thanks for hearing the gunfire and doing something about it."

"The skipper was the one who did it," Tony answered.

"Thanks, anyway," Warren said.

Tony repeated Warren's surname. "I know that name."

"My father —"

Tony shook his head. "That's not it. I know a pilot who knows you. He's from Brooklyn. I met —"

"Jacob Miller?" Warren asked, excitedly.

"That's him," Tony said. "That's him. We went out to the Coast together. He told me about you. In his book, you're a great guy."

"He's not so bad himself," Warren said.

"You better believe it!" Tony exclaimed.

"When you see him, you tell him we met," Warren laughed.

"If you see him first, you tell him yourself," Tony answered. "Hey, this is great. Maybe when all of us get back to Pearl, we'll have one hell of a celebration."

"Skipper, will you join us?" Tony asked, looking at Brisson.

"Sure, he'll join us," Warren said. "He and every man on the *Tarpon* will join us. Hell, we can't ever pay them enough for giving us back our lives."

"If the food and drink are free," Brisson laughed, "sure I'll join you. But what choice did we really have? None. You had the fuel. If the Japs had gotten it, we wouldn't have. To save ourselves, we had to save you."

"Listen," Warren said, "don't destroy the few illusions I have left. Let me believe that you saved us because we needed saving."

"And you just happened to be on the same side," Tony added.

"That too," Warren said.

"I better get back to the boat," Tony said, "and make sure the EO doesn't find some empty barrels to take a few more gallons just in case."

"As soon as we're topped," Brisson said, "you and the EO have 15 minutes to come on board here and shower down. Tell them to go easy on the water. We just about have enough for our own needs."

"Thanks, skipper," Tony answered, saluting him because they were in the presence of another officer, who probably wouldn't be familiar with the informality aboard the *Tarpon*.

Brisson waited until Tony was out of earshot before he said, "He's a good officer and knows how to make hard decisions."

"Sooner or later that's something all of us have to do," Warren responded.

"Speaking about hard decisions, that's Lieutenant Hacker coming toward us now," Brisson said, looking past Warren.

Warren turned around. Irene Hacker was smiling. She was a petite woman, with a good figure that even the baggy khaki pants and oversized shirt she was wearing couldn't hide. She didn't resemble Hacker in the least.

Brisson introduced them and said, "Please excuse me, I have some things to check out before we get underway again."

"I hope you had a good shower," Warren said, not able to think of anything else to say and, at the same time, not wanting to appear to be gauche or unfriendly.

"Delicious," she answered. "Three glorious minutes under scalding hot water with half a bar of Ivory soap was a dream come true."

Warren laughed.

"Tell me, Captain, is there any way I can bribe you to pack up the shower and soap and send it across to that excuse for a ship down there," she said, pointing to the low, dark shape of the *Tarpon*.

"In a week, 10 days at the very most, you'll be back in Pearl," Warren said, "and then you can even have a bubble bath and all that goes with it." Suddenly he found himself imagining her naked in a bathtub full of perfume-scented bubbles...

"Captain, is anything wrong?" she asked.

He felt himself flush but knew that in the darkness she couldn't see it. "I'm sorry," he apologized.

For several moments, they looked at one another without speaking; then she said, "I better get aboard the boat."

Warren put his hands on her arms. "Don't go yet... I —"

She scowled. "Don't do, or say, anything you'll be sorry for," she warned, twisting away from him.

He took a deep breath. "You're making a mistake," he told her.

"No, but you were about to," she said and, turning around, she started to walk away.

"Irene, your father was skipper of this ship," he said, following a few steps after her.

She stopped and faced him. "Is this some sort —"

Warren put out his hand and took hold of hers. "Come with me," he said.

She nodded.

Warren led her into the wardroom. "Sit down," he said and asked if she would like a cup of coffee.

"No," she answered quietly.

He stood in front of the coffee urn. She had a small, doll-like face, with dark blonde hair, almost brown, and Hacker's blue eyes; only the blue of hers was richer.

"Where is he?" she finally asked.

"He was buried at sea on January first," Warren answered.

She stiffened. "Killed in action?" she asked in a whisper.

"No," Warren said and explained what happened.

Irene bit her lower lip. She stood up and began to pace back and forth; then she stopped. "I didn't even know he'd been given command of a ship."

"I didn't think so at first," Warren said, "but he was a good skipper."

"Thank you for being honest."

"If you want anything of his —"

She shook her head. "Nothing," she said. "I scarcely knew the man. Now and then he was around and when he was, he was difficult to —" She stopped and tried hard to keep herself from sobbing.

Warren went to her and put his arms around her.

"This is so stupid," she said, talking into his chest. "So stupid."

Warren couldn't think of an appropriate response, but he found himself intensely aware of her.

"I must have wished him dead hundreds of times," she said. "But now that he is, I suddenly feel empty and alone." With tears streaming down her cheeks, she looked up at him and asked, "Was he really a good skipper?"

Warren nodded. "And a brave man too," he told her.

She managed a smile. "You are too, Captain," she said and kissed him lightly on the lips.

CHAPTER 25

Jacob was in the cockpit of his F4F, waiting for the flight deck address system to blare: "Stand clear of propellers... Start engines." It was dark. But a full moon was just setting and the flight deck was bathed in moonlight. Soon dawn would break. He checked his safety belt and his parachute harness; then he craned his neck and looked from side to side. The two pilots on either side of him looked relaxed, almost bored. But he was so nervous that he felt his stomach alternately tighten and churn. He was, as the saying went, "chewing buttonholes in his seat pack."

This would be his first strike mission over enemy territory since he'd become a member of Fighting Squadron Six aboard the Big E. On previous days, as the ship entered enemy-dominated waters, Fighting Six flew combat air patrol missions over the ship only to defend her against possible air attacks. But today all of Air Group Six was going into combat. Twelve VF6 aircraft in two groups would make bombing and strafing attacks on a Japanese-held atoll in the Marshall and Gilbert Islands. If any Japanese fighters rose to intercept them, they'd jettison their 100-pound bombs and fight air-to-air. This was going to be his first combat experience. He took a deep breath and slowly exhaled. He wished he had a cigarette. The wait seemed interminable.

Suddenly he realized the ship was turning into the wind.

"Start engines," the voice on the flight deck address system finally ordered.

Jacob hit the starter button; the shotgun cartridge in the starter fired and the engine coughed. The propeller made a partial revolution and stopped. The plane captain pulled out the spent round, inserted a fresh one, and held his thumb up.

Jacob pushed the starter button again. The engine coughed, sputtered, and came to life with a steady roar.

Ahead and on either side of him the exhaust from the engines of other planes flamed red, white, and then hot blue.

He would be the fifth plane out of the 12 scheduled to take off for the strike. Already three were in the air. The plane in front of him was rolled into position. On signal from the crouching deck officer it raced down the deck.

Jacob unlocked his plane's wings. The handlers spread them and, as they thumped into place, locked them. In answer to the taxi director's signals, he moved his plane forward and finally into take-off position; sucking in his breath, he waited for the launch signal.

The Launch Officer went down on one knee and extended his right arm toward the bow.

Jacob's left hand kept the throttle forward as far as it would go. He released his foot pressure on the brake pedals, lowered his toes to the rudder pedals, and was racing down the deck. In seconds, he was airborne, settling slightly toward the sea and the next instant climbing for altitude. He raised his flaps, cranked up his wheels, veered slightly to the starboard, and glanced over his shoulder back at the carrier, just as another plane cleared the deck. To his horror, he saw it stagger and plunge into the sea.

"Goddamn," Jacob swore, "he spun in!" But he couldn't think about the crash; now he had to concentrate joining up on the plane ahead of him.

He was wingman to Lieutenant John Yancy, a Mississippian, who had told him several days before, "I hate Jews more than I hate Catholics. You get your fuckin' chestnuts in a jam, you get 'em out, you hear. Because, I don't risk my ass for any son of Satan."

"And what if you get your fuckin' chestnuts in a jam?" Jacob had asked.

"Don't worry about me none," Yancy had said. "I got friends here who'll help me, if it comes to that."

Jacob had nodded and walked away.

The 11 VF6 aircraft circled the Big E and then headed toward the targets. Jacob put on his oxygen mask and at 15,000 feet the Flight Leader leveled off. Five aircraft would attack Wotje atoll; the remaining six would strike Maloelap. Orders were to maintain radio silence to and from the target until the captain decided not to. The pilots could use only hand signals to "talk" to each other.

Jacob checked each of the instruments in the cockpit. All of the readings were normal. He was close in on Yancy's port wing. The planes in the group were flying in a tight left echelon formation. At sea level it was still dark, but at 15,000 feet the setting moon and the rising sun were on opposite ends of the horizon, and there was sufficient light for him to clearly see Yancy, who faced him.

Jacob stuck his thumb up.

Yancy immediately looked the other way.

Speaking to himself, Jacob said, "Nice to know you're there, old buddy."

He listened to the steady throb of the engine and found the sound reassuring. A great many thoughts ran through his mind, but none of them stayed more than an instant before it was replaced by another.

Moment by moment, the sky around him was becoming brighter and brighter. He looked at his watch. It was 0515. In 15 minutes, they'd be over their target. The plan was to surprise the enemy as they had been surprised Pearl Harbor.

The Flight Leader began to nose down slightly and in a matter of seconds, Jacob saw a dark-hued speck in the ocean below, over which hung scattered white cotton-candy looking clouds. He concentrated on keeping his position on Yancy's wing. The atoll was beginning to have definition, especially around its irregular perimeter. He could see the clear blue water inside the atoll's lagoon and the white ring of surf on the outside of it.

The CO signaled his flight to open out and prepare to dive.

Jacob reduced the throttle and dropped back from Yancy's wing. All six aircraft were strung out in a long line, ready to push over and follow the leader. Jacob checked his altimeter: the needle moved through 12,000 feet. Suddenly, he felt disembodied and his other self was watching him. That he was actually going into combat for the first time struck him as being extraordinary, especially since it was going to happen on such a beautiful morning with the sun now above the horizon in the east and darkness still claiming much of the distant sky in the west.

"Soon," he told himself. "Very soon." And he looked ahead at Yancy's plane. Would this man really let him die if things got tough? The question flapped in the winds of his brain like some tattered ensign of doubt. Could this man, whose machine was only a few hundred yards ahead of his, be as much his enemy as —

The Flight Leader pushed over and began his dive.

The other self melded with Jacob's corporal being and he reached forward to the master armament switch and flipped it to its ON position. The red cover was raised and the switch indicated ON. He charged the two outboard machine guns; then the two inboard. His hand went back to the stick and his forefinger rested on the trigger, while his thumb caressed the button on the top of the stick that would "pickle off" the bombs. He was ready and pushed forward on the stick.

His eyes went to the altimeter — 10,000 feet and unwinding.

Jacob could see the leader barreling down at the target. The second and third planes and Yancy were in steep dives. The air screamed past him. The island grew larger and larger. He could see the runway and there were several hangars. Planes were on the runway. Men were running.

Jacob pointed his ship at a group of three dive bombers. The red circles on the wings of the aircraft grew larger. His eyes went to the altimeter. 2000 feet! The pull-out point. Puffs of black smoke blossomed in various sectors of the sky. Machine-gun tracers from the ground seemed to float up toward him.

Yancy pulled out of his dive and was clear.

Jacob's finger pressed the trigger. The four 50s began to hammer. Tracers were chewing into the parked aircraft.

Yancy's first bomb hit and exploded to the side of the runway.

Jacob pushed his own bomb release button and at the same time released the machine-gun trigger and eased back on the stick. He was level and low over the field. He came back hard on the stick. The Gs pushed him against the back of the seat.

"Climb, you fucker," he shouted, "climb!" He was gaining altitude. He looked back. Flames and black smoke were coming from one of the hangars and several of the aircraft.

The black puffs of antiaircraft fire seemed closer.

"We're going in again," the flight leader said, suddenly breaking radio silence. "Follow me. Keep the same interval on each other." He was climbing fast and turning back toward the atoll. "Pick your targets," the flight leader said. "I have that tanker in the lagoon."

"Planes on the runway," Yancy called out.

"Oil storage tanks," Jacob radioed.

The other pilots picked their aiming points.

"They'll be waiting for us this time... You're on your own," the captain said. He went straight in with his guns blazing.

Following Yancy, Jacob streaked down at the island. Just as he came over the lagoon, he banked sharply to the starboard and spotted four enemy fighters taxiing on the runway. In minutes they'd be airborne.

"Four Zeros on the runway," Jacob said, trying to keep the excitement out of his voice. Sweat soaked his shirt and dripped off the end of his nose.

"Go get 'em, Jake," the flight leader answered. "I'll be there in a minute."

Jacob centered the tail-end Zero in his gun sight.

The Zero and the three ahead of him were moving rapidly down the runway.

Jacob dropped his nose a bit to lead him and then he pressed the trigger.

The white tracers passed the Zero's nose. Suddenly the whole plane burst into flames and veered off the runway.

Jacob eased the stick back to take the next Zero in his sights and continued to fire his four 50s.

The tracers enveloped the plane and it slewed around in a great circle on the runway.

Jacob pulled up and, looking back, he banked hard to the port. The second Zero was on fire too.

"Good work, Jake," the captain called. "I'll try to get the other two."

"Going around for another run," Jacob answered, climbing out over the ocean to a thousand feet. There were black puffs of smoke all over the sky now and tracer trails from the ground crisscrossed one another, making a huge spiderweb that hung over the island.

"I've hit one, Captain," one of the VF6 pilots shouted.

Jacob craned his neck to look around; then suddenly, at three o'clock on his starboard side, he saw the plane explode and its pieces fall into the sea.

"Fighters coming up!" another pilot yelled.

Jacob climbed, searching for contacts.

"Yance, look out... He's on your tail," a pilot yelled.

"Where the fuck is that Jew boy?" Yancy answered.

Jacob banked over to the left and saw the two planes.

Yancy was doing a roll, frantically trying to shake the Japanese fighter off his tail.

At full throttle, Jacob streaked toward them. He put the Zero in his sight and pressed the trigger... The guns didn't fire. He was very close to the Zero and had time to recharge only two guns. He pressed the trigger again. The two guns chattered briefly, then stopped.

"Get him!" Yancy shouted. "Get the fucker!"

Jacob zoomed past the Zero. He could almost see the enemy's face. For an instant he was between Yancy and the Japanese guy.

"What the hell is wrong with you?" Yancy screamed.

Jacob wiped the sweat from his eyes, banked sharply to the right, and was going to come around for another try at the Zero, when suddenly the Zero's nose dropped and he broke off contact.

"Join on me," the flight leader said. "Join on me... Good work... We're going home... No more chatter. Radio silence. Let's go!"

Jacob looked back at the island. Several fires were burning and black columns of smoke were beginning to mushroom out over it. He started to climb and in a matter of minutes, slid into place alongside Yancy, who gestured to him with a clenched fist.

"Reb," Jacob said aloud, because it made him feel good to hear the words, "Reb, you take that and shove it up your ass." Then he raised his fist and shook it at Yancy.

Jacob circled the Big E. The signal flags, "FOX" for the letter F, were "Two-Blocked" at the yardarms to indicate that the ship was recovering her aircraft. He would be the last plane down. The adrenaline was still flowing, and he knew that once he was on board there would be a confrontation with Yancy. His flaps, wheels, and arresting hook were down, and his shoulder harness locked. He turned toward the ship and picked up the landing signal officer's orange paddles.

The LSO's paddles gave a series of signals and he corrected his approach to answer them.

The orange paddles were now being held straight on either side of the LSO's body.

A "ROGER!"

Jacob was at the cut point over the ship's stern.

The LSO made a quick slashing movement with the right paddle across his chest.

Jacob cut the throttle. Then the plane touched down and rolled forward. An instant later its hook grabbed an arresting wire and Jacob's shoulder harness kept him from being thrown forward into the instrument panel as his Wildcat came to a stop.

Jacob slid the wing-unlocking lever forward.

Plane handlers pushed the plane's wings back into a folded position and moved Jacob into a spot among the other parked aircraft on the forward part of the deck.

Jacob unbuckled his chute and, as he cleared the cockpit, he told the plane captain, "My guns stopped firing... I tried to clear them but couldn't."

"I'll get right on it," the man answered.

"I don't want to get caught like that again," Jacob said angrily, "I'll —" He looked toward the ready room, which was in the island structure, a few feet to the rear of one of the forward gun mounts.

Yancy was at the entrance, waiting for him.

"Let me know what went wrong," Jacob growled.

"Aye, aye, sir," the plane captain answered.

Jacob headed for the ready room.

"Okay, Jew boy, tell me what the hell you think you were doin'?" Yancy challenged, blocking the entrance.

Jacob's eyes became slits. "I'll tell you —"

The Klaxon sounded; then over 1MC, a voice said, "General Quarters... All hands man your battle stations... All hands man your battle stations!"

"We'll settle this later, Jew boy," Yancy said, stepping back.

The Big E's antiaircraft guns and those of her escorts began to fire to the starboard. The ship heeled to the port as the captain maneuvered to throw the bombers off their aiming points.

"Five Bettys coming in low on the starboard side," came over the 1MC.

In an instant the pilots in the ready room were thrown into panic. They'd rather be in the air than defenseless during an air attack. Several tried to hide under the tables, and others used chairs for cover.

"Crazy!" Jacob shouted at Yancy. "I'll take my chances outside." And he left the ready room.

The nearby mount was banging away at the incoming Bettys. Hot shell casings clattered onto the deck.

"They're nuts in there!" Yancy exclaimed, coming out of the ready room.

Jacob pointed to the incoming planes in a tight V, low on the starboard side, surrounded by antiaircraft bursts.

"Shit, we ain't hit one of those fuckers!" Yancy shouted.

The bombers swooped across the turning ship: bomb-bay doors open.

Jacob could see the bombs fall.

Split seconds later explosion followed explosion. Huge geysers of water shot up from the sea on the port side — but none of the bombs landed on the ship.

The planes roared away from the ship across her deck; the five-inch guns and machine guns fired furiously after them. Suddenly one of the bombers, smoking from an engine, swung away from the other planes to the left, circled back toward the ship, and began to come at the Big E as if it was going to land on its deck.

"The son-of-a-bitch is going to crash into the parked planes!" Jacob yelled.

The Betty was low, trying to line up with the flight deck.

Rear seat gunners in the parked Dauntless dive bombers trained their .30-calibers on the oncoming aircraft and were firing in unison with the ship's other guns.

The Big E heeled further as she answered a hard-right rudder.

The Japanese pilot tried to follow the turning ship and dropped lower and lower. He was hit. He almost veered off, but quickly straightened out.

The Betty slammed down on the deck and, as it skidded toward the port catwalk, its starboard propeller severed the tail section of a Dauntless before it fell into the sea.

Jacob saw the man, in what was left of the wrecked Dauntless, slump over his gun.

"Let's go," Jacob shouted and he began to run across the deck, with Yancy close behind him.

Flames sprang up in the catwalk and were spreading under the Dauntless.

Together Jacob and Yancy clambered up the wrecked fuselage and hauled the gunner out of the plane. There was an ugly gash across his forehead and he was bleeding profusely.

Corpsmen, carrying a wire stretcher basket, ran toward them.

"I'm all right," the man insisted, as he was put into the stretcher. "I knocked my head against the gun when the Jap crashed into my plane… Goddamn, I was scared shitless when I knew he'd hit me." Then looking up at Jacob and Yancy, he managed a smile and said, "Thanks, guys. Thanks. I wouldn't have gotten out alone."

The corpsmen lifted the stretcher and quickly carried the man into the sick bay.

Side by side, Jacob and Yancy walked back toward the ready room.

"I was about to tell you, my guns jammed," Jacob said, looking at the man.

Yancy grinned. "Jew boy, I should have known. You got balls, I'll say that for ya."

"So do you, Reb," Jacob answered. "So do you."

CHAPTER 26

Admiral Troost was on the bridge of the *Albany*. The heavy cruiser *Brockton* was on the starboard, the *Williamsburg* was on the port side and the destroyer *Emmens* was 1000 yards in front of the three cruisers. Their mission was to bombard the island of Wotje. Fighter bombers from the Big E had raided it earlier to suppress counter air attack and, even before the island came into view, the black smoke from the still burning fires hung over the island.

"Admiral, my aircraft reports no visible sign of shore batteries or air activity," Captain Hasse, skipper of the *Albany*, repeated over the navigation squawk box as the information was radioed from one of its scout seaplanes.

"Signal the *Emmens* to move to within 5000 yards," Troost, on his bridge, said, turning to his watch officer.

The WO relayed the order by phone to the signal bridge.

Troost raised his glasses and watched the *Emmens* execute his order. This combined air and shore bombardment operation on the Gilbert and Marshall Islands had been suggested from Washington by Admiral King, now COMINCH, the most senior man in the navy, to Admiral Nimitz, who had become CinPacFlt. Despite the losses at Pearl Harbor, King was very anxious to take the offensive in the Pacific. The idea submitted by his staff on January 2 was hotly debated in Washington and Pearl before it was finally deemed feasible.

One of the flag bridge phones rang.

Troost's watch officer took it. "*Emmens* is at 5000 yards... Reports no hostile fire... Several large craft in the lagoon."

"How far are we from the island?" Troost asked.

"14,000 yards," the watch officer answered.

"Tell the *Emmens* to remain at her present position," Troost said. "We'll join her and the four of us will move to 5000 yards to begin our bombardment."

The WO relayed the message.

"At least we won't have return fire," Troost observed, continuing to scan the island with his glasses; then looking at his watch officer, he said, "Put a signal in the air from me to all ships to stand by to form a column: the *Emmens* in the van, followed by this ship, then the *Brockton* and the *Williamsburg*... *Emmens* will guide... Speed 25 knots... Standard interval... Let me know when they have two-blocked their hoists."

"Aye, aye, sir," the WO answered, picking up the phone to the signal bridge.

Addressing himself to the bridge watch in general, Troost said, "We'll pass the island from south to north firing to port, reverse course, and fire from starboard as we run south." Then going to the squawk box, he asked, "Captain Hasse, what do you make the range?"

"Fire Control makes it 8000 yards," Hasse answered and added, "I understand the flag hoists in the air."

Troost nodded. The damage from the air strikes was becoming clear. Several buildings were on fire and two ships in the lagoon were burning.

After being advised that all of the ships understood the hoisted signals, Troost said, "Execute the signals now flying." In a matter of minutes he would order the captains of the individual ships to fire at will and it would be up to them and their gunnery officers to carry out the bombardment.

"Column formed, sir," the watch officer reported.

Troost scanned the shoreline with his glasses. He glanced at the clock on the rear bulkhead of the bridge.

"Range 5000 yards," a staff member at the flag bridge radarscope called out.

Troost glanced at the clock. As the clock's second hand touched 12, Troost picked up the radio microphone and, breaking radio silence, transmitted over the primary tactical circuit. "This is Red Rover, all ships of this task group commence firing at will." He moved to the chart table and looked down at a map of the island. Given its length, the ships would be able to fire effectively for five minutes. Then —

The silence on the bridge was broken as the *Emmens* commenced firing. Three rounds from her five-inch gun mounts burst beyond the beach, raising a sudden curtain of white sand into the air. She continued firing.

The *Albany*'s eight-inch gun turrets commenced firing. The thunder of the salvos was deafening, and the recoil sent a shudder through the ship. The *Brockton* and *Williamsburg* opened up.

Even with cotton in his ears, Troost found the noise deafening.

Fires sprung up ashore and in the lagoon. New plumes of smoke pushed into the sky.

Suddenly the watch officer pointed to the beach and shouted, "Look, Admiral, counter fire!"

There were red flashes on the shoreline. The Japanese had skillfully camouflaged three shore batteries.

The *Emmens* took a hit in her stern and a fire flared up.

The tactical radio circuit came alive with the *Emmens* reporting she was having rudder control problems. Moments later she reported, "I have dead and wounded. Damage control—"

A shell came screaming toward the *Albany* and slammed into the port side just below the navigation bridge. A tremendous explosion tore away the port side of Basse's bridge.

Troost couldn't raise Hasse on the squawk box and rushed down the ladder to the captain's bridge. Blood and debris were everywhere. Hasse and the chief quartermaster were lying on the deck.

"Get a doctor and some corpsmen up here on the double," Troost shouted; then turning to the helmsman, he asked, "Do you have rudder control?"

"Yes, sir," the dazed man answered.

Troost turned to the shaken OOD. "Hold your course and speed," he ordered. "Inform your executive officer to take command."

The guns from the three cruisers continued to pour salvos into the shore batteries.

Suddenly there were two huge explosions on the beach and the shore batteries fell silent.

Less than four minutes had passed since the firing began.

"Admiral, the *Emmens* reports she has regained rudder control," the squawk box from the flag bridge blared, "and can continue as guide. Damage is not severe."

Troost suddenly realized that the doctor and the corpsmen were attending to the bridge casualties. He picked up the PRITAC microphone. "This is Red Rover," he said. "Cease firing… Cease firing!"

A sudden silence fell over the sea.

The doctor came to Troost. "Admiral, I'm sorry to have to tell you the CO and the quartermaster are dead," he said. "The skipper —" The man shook his head. Hasse's chest had been torn open.

Troost nodded and returned to his own bridge. Though he actually liked Hasse, he couldn't deny his deep feeling of jealousy. There were times when Troost found himself wondering if Kate would ever love him as much as she had Hasse. And then he'd tell himself *it's none of your business — the only thing that really matters is that she needs and wants you with the same intensity that you need and want her.* More than once she'd told him, "You are a separate part of my life, something I want and don't have to share with anyone else." That was true. She didn't even share him with Gloria. Just as he was separate and apart for her, she was the same for him. She was a gift that only she could bestow...

Troost clenched his teeth and tore himself away from his personal thoughts. Now he had to get his ships the hell out of the area.

CHAPTER 27

"All stop," Warren said.

"All stop," answered the order telegraph watch.

Warren peered through the bridge window into the darkness made even blacker by a heavy fog. "I can't see a fucking thing," he complained and went out to the starboard open wing of the bridge. "One third back."

The signalman repeated the command.

"All stop," Warren called from the flying bridge. The *AKO-96* had been ordered to this particular cove on Mindanao, not far from Cagayan, by ABDAFLOAT to evacuate several high-ranking U.S. officers and Filipino officials and take them to Australia.

"All stop," the signalman repeated.

"Ahoy there, A kay oh 96," a man called from somewhere off the starboard bow. "Ahoy, A kay oh 96."

Warren cupped his hands in front of his mouth. "A kay oh 96," he answered. "Who are you?"

"I am Major Luis, Philippine Army. I have a message for you. Permission to come aboard?" the man asked.

"Permission granted," Warren called through his cupped hands. "Come alongside my starboard side." He could hear what sounded like the splash of a paddle.

"Skipper," the OOD called out, "a small boat is approaching on our starboard side. I can barely make him out."

"Will drop the hook and take him aboard," Warren said; then turning to the boatswain mate of the watch, he said, "Put a ladder over the starboard and take the major on board."

"Aye, aye, sir," the man responded.

Warren checked the Fathometer. There was 30 feet of water under the keel. He turned to the OOD. "Is the anchor ready?"

"Anchor detail manned and ready," the OOD answered.

"Stand by to let go anchor," Warren said.

"Anchor ready for letting go," the OOD reported.

"Let go anchor!"

Warren could hear the splash of the anchor and the rapid rattle of the anchor chain as it ran out.

"Post armed lookouts forward and aft," Warren said.

"Aye, aye, skipper," the OOD replied.

Warren stepped onto the bridge wing. "Is that man aboard yet?" he called down.

"Aboard," a voice below answered.

Warren nodded with satisfaction and stepped back inside the bridge. Then filling and lighting his pipe, he waited for the boatswain mate to bring the visitor to the bridge.

The door opened and a voice said, "I am Major Rudy Luis."

Even on the blacked-out bridge, Warren could see that Major Luis was a short, wiry man with a rifle slung over his right shoulder.

"Captain," Luis said, extending his hand.

"Lieutenant Troost," Warren answered, shaking the man's hand.

"I'm glad to see that you didn't have too much difficulty finding this place," Luis said. He spoke with a definite island accent.

"The fog is the problem," Warren answered.

Luis nodded and made a clicking sound with his tongue; then he said, "You're safe here as long as you wish to stay. This area is held by my men. Your ship is under my protection."

"Thank you," Warren answered. "But as soon as our passengers arrive, I intend to leave."

Again, Luis made a clicking sound with his tongue, but this time he did not nod. "I am to tell you those plans have been changed," he said. "General Mac-Arthur and the President of the Philippines were flown out earlier today."

Warren puffed hard on his pipe. He had no idea who his passengers were to have been. His ship was not really prepared to transport and protect such important men. He was glad the plans were changed, but now he wondered what was going to happen to him and his crew. The longer he stayed in the islands, the less chance his ship had of surviving. Sooner or later the Japanese would get him. "Where the hell does that leave us?" he growled, angry that ABDAFLOAT hadn't messaged directly to him and given him specific instructions.

Luis shrugged. "You and your crew are welcome to stay here," he said. "But if you do, we will have to strip your ship and use what we can of her for our own purposes."

The OOD suddenly started to cough, and several of the other men on the bridge cleared their throats.

"We'll sail as soon as the fog lifts," Warren said.

"Back to the Rock?" Luis asked, using Corregidor's nickname.

"No," Warren said. "The Japs are thick as fleas there."

"Where then?"

He took the pipe out of his mouth and uttering a deep sigh, he muttered, "I wish the hell I knew... Maybe, by the time we get to sea, somebody will tell me."

Despite the darkness, Warren could sense that every man on the bridge was looking at him.

Warren puffed on his pipe. Given the disastrous situation in the Philippines, remaining at sea until he received further orders would be the most logical action possible to preclude his ship and crew from either being destroyed or being captured by the Japanese.

At that moment a messenger from the radio shack entered the bridge and said, "Captain, here's a priority message for your eyes only."

Warren took the paper and read it hurriedly. A smile crossed his face. "We're ordered to return to Pearl!" he exclaimed.

The men on the bridge cheered.

"Mr. Luis," Warren said, "will you join me and my executive officer in the wardroom for a cup of coffee? It's all I can offer you."

CHAPTER 28

Troost and Gloria were in a room in the Sands, a hotel in the downtown section of Honolulu. Lillian was already out looking over the shops.

"I told you I'd come out here," Gloria said, smiling. "It took a bit of doing but —"

"I would have sent for you when the time was right," he said, knowing he was lying, that he'd have done nothing.

Gloria laughed. "Well, look at it this way: it's one problem you don't have to deal with."

Troost was sitting in a chair and Gloria was on the bed opposite him. "I came as soon as I got your message," he said. She wore a white dress and looked older than he remembered. "Aren't you going to ask how I got here?"

"No doubt you were flown."

She smiled. "But it was a perfectly awful experience; then when I finally did reach here, I was told you would not be available for several days."

He nodded. "I was —"

"At sea?"

"Yes… You should be reading about it in the newspaper in a few days."

"Have you heard anything more about Warren?" she asked.

Troost shook his head. "The situation in the Philippines is confused and very grave."

Gloria sighed. "Well," she said, "the most important thing now is to get us a decent place to live in. This place is really terrible and —"

Troost stood up. "You and Lillian are going to have to find the apartment —"

"I want a small house," Gloria said. "I have never lived in an apartment and I don't intend to start now. I know, if you wanted to, you could get us a house." She left the bed and approached him. "It would be for you as much as for us. You would have a place to return to after your missions at sea." She put her arms around him. "Andy, it would be so easy for you to do it."

He took hold of her arms and lowered them. "You and Lillian will have to find it," he said quietly.

Gloria walked to the window and turned to face him. "Is there another woman?" she asked quietly.

Troost didn't answer. In his 25 years of marriage, he'd had three love affairs. The last had ended some five years before.

"Where do we go from here?" she asked, when he failed to respond.

"I can't answer that now," he said, moving away from her. "I just returned. I have to —" He thought about Kate. By now she would have received official notification of Peter's death. "I have things that I must take care of. I'll try to come by later this evening. I want to see Lillian."

"That would be nice, considering you're her father."

Without comment, Troost picked up his hat.

"I must say," Gloria added bitterly, "there's nothing like a war combined with some adulterous sex to put a bounce in an old man's steps."

Troost flushed.

"Don't be angry, Andy. It was really a compliment. The war seems to have rejuvenated you. Perhaps it will do the same for me."

"If I can't come by," Troost said, going to the door and opening it, "I'll phone."

"Do that," Gloria answered.

Troost nodded, stepped into the hallway, and closing the door behind him, felt relaxed to be out of the room.

Later in his office, after Troost finished writing his report of the action against Wotje, in which he took full responsibility for ordering the close inshore bombardment, he sat back in his chair and had time to reflect on his meeting with Gloria. The truth of the matter was that he wanted out of the marriage. But there were several factors that mitigated against a divorce. The first was that Gloria wouldn't consent to it. Second, there was his career: her family had enough influence in very high places to affect it. And third, despite the way they related to each other, there were those many ties that two people build between them over years of marriage. He uttered a deep sigh and whispered to himself, "I love you, Kate…"

It was just 1800 when the phone rang. It was Commander Wallace phoning from Service Force CinPac Fleet to say, "I thought you'd like to know that your son's ship, the *AKO-96*, will be arriving the day after tomorrow. Her ETA is approximately 1500 hours. I'll let you know as soon as she's assigned docking space."

"Thank you," Troost said.

"Seems as if your son is something of a hero," Wallace said. "I don't know all of the details. But he has skippered the ship for months."

"Thank you again," Troost said.

"My pleasure, Admiral," Wallace answered and hung up.

Troost put the phone down and for several moments did nothing. Warren was never far from his thoughts.

The phone rang again.

He picked it up and said, "Admiral Troost here."

"I'd like to see you," Kate told him.

"6:30, give or take a few minutes," he said; then he asked, "Do you want to meet me —"

"There's no need for that now," she responded quietly.

Then he said, "Gloria and Lillian arrived while I was at sea."

"Oh! Perhaps it would be inconvenient —"

"No, I want to see you... I have good news I want to share with you."

"About Warren?"

"His ship will be in Pearl the day after tomorrow," Troost said. "But there's more. I'll tell you when I see you."

"I look forward to it," she answered.

Troost listened for the click on the other end before he put the phone down.

CHAPTER 29

Glen sat at a bar in a dimly lit cocktail lounge nursing a beer and listening to the jukebox play "I Got It Bad and That Ain't Good."

Earlier he had gone to see the *Arizona* and, standing on the pier, he wept for his brother Hank and promised to avenge his death. That there were the bodies of over a thousand men still aboard her was almost too much for him to believe.

Glen had arrived in Pearl the previous morning aboard the destroyer *Harium*. He was assigned to her immediately after completing his time at the Officer Training School at the University of California in San Diego. He was the ship's radar officer.

When the record stopped playing, Glen turned to the jukebox and saw a long-legged woman enter the room. She wore a floral-print skirt and a white blouse, open at the neck, and a white headband held her shoulder-length blonde hair in place.

Almost at the bar, she paused. There were three empty stools. One was next to Glen; the other two were at the other end of the bar.

She started toward one of the other stools then suddenly changed her direction and headed for the vacant stool next to Glen. He looked at her fingers: no engagement ring and no wedding ring.

"I'll have a very dry martini," the woman told the barkeep.

The barkeep, a young man with a pockmarked face and big yellow teeth, smiled at her. "Name's Jimmy," he said.

She didn't answer.

"How about another brew, Jimmy?" Glen asked.

"Yeah, yeah," Jimmy said. "Another brew... Hold your horses, Admiral."

She looked at Glen.

"Put a uniform on some guys," Jimmy said, "and right away they start ordering everybody around."

Glen flushed.

"Listen," Jimmy said, "I finish up here in 20 minutes and I know a great Chinese restaurant that —"

"Why don't you just make the martini, Jimmy, instead of trying to make time with my friend," Glen said.

The woman's eyes opened wide.

"Your friend?" Jimmy challenged.

Glen nodded vigorously. "You saw her come to this stool as soon as she saw me. Now give her the martini and get me my brew."

The barkeep looked questioningly at the woman.

She smiled and, putting her hand on Glen's, she said, "I just love the way he takes charge of things, don't you?"

"Yeah, yeah," Jimmy answered sourly. "Great, really great." He poured the martini into a glass and drew another beer. "That'll be a deuce," he said, putting the glass mug on the bar.

Glen put two silver dollars down and a 25-cent piece for the tip.

Jimmy scooped up the coins and walked away.

"Glen Lascomb," Glen said, lifting his beer.

"Lillian Troost," the woman answered, touching her glass to his.

They smiled at each other; then they began to laugh.

Kate was naked in Troost's arms. Light from a lamp on a night table touched the two of them but left the rest of the bedroom in semidarkness.

He ran his hand over her hair.

"What are you looking at?" she asked, touching the side of his face with the tips of her fingers.

"Your breasts," he answered, moving his hand over one and then the other. "They're lovely."

"I love you, Andrew," she whispered.

He kissed her on the lips and opened his mouth.

"If I didn't love you, I wouldn't be here with you," she said, after they separated. "Not before and not now."

"You don't have to explain anything to me," Troost said.

"The navy didn't come between Peter and me," she continued. "It's just that somewhere along the way, I realized that I needed something more than just being a navy wife."

Troost lay back and Kate nestled in the crook of his arm. For a while neither one of them spoke; then she said, "Five years ago, just before the twins went off to college, Peter was stationed in Seattle. There was this dinner and dance at the OC. Peter became interested in the sister of one of the officers. I was both jealous and concerned about his obviousness and decided to go home alone."

"Whatever it is," Troost said, "if it's causing you pain, you don't have to tell —"

"I want to tell you," she said forcefully.

He brushed her hair away from her face.

"One of the other officers followed me out to the parking lot," Kate said. "I knew him to say hello to. He was a captain. Peter had just made commander. He asked me if I would like to have something to eat. Because of Peter's actions I hadn't touched my dinner and, at that particular moment, even a hamburger and coffee would have been wonderful. He suggested we go in his car and I leave mine for Peter..." She took a deep breath before she continued. "He took me to a diner. I ate and so did he. We spoke about the navy; he even asked me about my twins. By the time we left the diner, it was 1:30 in the morning. When he started to drive, he suggested we go to a motel. At first, I thought he was joking. But he wasn't. He said he wanted to fuck me from the moment he saw me and then —" Kate shuddered and began to cry. "He pulled the car off to the side of the road, held me down, and raped me. I couldn't breathe... I felt as if I was suffocating... I couldn't even scream. I wanted to fight back, but I was afraid of what he would do if I did. I was too terrified to do anything..."

Troost caressed her bare shoulders. "I love you," he whispered, hoping that his words would somehow assuage her pain and at the same time knowing that nothing he could say or do would.

"When I told Peter about it," Kate explained, "he said that the best thing I could do would be to forget about it."

"Forget about it?" Troost responded.

"He said that if I brought the man up on charges, the burden of proof would be on me — that I would have a difficult time explaining to any of the officers in a court-martial why I agreed to go with him. Then there was the matter of his career to consider. It was dropped and never mentioned between us again."

Troost held her tightly to him. He couldn't begin to imagine someone violating her body. He kissed her forehead and the lids of her eyes. That someone took by force what she so willingly, so beautifully, gave to him, made him want to absorb her pain and free her forever from it.

"Besides Peter, you're the only other person I ever told," she whispered.

She put her hand on his chest. "Will you spend the night?" Kate asked.

Troost shook his head. "I need to see Lillian," he said.

"I understand," she answered.

He kissed her passionately. "I need you," he whispered.

"Take me."

CHAPTER 30

The *Tarpon* was five days out of Pearl, where she had delivered the nurses and Army Air Force pilots she had taken off the "Rock," and was once again headed west. It was just turning dark when Brisson gave the order to surface. Tony, the officer of the watch, scrambled up through the hatch behind Brisson as the conning tower broke the surface and made sure the four lookouts were in position.

"All ahead, standard," Brisson ordered.

Tony relayed the order to the engine room.

"All ahead standard," came the reply.

The diesels cut in for surface cruising and throbbed reassuringly.

Brisson checked the compass. "Steady as she goes," he said.

"Aye, aye, skipper," Tony answered, his eye catching the bow planes being folded against the hull.

"You have the conn, Tony," Brisson said, then turned and dropped gingerly down the hatch.

Tony made a quick sweep with his glasses. There was nothing that broke the constant seam of sea and sky.

The navigator requested permission for himself and the chief quartermaster to come topside to shoot the position of several stars.

"Permission granted," Tony answered, allowing himself to enjoy the beauty of the twilight and to think about Miriam. There were a dozen letters waiting for him from her when he returned to Pearl, and in one of them she enclosed a picture of herself in a green bathing suit. Just as he looked up at the sky, two shooting stars flashed across it from east to west and he wished that Miriam would fall in love with him.

"Leaving the bridge," the navigator said.

Tony nodded and started to make another sweep with his glasses. He moved them past port beam, when he saw a quick flash of light off the port bow. "Lookout, port side three points off the bow," he said.

A few moments, then he saw it again. "Now!" Tony exclaimed.

"Got it," the lookout answered. "Looks like a blinker signal on the horizon — could be 15 miles away."

Tony notified Brisson, who clambered up to the bridge in less than two minutes.

"Another light, to the right of the first," the lookout called.

Brisson said, "I have the conn. Everybody keep a close lookout between relative bearings two nine zero and three four zero."

After a few moments the radar watch reported, "Conn, several contacts — bearing zero two nine five to three zero five. Range 10,000 yards."

Tony checked the sector with his glasses. Nothing.

"All ahead, flank," Brisson ordered.

"All ahead, flank," the signalman engine room responded.

"Radar, can you give me their course and speed?" Brisson asked; then looking at Tony, he called down to the helmsman, "Come to course two seven five."

"Coming to course two seven five," the steersman answered.

"We'll run in closer on the surface," Brisson said.

Tony nodded. This was going to be it: his first taste of action. There were at least three ships out there. Maybe more. Undoubtedly Japanese. His lips and throat suddenly became dry.

"Range 8000 yards. Bearing three zero zero true. Course one two zero degrees, true. Speed one two knots," Radar reported.

Brisson said, after speaking to the sonar officer, "Their sound signature indicates they're enemy ships and they're large."

Despite the cool breeze caused by the 15-knot speed of the *Tarpon* through the water, Tony was sweating. Several times he ran his arm across his forehead. The next few minutes seemed like hours to him.

"5000 yards," Brisson announced. "All right, now we dive." He gave one long blast on the Klaxon and then shouted, "Dive... Dive... Dive."

The lookouts swung down from their perches between the periscopes and scrambled into the open hatch. Tony and the captain followed. The access hatch was dogged down.

"Bridge cleared — hatch secured," Tony reported.

The bow planes were already rigged out and the *Tarpon* was bow down.

Tony immediately took his place at the TDC.

The throbbing noise of the diesels was replaced by the hum of the electric motors. The air vents were being shut and the ballast tanks were being flooded.

Brisson was at the periscope. "Level off at six zero feet," he said.

"Level off at six zero feet," the diving officer answered from the control room.

"All ahead, two thirds," Brisson said.

"All ahead two thirds," the engine order telegraph watch answered.

Even as Tony watched the needle of the depth gage reach 40 feet, the sounds of the Japanese ship's screws rumbled through the water.

The DO ordered the bow plane watch to ease up on the bow planes. The boat responded. Her bow began to lift.

"Passing through four five feet," the DO reported.

The boat's rate of descent was slowed.

"Trim her," Brisson said.

The DO ordered ballast to be pumped from the forward trim tank to the after tank.

"Zero six zero feet," the DO reported.

Brisson stood very still, looked at his watch and said something in a very low voice to Chris, the XO. Then suddenly he said, "Dive control, come to periscope depth."

The boat responded.

"Periscope depth," the DO said.

"Up periscope," Brisson ordered, snapping out the handles and riding them up. He made a 360° sweep before he said, "Targets bearing zero one eight... Range 4000 yards... Three ships... Target angle, zero five four... Down scope."

Tony cranked the data into the torpedo data computer and read out the results to Brisson.

"We'll shoot from the bow," Brisson said; "then turn and shoot from the stern."

Chris gave the order to load the four bow torpedo tubes and "stand by to fire."

"Up periscope," Brisson said, squatting down to meet it and again riding it up. This time he immediately focused on the targets first. "Bearing three zero zero, true... I make out three ships close together... Down scope." He snapped the handles closed and stepped away.

Tony called out the information generated by the TDC.

"Three minutes, skipper," Chris said.

"Up periscope," Brisson ordered. "Tell the SO to ping once on the targets."

Tony could hear his heart beating.

"Bearing two nine five... Target angle zero four zero," Brisson said.

"Range 2200," the sonar man reported.

Tony felt the tension in the conning tower stretch to rubber-band thinness.

"Stand by to fire," Brisson said.

Chris relayed the order.

"Sonar, ping once," Brisson said.

"Range 2000," the sonar watch called out, as the sonar echo returned to the boat.

"Bearing, two eight five," Brisson said, peering through the periscope.

"Fire one," Brisson ordered. "Fire two!"

Tony felt the *Tarpon* shudder ever so slightly as the torpedoes left their tubes.

"Fire three and four," Brisson ordered.

More seconds passed.

"All fish running on course," sonar reported.

Tony watched the clock on the TDC — ten seconds.

An explosion rumbled down on the *Tarpon*. A second explosion came five seconds after the first.

"The big one is on fire and listing to her port side," Brisson said, with his eyes against the periscope.

The third explosion and the fourth came within two seconds of each other.

"Bingo... Another hit!" Brisson announced. "Down periscope... Rig for depth charges... Take her down fast to 200 feet."

"Target bearing two zero," the SO said. "Destroyer type... Moving very fast... Closing."

The *Tarpon*'s bow tilted sharply down.

"She's echo ranging on us, skipper," the sonar watch reported.

"Passing through 80 feet," the diving officer called out.

"She's directly above us, skipper," the sonarman reported.

Prickles broke out on Tony's back.

"Left full rudder," Brisson ordered.

Sweat soaked through Tony's shirt.

"Three cans on the way down," the SO said.

Chris turned very pale.

The first explosion thundered overhead and shook the boat from stern to stern. The second can caught the port side. Again, the boat trembled in agony.

The lights went out then came back on.

"Skipper, two men in the forward torpedo room are injured," the torpedo officer reported.

"Harly, to the after torpedo room," Chris shouted into the control room, where the pharmacist mate was doubling on an emergency telephones to engine room.

The third can detonated under the stern, lifting it upward and throwing all hands off balance.

The red signal light on the phone connecting the control room to the after engine room began to flash.

Chris answered. "Skipper, engineering reports a ruptured hydraulic line… Damage control is working on it now."

"Passing 100 feet," the DO said.

The pinging faded out of the hull. But the thrumming of the destroyer's screws was loud and clear.

"He's making another run," the sonar reported. "Two more cans."

Tony clenched his teeth. He looked at the men around the TDC. His fear was reflected in each one of their faces. Not one of the boat's crew had ever experienced a depth charge attack. They were all new to the terror. A thunderous explosion outside the laboring boat knocked him against the bulkhead.

"Passing one two five feet," the diving officer reported, his voice tight with fear.

Before Tony could pull himself up, another explosion hammered against the starboard side.

"Left full rudder," Brisson ordered.

"Left full rudder," the helmsman responded.

"Control, level off at 150 feet," Brisson said.

Chris started to relay the order, faltered, and had to begin again.

"Coming to 150 feet," the DO answered.

"Target moving away," the sonar reported. "Bearing two six zero."

Tony heard the feeling of relief in the man's voice and felt the tautness go out of his own body. He looked at the conning tower clock. Less than 45 minutes had passed since the Japanese signal lights were spotted. He took a deep breath and, as he slowly exhaled, the DO called out, "150 feet, skipper."

"Helmsman, come to two six zero," Brisson ordered.

Tony stiffened. It seemed as if the skipper was going after the Japanese destroyer. He looked at Chris, who was saying something to Brisson.

The skipper responded with a vigorous shake of his head.

"I have lost contact with target," the sonar reported.

"Dive Control, bring her to periscope depth," Brisson said. "We'll go up and take a look around. If we don't have any company, we'll surface and finish recharging our batteries."

Tony relaxed again. The men around the TDC broke into smiles. Minutes later the *Tarpon* surfaced, and he and Brisson were back on the conning tower bridge. Miles away, toward the southwest, a small portion of the sea and sky glowed red. The enemy ships were still burning.

"From here," Brisson commented, "it almost looks pretty."

Tony had other thoughts and, though he wasn't a religious man, he crossed himself and said, "But it also looks a lot like the mouth of Hell, doesn't it?"

For several moments Brisson remained silent; then, in a low voice, he answered, "Very much like the mouth of Hell. Thank you for — for bringing a new perspective to me." Then he said, "I'm going below. You have the conn."

"Aye, aye, skipper," Tony responded.

CHAPTER 31

Warren sat across the table from Irene Hacker in Society Sal's, a small French restaurant. The wavering light from a candle in a green wine bottle flickered across her face. She was in uniform and there was considerably less strain on her face than when he had seen her aboard the *AKO-96*.

They met outside the restaurant, acknowledged one another with a nod, entered, and were shown to the table by the hostess.

Warren ordered a scotch for himself and a rum and coke for Irene. Neither of them made any effort to speak.

Irene studied the menu, while Warren studied her.

Finally, looking over the top of the menu, she asked, "Have you decided what you want?"

Without hesitation, he answered, "You."

"Onion soup and the medallions of veal with mushrooms for me," she said.

"That sounds good to me," Warren responded.

"What?"

"I'll have whatever you have," he said, offering her a cigarette from a case.

She nodded and took one.

Warren held the cigarette lighter for her and then lit his own.

"How did you find out about this place?" she asked.

Warren looked around. The walls were red brick. There were potted plants in the corners. "Don't you like it?" he asked.

She smiled. "I'll let you know after I've eaten," she said. "But how did you find out about it?"

"I asked one of the guys at the BOQ," Warren explained.

The waitress brought a basket of hot French bread to the table and two small cups filled with butter. "One is regular, the other is flavored with garlic," she explained; then she asked if they were ready to order.

"Both of us will have the onion soup and the medallions of veal with mushrooms," Warren said.

"And would you care for wine?" the woman asked.

"A carafe of the house white —"

"I'd much prefer the red," Irene said. "Though of course white goes with veal."

"Make it a carafe of red," Warren said, looking up at the waitress.

She nodded, smiled at him, and left the table.

"I'm glad you agreed to meet me," Warren said, moving his eyes to Irene.

"More out of curiosity than anything else," she answered. "I'd have to admit that I didn't expect to ever see you again, let alone have you call and invite me to dinner."

Warren stubbed out his cigarette. "I wasn't sure I'd ever see Pearl again."

The waitress brought the soup to the table and then the carafe of wine.

Neither spoke until they were finished with the soup. "I'm glad you got out," Warren said finally. "Things were very bad when I left. I was supposed to take MacArthur and some others to Australia, but they were flown out instead."

"I have bad dreams about Corregidor," she said, looking down at her empty soup plate, "and worse feelings about being safe here." She raised her eyes.

He reached across the table and squeezed her hand.

"I left some very good people —" Her voice cracked and she turned her head away. "Excuse me," she said, "I'm sorry."

Warren lit another cigarette and blew a cloud of smoke toward the ceiling. He had his nightmares too. He'd see Rawlins's head, or what was left of it, or he'd be on the ship's bridge again when she was attacked by bombers.

A moment later and more composed, Irene asked, "Would you mind if I had a glass of wine now?"

Warren poured.

A busboy came to the table and collected the soup plates.

"Was there someone special?" Warren asked, putting into words what he intuitively knew.

She nodded. "A major. We were going to be married. He was still on Bataan when I left Corregidor. He's a doctor. I don't think he ever left Bataan."

Warren remained silent. That afternoon there were rumors that Corregidor was about to surrender.

The waitress came with their entrees and, when she left the table, Warren said, "If it tastes as good as it smells, it will be delicious."

They began to eat.

Warren offered to pour Irene more wine and she held out her glass.

"You didn't have much of your scotch," she commented.

"I really don't care much for drink," he said.

"Then why did you order it?" she asked.

"Foolish, I guess," he said; then looking at her, he added, "It was the thing to do."

"Because of me?"

He nodded.

Once more the conversation between them lapsed until Irene said, "There was no need to try to impress me. Whether you drink or don't is your business."

"I know that," Warren answered; then with a slight smile, he added, "I'd much prefer it if you didn't drink."

Irene frowned.

He touched the carafe. "That won't bring your major or anyone else you knew back."

"How dare you say that to me!" The candlelight heightened her flush. "What do you know about losing people?"

"I already know a great deal about losing people," he said. "Your father … the man who killed him … several other members of my crew." He paused and took a deep breath.

"I'm sorry," she said, "that was a stupid thing to say."

Warren looked straight at her. "I also know about alcoholics; my mother is one." The words were out before he could stop them. He saw his mother the evening he arrived. She had a drink in her hand and told him that his father had another woman. Not that he disbelieved it, or resented it, but wondered, if it was true, why his father had waited so long to have an affair.

"Why did you tell me that?" Irene asked. The flush in her face was gone now.

He touched the carafe again. "Because this can't ever give you what you need," he said.

She cocked her head to one side. "And what is it you think I need?"

"Love," Warren answered.

She uttered a derisive snort. "You mean you want to bed me, isn't that it, Lieutenant?"

Warren's cheeks became hot. The women he knew didn't use that kind of language, even though they were probably thinking it.

She smiled at him. "I just wanted to put it in perspective."

Warren rested his elbows on the table. "I wouldn't have tried to see you, if I didn't want to, as you just said, 'bed' you."

"Well, at least you're honest," she responded.

"But I can also give you something —"

"Just what the hell can you give or think you can give, me?"

"The feeling of being needed," he said quietly. "The courage to live and not to think that you somehow cheated, because you aren't a prisoner of war or dead."

She gave him a long, hard look; then she said, "My, my, my! I never knew that you could do all that and get a woman pregnant, too."

Warren didn't answer. But he meant what he said: he could give her those things.

"I noticed you said nothing about love, I mean real love."

"It might come," he responded.

She picked up her glass and drank the remaining wine from it. "You don't happen to give a guarantee that your service will work, do you?" she asked.

Because she was making him feel stupid, he said, "I think we had better drop the subject."

"You're angry, aren't you?"

"Let's say —"

"Frustrated? Annoyed?"

"The first time I saw you aboard the Nine Six, I wanted you."

"That was probably because you were at sea too long," she said.

"No. Because, despite the way you were dressed, I liked the way you looked and the way you handled yourself when I told you what happened to your father."

The busboy returned to the table to clear the plates away; then the waitress returned to suggest they try the house dessert, which was a chocolate mousse topped with whipped cream.

"Sounds wonderful!" Irene exclaimed.

"One mousse," Warren said, "and nothing for me."

"Coffee?" the waitress asked.

"Demitasse, if you have it," Irene answered.

"I'll have one too," Warren said and, when they were alone again, he told Irene, "I'm sorry the evening was such a flop. I really wanted to make it good for both of us."

"Yes, I know that," she responded. After the waitress returned with the dessert, Irene asked Warren. "Will you be assigned to another ship soon?"

"I've been accepted for PT boat training," he said. "That's six weeks long; then I'll be assigned to a squadron."

"Six weeks in Pearl?"

He laughed. "More or less."

Without commenting, Irene began to eat, while Warren found himself becoming more and more ill at ease. He was very attracted to her, even though she seemed to be more remote than when he first saw her.

"The food here is very good," Irene said, putting the small demitasse cup down in its saucer.

He wanted to say *I didn't think you noticed*, but instead, he agreed and added, "It's worth coming back to."

"Yes," Irene answered; then with a mischievous twinkle in her eyes and a half-formed smile on her lips, she asked, "But will you invite me?"

He did a double take.

"Of course, you might not want to after tonight?" she challenged.

"Why don't you let me decide that," Warren answered.

"I share a small apartment with another nurse," Irene said. "We could go there. She's on duty from 2000 to 0400 and, because of the curfew, she won't be back until 0800. That will give you enough time to decide —"

"I don't have to go to bed with you to decide whether or not I want to see you again," Warren said. "I want to see you."

Irene reached across the table and took hold of his hand. "Come home with me," she whispered.

"Are you sure that's what you want?"

"I'm sure I want to be with you," she answered.

CHAPTER 32

Troost was asked to attend the night briefing at Admiral Sprat's request. It was held at CinPacFleet Headquarters in the large conference room. This was Troost's second visit to the room. There was, as there had been before, a yellow pad, a pencil, and a glass on the table in front of each chair; two large pitchers of ice water, one at each end, were placed to be within easy reach of everyone.

In addition to Troost and Sprat, Admiral Floyde, commander of Task Force Seventeen, was there with several captains and commanders.

Admiral Gower was absent. Troost had heard that the admiral was ill. He'd little doubt that the briefing would be about the recent battle in the Coral Sea, during which the *Eire* was lost and the *Gettysburg* badly damaged.

As soon as everyone was settled, Admiral Nimitz gave them permission to smoke; then he surprised everyone by not immediately mentioning anything about the recent events in the Coral Sea and instead told them, "All intelligence sources agree that two Japanese task forces are at sea. One is estimated to be heading to the Aleutians and might assault Attu and Kiska and attempt an invasion. The other and larger of the two is clearly heading for Midway Island. Commander Layton will explain this in detail." And he nodded to the junior officer.

Layton, everyone knew, was one of the few men whom Nimitz retained from Kirst's staff. His reputation for precise work and analytical thinking was well known.

He stood up. It was obvious he was nervous and was forced to clear his throat several times before he finally said, "Initial air attacks on Midway could occur on the morning of June fourth. The carrier strike force probably will approach Midway from the northwest on a bearing of about three hundred degrees, and launch at about one hundred and seventy five miles from Midway, at some time in the early-morning twilight."

Layton continued, "Our sources indicate that the entire fleet is divided into two groups: the southern force, which includes transports and a second carrier force, consisting of the light carrier *Ryujo* and a new fleet carrier, whose name is indecipherable. But the main carrier force, designated Carrier Force One, will be the one to strike Midway. It is commanded by Vice Admiral Chuichi Nagumo, who commanded enemy forces at Pearl." He paused, poured a small amount of water into a glass, and drank it. "The entire operation has been planned and is under the overall command of Admiral Yamamoto. Carrier Force One consists of the carriers *Akagi*, *Kaga*, *Hiryu*, and *Soryu*, with a screen of two battleships, three cruisers and eleven destroyers." Finished, Layton nodded at Nimitz and resumed his seat.

Nimitz stood up again. "I need not tell you men that this is a most serious situation," he said. "The Japanese forces are very powerful, and far stronger than those I have available to commit against them. But now we know the Japanese battle plan. That gives us an advantage which we must exploit to its fullest. If we fail to stop the attack and lose that island, the Hawaiian group and the west coast of the mainland will be in grave danger..." He paused a moment; then looking at Sprat, he continued. "Admiral Gower is in the hospital."

The men at the table suddenly shifted their positions.

"He has recommended that command of our carrier force be turned over to Admiral Sprat. Even though Admiral Sprat is not an aviator, I have full confidence in him and he will replace Admiral Gower," Nimitz said. "But that leaves Sprat's command vacant."

"Sir," Sprat said, "Admiral Troost is an experienced destroyer man."

At the mention of his name, Troost almost dropped his pipe. He was the most junior of the flag officers present, and there were others in CINCPACFLT Headquarters who were at least as qualified.

Nimitz rubbed his chin, moved his eyes to Troost, and after a few moments' thought, said, "I read your report of the surface strike on the Marshall-Gilbert. Overall you did very well."

Troost flushed. He could hear his heart pound.

"All right, Admiral Troost," Nimitz said, "you're in command of the support force."

Troost realized he was the center of attention. He flicked his eyes over the faces turned toward his. On several there was more than a hint of envy. With those few words, Nimitz not only gave him one of the most important commands in CinPacFleet, but also made him a target for more senior flag officers of the "black shoe" community who aspired to the ComCruDesPac command.

Nimitz smiled at Troost.

"Thank you, sir," Troost said. "I'll do my best."

Nimitz turned his attention to Sprat and to Floyde, who would be the overall commander of the U.S. forces at sea. "Now, gentlemen, you are to go to sea as soon as possible with everything we have and that will include the *Gettysburg*. I'm assured she'll be ready when we need her. Sprat and Floyde, it will be up to you and your men to stop the Japanese at Midway…"

The next few days and nights were hectic for Troost. He worked closely with Admirals Sprat and Floyde, Lieutenant Commander Layton, and the operations officers from Task Force 16 and 17 to produce CinPac Operations Plan No. 29-42 for the defense of Midway. The plan was based on two premises: the first was that the American force was inferior in numbers; the second was that Sprat would have had the advantage of knowing where and when the Japanese intended to strike. Having this information would allow him to surprise the attacking force. But it was recognized by everyone who participated in the preparation of the plan that luck and timing would play a vital role in its success or failure.

Troost managed to spend some time with Kate, and though he never mentioned the Midway operation to her, he had the feeling she knew something very important was coming up. Then on the night of May 27, he was late getting off the heavy cruiser *Appalachia*, the ship from which he chose to command, and when he finally arrived at Kate's house, he found her standing in a darkened living room looking out at the night-shrouded garden.

"You'll be leaving soon," she said, without facing him.

Her words stopped him in his tracks.

"I've felt it for a while," she admitted, still not turning toward him.

"I'll be back before you realize I'm gone," he said, closing the distance between them and putting his arms around her waist.

She leaned back against him.

"When?" she asked.

"Dawn tomorrow," he answered, nuzzling the side of her face and delighting in her scent.

She put her hands over his. "I thought I'd never experience certain feelings again," she said in a low voice and turned her face toward his. "I feel alive in a way that I haven't in a long time. And I'm so afraid that it will vanish again," she confided, "that I find myself wondering if I'm not making more out of our relationship than really exists."

He brought her gently around to face him. "I don't know what you think really exists," he said, "but I'll tell you what exists for me. A warm, loving, sensitive woman, who is able to physically express her love, who has become the single most important part of my life. A woman who has made me feel emotions and sensations I haven't felt for years, or never really felt." He took hold of her face between his two hands and brought it close to his. "All of that exists for me," he said kissing her passionately on the lips.

"I guess," she said, "I'm afraid of it suddenly ending."

"I'll make sure it doesn't," he said.

She reached over to the drawstring and drew the curtain closed.

Troost switched on a lamp.

"Are you hungry?" she asked.

"Absolutely starved," Troost answered.

CHAPTER 33

It was the kind of bar Jacob would have never entered on his own, but when he was with Yancy everything and anything was possible. The bar, Sing Tau, was on the edge of Chinatown, and though most of the patrons, from what Jacob could see, were officers, it was a scummy-looking place, with sawdust on the floor, yellow walls streaked with dirt, and an atmosphere clouded with cigarette smoke and the smell of sour beer.

"It's almost curfew time," Jacob said, squinting hard at Yancy, who had one hand wrapped around a glass of bourbon and soda and the other inching its way toward the breast of a woman he'd met an hour before.

"Curfew, curfew… I don't care about curfew," Yancy answered. He grinned stupidly at Jacob. "What I care about is this luscious bit of womanhood." His southern accent became more pronounced.

The woman giggled. "Does he always talk so funny?" she asked.

"Only when he's sober," Jacob told her.

"All I need honey," Yancy said, "is a little bit of lovin' and I'll be ready to take on the whole Jap navy." His hand reached her breast.

She pushed it away.

"What's a little squeeze between friends?" Yancy asked.

"I think it's time for you to leave, Miss," Jacob said in a low voice. "He's a terror when he gets horny and he's getting horny very fast."

The woman looked at him as if he was out of his mind.

He nodded.

She disengaged herself from Yancy's arm.

"Say, where you goin', you little ball of fluff?" Yancy asked, trying to grab hold of her again.

Jacob came between Yancy and the woman. "She 100 bucks," he whispered into Yancy's ear.

Yancy's eyes went wide. "100 just to fuck?" he roared.

Except for the sound of the jukebox, the bar became absolutely silent.

"I ain't never paid for it in my life an' I'm not about to now, even if there is goddamn war on," Yancy declared.

"Shit, man, don't a hero always get it free? Sure they do… I'm goin' be a big goddamn hero… My daddy wants me to be a hero, an' that little bundle of fluff is just waitin' for me to be a hero, ain't ya?"

"You're right," Jacob said and signaled the barkeep.

Jacob put 10 dollars on the bar. "That should cover it," he said.

"More than cover it," the barkeep answered.

"Okay, Yance, we're going to shove off," Jacob said, opening the door and gently pushing Yancy out into the night.

Glen reveled in Lillian's naked body. It was lithe. Her skin was soft and she always smelled good, everywhere. He held her tightly against him. If there was a heaven, he was absolutely certain it would have to include a woman like Lillian for him.

"You look as if you're deep in thought," Lillian said, gazing up at him.

He kissed her chin. "The only thing I'm deep in is you," he said grinning.

She smiled and traced a small circle on his bare shoulder. "I like that. Glen, have you ever thought about us?" Lillian asked, simultaneously wrapping her bare arms around his neck and her bare legs around his.

"Sure, baby," he answered, wondering if she wanted it again. The second time around she was slower coming than she was the first, and he had to be back to the ship before curfew.

"I mean, not just about how good it is in the sack between us," she said.

The question made Glen uncomfortable. It had a familiar echo, so familiar that he was beginning to lose his erection. She must have felt it dwindle, because she started to move against him.

"Do you?" Lillian asked.

"Sure."

"So do I," she said. "I really think about us. I think about us so much that I want you to meet my folks."

"Folks?"

She laughed. "Yes, my father, Admiral Troost —"

"Admiral Troost!" he exclaimed. His erection completely collapsed. He bolted up, almost throwing Lillian off the bed. "I didn't know he was your daddy."

"Well, didn't you see we have the same last name?"

"Sure, but lots of people have the same name."

She laughed. "I even have a brother in the navy. Lieutenant Warren Troost."

"Christ!" Glen exclaimed. "I've been screwing an admiral's daughter." He shook his head with disbelief. This could ruin his career even before he had one. He reached for the pack of cigarettes on the night table and took one out for himself.

"I'd like one, please," Lillian said.

He held the lighter for her, then lit his own.

Lillian had pulled herself up to a sitting position and was leaning against the back of the bed.

"I have to leave before curfew," he said, swinging his feet off the bed and planting them on the floor.

"We've got to talk," Lillian said, blowing smoke out in front of her.

"Does your father know about me?" Glen asked.

"Not yet — but my mother does."

"Christ!" he swore again.

"She was the one who suggested that I introduce you to my father, when I mentioned that I thought we'd make a nice couple."

"Nice couple? What does that mean?" Glen asked, putting on his skivvies.

"Married," she said.

"Married?" he repeated. "I'm already married."

Lillian gasped and began to cough.

"I thought you knew that," Glen said, putting on his pants.

"You neglected to mention it," she cried.

Glen shrugged. "C'mon, it wouldn't have made any difference to you. You wanted it from me as much as I wanted it from you."

"Well, we got it," she hissed. "We fucking well got it!"

He moved closer to the bed. "Got what?"

She rubbed her bare stomach. "Guess what you put here?" she challenged.

Glen tried to speak, but couldn't get his thoughts in gear with his tongue. Finally, he said, "My wife is going to have a kid."

"That's her problem," Lillian said and, patting her stomach, she added, "Mine is right here and so is yours."

"You can't prove it's mine," Glen said, reaching for his shirt. He was anxious to be out of the motel room and away from her as quickly as possible. "You're with other guys —"

"You're a bastard!" she exclaimed, stubbing out her cigarette in the ashtray on the night table.

"You weren't a virgin when we met."

"What am I going to do?" she asked, suddenly crying.

Glen was completely dressed. "Find a doctor and get rid of it," he said.

"If I had known you were married —"

"I'll pay for the doctor," he said, going to the door.

"You're a son-of-a-bitch!" she screamed. "A real son-of-a-bitch!"

Glen shrugged, then squaring his shoulders, he opened the door, and without answering or looking back at her, he left the room. He was sorry he was married to one woman. He wasn't going to be sorrier by far and divorce her to marry a second.

CHAPTER 34

At 0430 on the fourth of June, the pilots of the Big E and the *Gettysburg* answered the call to general quarters. Jacob and Yancy sat close together in the fighter ready room and listened carefully to the briefing on the weather conditions and tactics. Then as they sat around and waited for the order to man their planes, some of them talked about the Japanese strike on Dutch Harbor in the Aleutians and the 1200 RAF bombers that had attacked Cologne.

Jacob had written to his parents the night before. Though he said nothing about the impending battle, he knew his father and mother were wise enough to read between the lines. He looked at Yancy and then at some of the other men nearby. Most were his age. Some would not be there by the time night fell.

"Okay." Yancy suddenly boomed, "I'm willin' to bet any sucker that I get me at least two meatballs before today is over. Do I have any takers?"

"Hey, Reb," one of the other pilots answered, "what odds?"

Yancy looked at Jacob. "What odds, Jake?"

"Don't bet him," Jacob answered.

"What you talkin' about? I can't back down now."

"Okay, okay... Make it even money. He won't take it."

"Even money?" Yancy whispered.

"Reb, I'm waiting on your offer," the pilot said.

"Just hold your cotton-pickin' horses," Yancy answered. "I'm talkin' to my banker... Jake, you sure?"

Jacob nodded. He didn't like the bet.

"I was hoping to make a few bucks to spend next time we're in Pearl," Yancy explained.

"Even money," Jacob repeated.

"Even money," Yancy called out.

"Shit, that's no bet at all," the other man responded.

"Take it or leave it," Yancy said, feigning a total lack of interest.

"Hell, just to show you that I don't believe you'll get one meatball, I'll put up a C," the pilot said.

"You said he wouldn't take it," Yancy whispered.

Jacob shrugged. He wanted to say, *He's dumber than you are*, but he kept his mouth shut.

"Do I take it?" Yancy asked.

"You don't have a choice, unless you want to be the laughingstock of the week."

"All right," Yancy said, "you're on. Pony up the C-note and my banker here will hold it."

"What happens if your banker doesn't make it back?" the pilot asked, standing over Jacob.

"Hey, you gotta be jokin'," Yancy said. "He's one of God's Chosen. He'll make it back all right."

Jacob folded each of the 100-dollar bills and inserted one in his right shoe and the other in his left; then he said, "If I don't make it back, I owe each of you 100 dollars."

Yancy gave him a questioning look; then he roared with laughter. "By Christ, I love this son-of-a-bitch!"

Troost was on the flag bridge of the *Appalachia*. At 0657 the sun came up over the eastern horizon. It was a clear, balmy day with a stiff southeast breeze and a few scattered clouds at 4- to 5000 feet.

According to the last position check given to him by a member of his staff, they were 290 miles to the north and a bit to the east of Midway. They were within perhaps a couple of hundred miles of where the Japanese carriers were steaming. If they found the Japanese ships first — Troost suddenly remembered the lines from Shakespeare's *Henry the Fifth* — *The game's afoot: Follow your spirit; and upon this charge cry "God for Harry! England and Saint George!"* He did not allow himself to think what would happen if the Japanese found them first.

At 0734 word came from the staff communications officer that a PBY patrol aircraft from Pearl had sighted enemy aircraft.

Troost made a visual check of the destroyer screen and cruisers supporting the carriers *Endeavor* and *Bee*. Every ship was in its assigned station around the carriers.

At 0745 the communications officer reported intercepting another contact report from the patrol plane.

"Many planes," the pilot of the PBY said. "Heading toward Midway, bearing three two zero, distance one five zero from the island."

"Captain Haines," Troost called on the squawk box, "did you receive that word?"

"Yes, sir, Admiral," Haines answered. "We are ready if they come our way."

Troost quickly checked the chart.

"Puts them about here," Troost said to his staff watch officer, "some 130 miles west of us. But where are the carriers?" He moved away from the chart table and, though his insides were churning, he forced himself to look calm.

At 0830 another message came in from the PBY: "Two enemy carriers and battleships... Bearing three zero...

Distance one eight zero from Midway... Course one three five... Speed two five."

Four minutes later, Admiral Sprat ordered the task group carriers to launch torpedo aircraft and turned the group into the wind.

Troost moved outside, picked up his glasses, and watched his ships make the turn, even while keeping their stations relative to the *Endeavor* and the *Gettysburg*. The game was afoot and they had been lucky. For the moment, they had the advantage.

"Pilots, man your planes... Pilots, man your planes," came over the ready room squawk box. It was the third time since 0400 hundred that they had gone to their planes, and each of the previous commands was a dry run.

On the way out, Jacob heard one of the pilots say, "We're going to kill the Japs by running back and forth to our planes."

Jacob climbed into the cockpit of his F4F, settled in the seat, slipped into his chute easily, adjusted the safety harness, and buckled up. There was activity all around him.

The *Bee* was on the *Endeavor*'s port side 1000 yards away. She too was preparing to launch. The group increased speed to 30 knots. On the flight deck of the Big E, Devastators loaded with torpedoes and SDB dive bombers with 1000-pound bombs were lining up to be catapulted into the air. The fighters would go off first; some to relieve the CAP, others to cover the attack aircraft.

The Flight Leader of Jacob's fighter group was taxied into take-off position. The fighter group was assigned to fly high cover on the dive bombers.

The plane captain pushed the starting cartridge into the starter of Jacob's Wildcat and gave the signal to fire it, as the words "start engines" sounded across the flight deck.

Jacob pressed the button. The engine coughed. The prop began to turn. Smoke came from the exhaust. The prop made several slow revolutions, then rumbled into life. He unlocked the wings.

The handlers spread and locked them.

Jacob taxied to his take-off position.

The signal came!

At full throttle the Wildcat raced down the deck, lifted off, and started to climb. In a matter of moments, he was in formation alongside Yancy, who grinned and gave him a thumbs-up sign.

By now, the TBs were boring in on the *Kaga*. Jacob heard the voices of the various pilots as they swooped down on the wildly twisting and turning carrier to get a shot at her and were themselves shot to pieces.

Four planes survived and were on their way back to the *Gettysburg.*

"Okay," the flight leader said over the radio, "those Jap bastards got first round, but there's more coming up."

Jacob's flight was flying at 20,000 feet, high enough to drop down on the more maneuverable Zeros, should they attack the SBDs below them.

"Skipper," one of the pilots called to the flight leader, "I'm having some trouble with my oxygen supply."

"Anyone else?" the Flight Leader asked.

Two other pilots reported having similar problems.

"We're going down to 15," the Flight Leader said.

Jacob eased the stick forward. The nose of his plane dipped. Below were scattered cumulus and, below that, the dark blue of the Pacific.

At 15,000 feet, Jacob's flight leveled off and he checked the fuel gage. It was getting low. They were rapidly reaching the point of no return, as the SBD flight leader searched for the Japanese Carrier Force in the direction of Midway.

Jacob turned his head to the port side and glanced down. There was the white furrow of a ship plowing through the water. "Skipper," Jacob radioed, "look down to your left. A ship is moving toward the northeast."

"Got it!" Jacob's flight leader answered.

"See it," the SBD skipper said, without having to be called. "I now see four carriers."

At 1150 the SBD flight leader's voice again came over the radio. "Attack... Aim good!" he exclaimed, already rolling into his steep dive-bombing run.

The other SBDs opened into a long line and followed him down.

Jacob watched the SBDs hurtle down toward their targets. Almost instantly small puffs of antiaircraft bursts surrounded the diving SBDs. As the bombs were released, he saw huge flames burst out of the turning carriers below.

In a matter of minutes, the *Kaga* and *Akagi* were in flames, and dive bombers from the *Gettysburg* wrecked the *Soryu*.

A dozen Zeros managed to get into the air.

"Go get them," Jacob's flight leader said, peeling off into a dive.

Jacob charged the guns, flipped the "Master Arming" switch on, and rolling over to the starboard, followed Yancy down.

Yancy broke out of the dive and picked up one of the Zeros. "Son-of-a-bitch, my guns jammed... Stay with me, Jake," Yancy shouted.

Jacob turned to close in on Yancy. A Zero suddenly swung into his sights. He pressed the trigger. His tracers left smoke trails from the wings of his plane to the target... One second

… two … three… The Japanese plane exploded. He kicked his plane over to the right. Where was Yancy?

In the melee, another red meatball zoomed by him and he suddenly found another Japanese in his gun sight reticle. He fired a quick burst.

Flames gushed from the enemy's starboard wing. "I'm hit, skipper," one of the pilots yelled. "I'm going down."

Jacob saw the pilot leap from the burning plane. "Open," Jacob shouted. "Open the fucking chute!"

The man fell into the sea.

"Jake, you got one coming in on your port side," Yancy called out. "I got my guns cleared. I'm coming in."

"See him, Reb," Jacob answered and threw his fighter over in a tight turn to the left until he was closing head on with the Japanese plane. He pressed the trigger button; his guns chattered and he pulled back the stick as the Zero flashed below him.

"He's smoking, Jake," Yancy yelled. "You're hot today."

Jacob rolled to his right and saw the smoking plane smash into the sea.

The remaining Zeros broke away. The engagement was suddenly over.

"Let's head home," Jacob's flight leader said. "Join on me."

Jacob was wet with sweat and, raising his goggles, he drew his arm across his eyes to wipe them clear. Suddenly, he felt the adrenaline flowing, as if he could run for miles and miles.

Almost before he realized it they were over the American ships. Down below, the *Gettysburg* was burning.

Suddenly Yancy's voice came over the radio. "Jake, you see anything wrong with my plane?" he asked.

"Nothing on your left side," Jacob reported. He dropped behind and below. "Looks good from down here," he said;

then he eased away and came up on Yancy's starboard wing. "Looks like you took a hit in the right side of your engine cowling, Reb."

"My engine is running rough," Yancy said.

"I hear you," the skipper said. "Yance, are you going to ditch?"

"Negative," Yancy answered. "I'll bring her in."

Jacob saw a thin fan of fluid trace its way along the fuselage, coming from the edge of the engine cowling. "You're losing hydraulic fluid," he told Yancy.

They were at 500 feet and parallel to the carrier.

"Comin' in with a bad engine," Yancy radioed, talking to the air boss on the ship.

"Crash equipment standing by," came the answer. "Take it nice and easy... The LSO knows about your problem."

Jacob was the next aircraft behind Yancy. He checked his altimeter: he was 100 feet above the sea. He saw Yancy's Wildcat over the stern and saw the LSO signal "Cut."

Yancy flared for a landing and engaged an arresting wire. Then suddenly his landing gear collapsed. The plane skidded to the port side. One of the wings was sheared off. It hung suspended over the side of the ship by the still attached arresting wire.

Frantically the LSO waved Jacob off, and as he passed close over the carrier's port side, he saw Yancy's plane burning and teams of rescue personnel and fire fighters swarming over it.

The air boss came on the radio. "Jake, we know you're low on fuel. Stretch out your approach pattern ahead. We'll clear the deck by pushing the plane over the side... Do you read?"

"Loud and clear," he answered.

Jacob made two more approaches before he was taken aboard. As soon as he was parked, he scrambled out of the cockpit, climbed out on the wing, and jumping to the deck, raced down the ladders and through a maze of passageways to the deck below the hangar deck, where the sick bay was located.

A doctor and several corpsmen were working on Yancy.

Jacob moved close to the bed.

Yancy's face, arms, and chest were burned. In some places the skin was charred. A ribbon of blood streamed from the right side of his lips.

Jacob looked questioningly at the doctor.

The man shook his head.

"Hey, Yance?" Jacob said, fighting the tightness in his throat.

Yancy's eyelids fluttered.

"It's me, Jake."

"Can't see," he said softly. "Can't see."

Jacob fought back the tears.

"Hold me, Jew boy... Hold me tight!"

Jacob reached down and gathered Yancy in his arms.

"Tell my daddy I tried," Yancy whispered. "Will ya tell him that?"

"Yes, I'll tell him," Jacob answered.

Yancy nodded. "You're best there is," he said. "The best!"

"He's gone," one of the corpsmen said.

Jacob nodded and gently put Yancy's body down in the bed. "He was my friend," he said, his eyes filling with tears. "He was my friend..." Jacob stood up and, rocking slowly back and forth on the balls of his feet, intoned the Kaddish, the Hebrew prayer for the dead.

CHAPTER 35

Jacob was in the fighter ready room. One by one the men of the fighter group came over to him and either grabbed his shoulder or mumbled something about Yance being a good guy.

Then suddenly the squawk box blared, "Incoming enemy planes... Incoming enemy planes... Range, 60 miles." Moments later the same voice ordered, "Pilots, man your planes... Pilots, man your planes..."

Jacob raced from the ready room with the others, and within minutes he was in the air circling the ship.

The flight director in the carrier's CIC radioed Jake, "Vector three two zero... Buster!" Other sections of fighters were being vectored to meet the incoming enemy.

At full throttle, Jacob turned into heading and immediately spotted his target, a Kate, low on the water, carrying a torpedo. He turned toward the Japanese and attacked.

The rear gunner blazed away at him.

He pressed the trigger in a long burst and saw the gunner slump forward. He pulled up, turned, and came head-on at the Kate. A short burst turned the plane into a ball of flames. Immediately, Jacob sighted another Kate, this one somewhat higher than the first.

The Japanese pilot dived toward the water.

But Jacob was on his tail. His guns blazed.

The plane dropped into the sea, cartwheeled twice, and exploded.

Jacob climbed rapidly back to 5000 feet and called his flight director to report he was ready for another vector. Suddenly, smoke started to pour out of his engine. "Shit! That fucking gunner got me before I got him!" His mind raced. He had to abandon his Wildcat. He jettisoned the canopy, unbuckled his harness, and rolled the burning plane upside down. Then he dropped from the seat, and in the next instant he was clear of the plane.

Everything was quiet. Jacob didn't feel as if he was falling, though he knew he was. He wrenched the ripcord. Moments became links in a long chain of time...

The pilot chute suddenly billowed open and he was jerked violently upright; then he began to drift silently down toward the sea.

Jacob watched his Wildcat crash into the ocean and vanish in a burst of flame.

The *Gettysburg* was burning and listing to port.

Glen's ship, the *Harium*, was alongside to aid the salvage parties. During the attack, the guns of the support ships shot down two of the attacking dive bombers. But many made it through the intense antiaircraft fire and managed to score two direct hits on the carrier. She was so badly damaged that Admiral Floyde gave the order to abandon ship. But now salvage and repair parties indicated she could be saved and towed back to Pearl Harbor.

Glen was at the phone bank on the bridge. "Number one mount," he called.

"Number one —"

Suddenly the 1MC blared. "Torpedo ... torpedo ... coming in on starboard beam."

The Klaxon screamed.

Two explosions rocked the *Gettysburg*, and a third lifted the *Harium* out of the water, mortally damaging her.

Glen was hurled to the deck.

Several more heavy explosions followed.

Glen did know which ship they came from. He crawled along the slanting deck. The OOD lay against the gyro repeater. The right side of his head was smashed in. Two of the others from the bridge watch were unconscious. He pulled one of them to the door and pushed him outside; then he crawled back and got the other.

Another explosion deep inside the *Gettysburg* sent flames shooting above the island.

There were men already in the water.

"Get these two," Glen shouted, dropping one and then the other man over the side.

Glen climbed down a crazily tilted ladder to the main deck, where a half dozen men were ready to go over the side.

"There are guys down below," one of the men told him. "I could hear them yelling." And then he jumped into the water.

"Let's get the guys below!" Glen shouted, already leading the way inside. Smoke was everywhere and flames were flaring up.

On the second deck, Glen heard a man shout, "Here ... we're here."

There were three of them. The Chief Engineer Officer and two of his men.

"We're the only ones who were able to get out," one of the men said. "The boss is hurt bad. I got a busted arm and Tim can't straighten up."

"Get these guys the hell out of here," Glen said, taking hold of the EO and slinging him over his shoulders, fireman-style.

By the time they reached the first deck and were outside again, they could hardly breath.

"Get off that ship," a man shouted from the deck of the destroyer *Linden*, which was alongside to assist. "Get off that ship!"

Glen waved and coughed until his gut hurt. "Jump," he told the men with him. "Jump."

They went over the side.

"The EO is going over," Glen shouted, dropping the man into the water. Then he jumped. He went under, came up, and clearing his eyes, grabbed hold of the EO and started to pull him toward the *Linden*.

There was just enough room in the small, bright yellow rubber raft for Jacob. That he somehow managed to free himself from the parachute, inflate his own one-man life raft, and then climb into it, was an unparalleled miracle, as far as he was concerned, and it left him completely exhausted. It felt incredibly strange to have the world reduced in a matter of minutes from the vastness of the sky to the cramped space of a bobbing rubber raft on an ocean whose own immensity stretched from horizon to horizon.

Jacob shifted his position and looked up at a sky so blue it actually hurt his eyes. It was absolutely empty. The planes were gone. There wasn't the slightest sign anywhere, not even debris on the water, except for himself, of the ferocious air battle that had taken place there only a short while ago.

With scarcely any effort, Jacob could imagine himself dying in the raft. It would be a slow death, unless a storm came up and the raft was overturned or swamped. He pursed his lips and began looking around for things that would help him survive. He had a knife, his .38. In his survival sea-pack he knew he had some fishhooks and line, also a canteen of water.

Jacob looked up at the sun. The lack of water was his most serious problem. A man could live for days without food but not very long under a tropical sun without water, although his parachute would give him some protection from the sun.

Jacob suddenly realized that a man was swimming toward him. Using the raft's two stubby paddles, he turned and paddled in the direction of the man, shortening the distance between them. Then he clearly saw him, stopped paddling, and yanked his .38 from its holster. "Don't come any closer," he shouted, waving the .38 at him.

The man stopped and began to tread water.

Up to that moment, he hadn't thought again about Yancy once. His own predicament occupied every nook and cranny of his brain. But now it was different. The enemy was in his sights and Yancy's burned body was in his mind.

"If you're going to kill me," the man said in perfect English, "do it now."

"Don't come any closer!" Jacob shouted. He needed a few moments to think. He didn't expect the man to speak English.

"Shoot me," the man called out. "It's a better way to die than to drown."

Jacob suddenly remembered his father said never to do anything he'd be ashamed to tell his son about. "I can't do it, Yance," he whispered aloud. "I can't do it even for you. I can't kill an unarmed man." He lowered the .38 and called out, "I'll paddle toward you. Grab hold of the raft."

"My name is Yashi Kurokachi," the man said, taking hold of the raft and looking up at Jacob. "Lieutenant Kurokachi."

"Lieutenant Jacob Miller," Jacob answered.

"I've been in the water for about two hours," Kurokachi said.

"About the same for me, only it seems longer," Jacob answered.

"Have you any water?" Kurokachi asked.

"None."

"Tomorrow will be very hard," Kurokachi said, "if we survive the night."

"We might make it," Jacob responded, though he was beginning to have his doubts.

Just then he saw the black smudge against the blue sky to the northeast. Pointing to it, he said, "I think we just got lucky, Lieutenant Kurokachi."

"Lieutenant (JG) Miller reporting as ordered, sir," Jacob said, standing in front of Admiral Sprat's desk. He stood at attention, his eyes straight ahead.

"Please, sit down," Sprat told him, pointing to the chair at the side of the desk. "Are you feeling well?" he asked.

"Yes, thank you, sir," Jacob answered. "I was only in the raft for about three hours before I was picked up."

Sprat offered him a cigarette and then took one for himself before he said, "I was sorry to learn that you lost a good friend during yesterday's action." He held the lighter for Jacob before he lit his own cigarette.

"Yance — I mean Lieutenant (JG) John Yancy was a very special kind of man," Jacob responded. "I never knew anyone like him before, and I probably will never know anyone like him again."

Sprat nodded and said, "I was also informed that before you were shot down, you downed four enemy planes."

"Yes, sir," Jacob answered.

"Before it is officially announced," Sprat said, "I thought you'd like to know that I'm recommending you for the Distinguished Flying Cross."

Jacob's jaw went slack.

"Believe it, Lieutenant," Sprat said. "I'm also promoting you from a JG to a full lieutenancy."

Jacob swallowed a mouth full of smoke and began to cough.

Sprat got up, poured water into a glass from a pitcher, and handed the glass to Jacob. "You did splendid work out there today. I'm proud to have you in my command."

"Thank you, sir," Jacob managed to answer. He was still too stunned to think clearly.

"When we hit Pearl," Sprat said, "you're going to get a lot of attention from the newspapers. Do you think you can handle it?"

"I think so, sir," Jacob answered.

"Yes, I think so too, Lieutenant," Sprat said. "I have a gut feeling you're the type of man who can handle just about anything that comes his way."

"Thank you, sir. I hope I deserve your confidence."

"You've earned it," Sprat said. "Now I have one other thing to tell you, but it must be kept a secret between us, though eventually it too will be part of the news."

Jacob nodded.

"The pilots who took part in this operation will be rotated back to the States for a few months to teach the things you've learned out here to other pilots."

"That's going to make the men smile," Jacob responded, smiling himself.

"By the way," Sprat said, "I was also told you managed to take a Japanese prisoner."

"We just happened to be in the drink together," Jacob answered. "He went down a few minutes before I did. He's convinced that I was the one who shot him down."

Sprat laughed; then he asked, "Tell me, why didn't you shoot him?"

Jacob stubbed out his cigarette in the ashtray. "Admiral, do you want an answer you could quote, or do you want what Yancy would say was the fucking truth?"

"The fuckin' truth!"

"We were out of it, sir, at least for the time being, and for a while there, it looked as if it would be forever. The war was being fought all around us, but we were just two men trying to stay alive."

"Suppose he had tried to kill you?"

"I'd have shot him, sir," Jacob answered without hesitation. "But he never made a move in that direction. He wanted to live as much as I did, and I wanted him to live."

"But he is your enemy," Sprat said.

"Was, sir," Jacob answered. "He was my enemy and —"

"Yes, and what?" Sprat pressed.

"I guess I remembered something my father told me," Jacob said, looking directly at Sprat. "He said that I should never do anything I would be ashamed to tell my son. Had I shot Mr. Kurokachi in cold blood I'd be ashamed to tell my son or anyone else about it."

"Have you a son?"

"I don't even have a wife yet, let alone a son," Jacob answered.

Smiling, Sprat said, "You must have one hell of a father."

"I have, sir."

"And he has one hell of a son," Sprat said, extending his hand.

Jacob shook Sprat's hand. "Sir, may I have permission to speak with Mr. Kurokachi."

Sprat raised his eyebrows.

"He does have a wife and two sons," Jacob said. "I can get word to them through the Swiss Consul that he's alive and well."

"But the International Red Cross does that."

"Something more personal would be much more meaningful," Jacob answered.

"I'll issue the necessary instructions to Colonel Rich," Sprat said, standing.

Jacob stood up. "Thank you, sir," he said.

"If the opportunity ever comes," Sprat said, "I'd like to meet your father. It's not every father whose son remembers what he has taught him."

CHAPTER 36

On Sunday afternoon, Troost sat in the living room of the house that Gloria somehow managed to rent. Ten days had passed since the Battle of Midway, and already he was involved in strategy conferences having to do with new operations against the Japanese. The battle, according to Layton and others in NI, in addition to giving the United States a significant victory over the Japanese, might well prove to be the turning point of the war.

"Well, just don't sit there," Gloria chided, "say something, anything."

"Sorry," Troost answered. "I was thinking about something."

"Or possibly someone else?"

"Gloria, let's not start. I came here for Sunday dinner and to see my children," Troost said.

"Sorry. It's hard for me to resist when I see an opening," she told him; then she asked, "What do you think of the house?"

"Seems fine to me."

She smiled. "You haven't even seen the rest of it."

"Whether you and Lillian like it is what matters, not what I think about it. I won't be staying here under any circumstance."

"Oh!"

"C'mon, Gloria, that isn't anything new," he said, taking his pipe and tobacco pouch out of his pocket and carefully filling the pipe bowl.

"You're absolutely right," she answered. "But to hear you say it so definitively — well, it does produce the teeniest twinge of regret to know that we will not be sharing our golden years together."

Troost puffed on his pipe. If Lillian inherited her acting ability, it came from Gloria and not from him.

"The view from here is absolutely spectacular," Gloria said, going to the window and looking out at the ocean. She faced him. "I do have something very important to talk to you about before the children arrive."

Troost took the pipe out of his mouth. He knew there had to be a very specific reason why he was asked to dinner. "I'm listening," he said.

"Lillian is pregnant," Gloria said.

Troost almost started out of the chair, stopped himself, put the pipe back in his mouth and puffing violently on it, growled, "Probably that damn acting teacher!"

"One of your men, darling," she said.

"What the hell are you talking about?" he asked, taking the pipe out of his mouth.

"Temper!" she cautioned.

"What do you mean one of my men?" Troost questioned.

"That young man who was awarded the Navy Cross and was promoted to lieutenant —"

"Glen Lascomb?"

Smiling, Gloria nodded. "He's the one. Of course, she wasn't a virgin when she went to bed with him, but he did neglect to tell her he was married and soon to be a father."

"Christ!" Troost exclaimed, almost leaping out of the chair. "What the hell is wrong with that girl?"

"Like father, like daughter," Gloria responded glibly.

Troost glared at her.

"There must be something you can do about it," Gloria said. "After all, Lillian is your daughter and —"

"Lascomb repeatedly risked his life —"

"Your daughter is carrying his child," Gloria snapped. "He must shoulder some responsibility."

"My God, does she hop into bed with every man she meets?"

"Her sexual behavior is not the issue," Gloria said.

"The man is a good officer."

"And that's where you intend to leave it?" she asked.

"What would you have me do?"

"Punish him. Make him pay. Don't you have any feelings? Your daughter is carrying that man's baby."

Troost took his pipe out of his mouth. "Yes, by Christ, I have feelings… I wonder whether Lillian has a brain."

"That's not the issue!"

"Does she really think any man is going to announce he's married and about to become a father before he gets in the sack with her?"

"You don't have to shout," Gloria said.

Troost walked to the window, looked out at the ocean and the surf breaking along the beach, and in a low, steady voice, said, "Have you any idea what it means for a man — not really a man, Glen is 23 — to go down into a burning ship and have men follow him and obey his orders?"

Gloria didn't answer.

Troost faced her. "Our son would do it," he said passionately. "He has done other things just as brave. Bringing his ship back to Pearl was one of them. Gloria, I'll certainly talk to him, but not on an official level. I'll also talk to Lillian."

For a few moments, neither of them spoke; then Gloria said, "You know, Andrew, you're really a very kind man."

Totally surprised by her words, Troost felt exposed, and to protect himself, he turned to the window again.

Jacob, Warren, and Glen met in the lobby of the Hali Kalani. It was Jacob who brought them together. He tracked Glen down after reading about him in the newspaper, and he found Warren the same way.

Almost immediately after Jacob introduced Glen to Warren, Glen said, "If you men will excuse me, I'm suddenly not feeling too well. I have to make a quick trip to the head."

"I'll be right back," Jacob told Warren and followed Glen into the men's room.

"That's one Troost too much," Glen said.

"What the hell are you talking about?"

Glen explained the situation between himself and Lillian. "The Admiral has already had a fatherly talk with me."

Jacob laughed.

"It's not funny," Glen groused. "You tell your friend that I died and flushed myself down the toilet."

"My guess is that he doesn't know a damn thing about his sister's condition," Jacob said.

"How can you be sure?"

"Things like that aren't up for general discussion in that kind of family. Besides, Warren doesn't live at home."

"What do you mean by that kind of family?" Glen asked.

"Think of your own family," Jacob told him. "If you had an unmarried sister and she became pregnant, would you know about it?"

Glen thought about Lucy for a few moments. She told her folks and his she was pregnant, but he was sure no one else knew. "Maybe a few years afterward," he said, "unless she had the baby, and even if she did, she'd be sent away to have it long before anyone would be able to tell she was pregnant."

"That's the way it would be in the Troost family," Jacob told him. "Warren doesn't know a thing about it."

"Okay, I'm game."

The two of them left the men's room together.

"Are you feeling better?" Warren asked.

"Much," Glen answered, "much better all around."

"Good. Now let's find a table," Jacob said, "and talk."

"Food or drink?" Warren asked.

"I'm starved," Jacob said.

"I don't see why we can't do both," Glen commented, heading for the restaurant area.

Escorted by a hostess, the three of them settled at a table for four away from the dance floor, which was crowded with couples moving to the sensuous beat of a tango.

The waitress came and asked if they wanted something to drink.

"Nothing for me," Warren said.

"I'll take a Johnny Walker Black on the rocks," Glen said.

"A dry martini —" Jacob started to say; then changing his mind, he said, "A bourbon."

"That's not what you used to drink," Warren commented.

"A guy from Mississippi latched me on to it," he said.

"Hey, this is great!" Glen exclaimed. "Too bad Tony isn't here."

"Submarine, isn't he?" Warren asked.

"You know him?" Jacob questioned. "Last name —"

"Trapasso?"

"That's him," Glen said. "But how the hell did you meet him?"

"I refueled his sub after it came out of Corregidor. It saved my ass. A Jap patrol boat was just about to finish us off, when the *Tarpon* sunk her."

"That's really one for the books. You meeting Tony that way," Jacob said.

"He said he knew you," Warren responded.

"Any idea where the hell he is?" Glen asked.

Warren shook his head.

The waitress brought the drinks to the table and said, "The drinks and dinner are on the house tonight," she said and gestured toward another table.

The three of them turned. There were four people. Two men and two women. One of the men was a civilian in black tie; the other was a commander. The women wore gowns. One was a blonde and the other brunette. Both were beautiful.

"Who are they?" Warren asked.

"Members of the press and Commander Horace Dean, CinPac's press liaison officer," Jacob explained, smiling and nodding at them.

"Who's the blonde?"

"Connie Burke. She's a reporter for the *New York Post*, and the other one, Beth Fields, is a freelance magazine writer."

"They're gorgeous!" Glen exclaimed. "What do you think, Warren?"

Warren looked toward the women and then at Glen. "They're beautiful all right, but out of your league."

"I guess I should go over and thank them," Jacob said, standing.

"I'll join you," Glen offered.

"I might as well go along," Warren said.

The three walked over to the table.

Jacob introduced Warren and Glen, and the man in black tie said, "Charles Green. NBC news." He shook hands with each of them.

"Lieutenant Miller, why don't you and your friends join us?" Miss Burke asked, smiling at him. She had blue eyes, straight white teeth and, it appeared from the décolletage of her black gown, lovely breasts.

"We haven't seen each other for a long time," Jacob explained. He really wanted to tell Warren about Yancy.

"Please," she said in a very soft voice.

"What about it?" Jacob asked, looking at Warren and Glen.

"It's okay with me," Glen said, leering wolfishly at Miss Fields.

Warren nodded.

Green summoned the manager and two tables were quickly joined together.

"Have you men eaten yet?" Commander Dean asked.

"No, sir —" Jacob started to say.

"Please, while we're at the table," Dean said, "let's dispense with the military formalities."

"We haven't eaten yet," Jacob said.

"Excellent!" Green exclaimed. "I'll have the manager ask the chef to do a special —"

"There's really no need," Jacob told him.

"Nonsense," Green responded. "There's every need. You men are heroes."

Suddenly the music stopped and the spotlight swept across the floor to the table.

"Ladies and gentlemen," the band leader said, "we're honored to have as our guests here tonight three very important Americans. Lieutenants Warren Troost and Jacob Miller and Lieutenant (JG) Glen Lascomb."

A spontaneous burst of applause filled the room. The three of them stood up.

"I feel like an ass," Warren whispered, while smiling.

"Don't let it show," Jacob answered.

"Lieutenant Miller, will you please come up here and say a few words to the people here tonight?" the band leader asked.

Jacob hesitated.

"Your show," Commander Dean said.

Jacob walked to the bandstand.

There was another burst of applause.

The spotlight poured over Jacob.

"First, Lieutenant," the band leader said, "let me congratulate you on behalf of all of us here and on behalf of the American people for taking out so many of the enemy." And he stuck out his hand. Reluctantly, Jacob shook it.

"I also happen to know that you were shot down," the band leader said. "Would you share with us some of your thoughts that you had while you were waiting to be rescued? Did you think of your mother and father — perhaps your sweetheart?"

Jacob wasn't going to let the opportunity pass to make everyone in the room think about the war from a slightly different perspective.

"I know it must be hard for you —"

"It's not hard at all," Jacob answered and in a loud clear voice, he said, "I wasn't alone."

"You mean you knew that God —"

"Lieutenant Yashi Kurokachi was with me," Jacob said. "He was shot down before I was. He was rescued with me, and someday when this war is over, maybe we will have the opportunity to meet as friends."

An awesome silence filled the room.

"Well, thank you, Lieutenant, for your most interesting comment," the band leader said and immediately gave the band the downbeat.

Jacob walked across the dance floor to the table.

"That will be in all the newspapers tomorrow morning," Commander Dean commented, his voice tight with anger.

Jacob sat down and looked at him. "Kurokachi is a man just like me," he said. "Neither of us is a killer. When it comes right down to it, Commander, most of us are scared shitless."

"Jake, why don't you come with me," Miss Burke said, standing up.

Jacob looked questioningly up at her. She went around to the rear of his chair. He could smell her perfume.

"Go with her," Warren said softly.

Jacob looked at Glen.

"We'll catch up with you another time," Glen told him.

"Come, Jake," she urged, gently taking hold of his hand and drawing him out of the chair.

"I'll see you guys," Jake said.

"Sure thing," Warren answered.

"Sure thing," Glen echoed.

"A penny for your thoughts," Connie said as they stepped into a garden adjoining the hotel lobby.

"I made an ass out of myself," he answered, "and I spoiled a perfectly good evening for a lot of other people."

"Something was bothering you," she answered.

He blew a cloud of smoke toward the sky. "I guess I didn't like what the band leader said."

"But that's what it boils down to, doesn't it?" she responded, "taking out the enemy?"

"That's exactly what it boils down to," he said, blowing more smoke into the night.

"I'm going back to New York in a week. I know you're going back the day after tomorrow. I'd like to see you when we're back there."

He looked at her. "Isn't something confused here? Shouldn't I be the one to say that to you?"

"You didn't know I was going to be there, but I knew you were."

"You're not supposed to know that," he said with a smile.

"I only told you because, as the regs state about classified information, 'You have a need to know'."

He slid his arm around her bare shoulder. "How could I refuse you?"

"I'm trying to make it as hard for you as possible."

"You've succeeded," Jacob said. "Suppose we make a date now... I'll meet you on June 25th at 1900 — I mean seven o'clock — in the lobby of the Plaza."

"It's a date," Connie answered.

"Sealed with a kiss," he said, bending down and kissing her on the lips.

CHAPTER 37

The *Tarpon* was on the surface 100 miles to the east of Attu. Though it was summer, a sudden storm came roaring out of the Arctic, bringing with it intense cold, mountainous waves, and ice that had to be chopped away.

Tony came down from the bridge through the conning tower hatch, pulled off his face mask, and shaking his head, complained to no one in particular, "It's murder up there." He was a different-looking man than he had been months before when he first came aboard the *Tarpon*. Now he was bearded, and in his eyes there was no longer the look of a young, inexperienced officer. This was his fourth patrol.

He pulled off his foul-weather gear, looped it over his arm, and was just about to leave the bridge, when the boat's bow dipped, and a torrent of water gushed into the conning tower and sluiced through the open hatch and down into the control room.

"Fire!" someone shouted moments later from the control room.

Tony hit the Klaxon button, waited until its blare stopped, and switched on the 1MC. "Fire in the control room… Damage control, fire in main control." He handed his gear to a nearby sailor and dropped through the hatch into the control room. Electric arcs and blue flames sputtered out of the main power cable.

Brisson appeared on the scene. "Get that fire out," he ordered, pointing to the large fire in the corner.

Smoke and fumes were rapidly filling the compartment, Keffer, the chief electrician's mate, used the fire extinguishers on the flames, but more fire continued to burn.

"Fire in the forward battery room," a man shouted.

"Tony," Brisson yelled, "get damage control to the forward battery room."

"Skipper," Keffer said, "we got the fires we can see, but there's a lot of burning goin' on that we can't see."

"Pull the forward battery breaker and forward power switch," Brisson said. "I want to reduce the electrical load forward."

Keffer said, "Right away, sir."

Brisson went up to the conning tower.

Tony followed him.

"Conn, the smoke and fumes forward are driving damage control back," the DCO reported.

"Abandon forward battery and torpedo room! Seal them off," Brisson ordered.

Smoke and fumes poured into the conning tower from the control room below.

Tony couldn't talk without coughing. His eyes burned.

"Forward battery and torpedo room abandoned and sealed," the DCO called up from the control room.

"Secure engines," Brisson ordered.

The engine signalman used the phone to relay the order. "Secure engines answered," he said, putting the phone down.

Brisson switched on the 1MC. "All hands — dead!" he exclaimed; then he said, "Pass the word, abandon the control room. Seal it off."

Tony relayed the order. The hatch between the conning tower and the control room was sealed off. "All hands lay aft," Brisson ordered.

Tony watched the gyro compass short out. The electrical steering system went out and the engine order annunciators were knocked out of commission.

"Radio transmitters are out," the communications officer reported.

The electrical controls for diving planes were shorted out.

"Conn," the XO shouted, "what the hell is going on down there?"

Brisson said, "Tony, we've got to get back into the control room," he said. "We'll use the rescue breathers."

Tony nodded, pointed to three men, and said, "Let's make a try for it." They opened the hatch and within moments were driven back. "Get that hatch shut," Tony yelled.

The hatch was slammed down and secured again.

"Skipper, I think we can do it if we charge the escape lungs with oxygen."

Brisson nodded. "It's worth a shot."

Tony charged the escape masks with oxygen and gave the order to open the hatch to the control room. He took a deep breath and dropped into the smoke-filled room.

The three men with oxygen-charged rescue breathers followed him.

Using a flashlight, Tony located the valve control bank. He flipped the levers to partially blow number three main ballast and bring the boat level.

One of the men pointed to his escape lung.

Tony nodded. Their oxygen supply was getting very low. He held up two fingers and, pointing to the auxiliary induction valve, he made a circular motion with his hand.

The men understood and immediately closed them off.

Tony was sweating. His lungs were starved for oxygen. There was a ringing in his head. He pointed to the hatch.

One of the men pushed it open and climbed out of the control room. The second man lost his footing and had to be pushed up and out. The third man seemed to take a very long time to climb into the conning tower. Finally, Tony started up. He felt himself slipping into a soft grayness and —

He was on the deck and someone was putting a replacement rescue mask on his face. Within moments his oxygen-starved lungs began to relax and the ringing in his head stopped. He nodded and sat up. "I'm okay," he said, taking the rescue mask off.

Brisson reached down and pulled him to his feet. "We've got to get our engines started. We're drifting too close to the beach."

Tony nodded and walked to the telephone bank.

"We'll try to suck air into the induction outlets aft," Brisson said. "Stand by."

Tony picked up the phone to the engine room. "Stand by for a cold start."

"Standing by," the EO answered.

"Start."

"Start," Tony repeated.

Nothing.

"I don't have electrical power for the engine starters," the engineering officer reported.

"Try it again," Brisson said.

"Give it another try," Tony said into the phone.

"Not working, skipper," Tony said.

Brisson pursed his lips. "We've got to get electrical power to the engine room. You think you can go back into the control room and try to get it going from there?"

"I'll need the help of an electrician's mate this time," he said.

Brisson looked around the bridge.

"I think I can do it," the chief quartermaster volunteered.

"Okay, the chief will go with you," Brisson said.

Tony put the oxygen-charged rescue breather on again and dropped through the open hatch into the control room. The chief followed. There seemed to be less smoke than there was before. Tony held the flashlight on the electric control panel.

The chief nodded and began to work, stopping now and then to wipe the sweat from his brow.

Tony waited, his breathing becoming more labored with each passing second.

The chief pointed to the master control switch. Tony put his hand on it. The chief made a downward gesture with his right hand. Tony threw the switch.

A green light indicated that power was flowing to the engine room.

Tony and the chief hurried back to the conning tower. The chief went out first. Tony started up, when suddenly he saw a burst of flame in a corner. He tore the mask from his face. "Fire!" he shouted. "Fire!"

A fire extinguisher and freshly charged rescue masks were dropped down to him. He put the mask on and squirted foam on the fire. The fire was building. He retreated to the hatch and climbed out. "Seal it off," he said to the sailor standing by. "Skipper, it's out of control."

The phone to the after torpedo room rang.

Tony picked it up.

"Conn," the TO said, "we're taking a lot of smoke back here. Some of the men are getting sick."

"Stand by," Tony said and repeated the message to Brisson.

"Everyone topside," Brisson said. "Maybe if we close the conning tower hatch, we'll kill the fires below."

"All hands topside to the bridge… All hands topside, to the bridge."

The wind and sea tore at the men. In seconds their clothing was soaked and their bodies numbed by the cold.

One man was almost washed overboard by a huge wave that broke on the *Tarpon*, but the chief grabbed hold of him.

An hour and a half passed before Brisson ordered the men back into the boat.

"We've got to get our diesels going," Brisson said. "This time we'll try from the control room. Tell the EO I want to re-establish an engineering watch in the control room and get those engines started."

"Skipper, before anyone goes in there, we better check it out," Tony said.

Brisson ordered the hatch opened.

"If I can manage without a mask, the EO and his men will be able to," Tony said, lowering himself into the control room. It smelled of burnt rubber and cork. But the fire he tried to kill was out and the smoke wasn't nearly as thick as it had been before. He climbed out of the hatch. "It's not great down there, but it can be tolerated."

Thirty minutes after the EO and his men went into the control room, the diesels coughed to life.

"All ahead standard," Brisson ordered.

"All ahead standard," the engine order telegraph watch answered.

"Reset the bridge watch," Brisson said. "We'll make port under our own power."

"Aye, aye, skipper," Tony answered.

CHAPTER 38

Jacob managed to get a flight from San Diego to Chicago but couldn't get one from Chicago to New York and had to settle for a one-way ticket on a "milk train" between the two cities. It was six o'clock in the morning when he arrived at Grand Central. He left the train, walked up the ramp, and crossed the concourse to the Lexington Avenue side. He stopped at a newsstand and bought a *New York Times*; then going outside, he got in the first taxi in the queue along the sidewalk outside the station.

"Brooklyn," he told the driver.

The cabbie turned around. "Where in Brooklyn?"

"Chester and Lott Avenues."

The man faced front, pulled down the flag, turned on the ignition and shifted into first.

Jacob leaned back and closed his eyes. The train ride had taken 22 hours, and during that time he doubted he slept more than three hours, and never more than a half hour at a time. The train was full of men in uniform, some like himself going home on leave. But of all the men he met, he was the only one who had experienced combat. In some strange, indefinable way, that fact set him apart from the other men. It was as if, in their eyes, he knew some great secret or possessed a superior wisdom.

"Comin' home on leave?" the cabbie asked.

Jacob opened his eyes. "Yes," he answered. Even at that early hour, the city was warm and muggy.

"Best way to go where you're goin'," the man said, "is across the Williamsburg Bridge, then follow the El until —"

"You go the way you know best," Jacob answered, picking up the *Times*. The British were holding the Germans at a place in Egypt called El Alamein. His eyes skimmed over a story about a fire aboard the *Tarpon*, an American submarine on combat patrol in the North Pacific, until they picked up the name Tony Trapasso; then he began to read it. The *Tarpon*'s captain, Commander Brisson, said, "Ensign Trapasso repeatedly risked his life to save the boat and its crew. I have recommended in my official report of the situation that he be promoted to the rank of lieutenant and be awarded the Navy Cross for outstanding valor above and beyond the call of duty..." Jacob smiled. He was almost certain that Miriam didn't know anything about it yet.

"I got a nephew in the marines," the cabbie said. "Been in it since before the war. He's a sergeant."

"I guess almost everyone has a relative or friend in the service," Jacob answered, deciding that sometime later in the day, he'd phone Tony's father and congratulate him.

"Yeah, if I were younger, I'd join up," the man said. "Hell, a guy can have some time, if he's smart." The cabbie glanced over his shoulder at him.

"That's not exactly what the war is all about," Jacob answered and immediately turned his attention again to the *Times*.

That early in the morning the ride from Grand Central to the building where his parents lived took 40 minutes and by 6:50 he was standing on the sidewalk outside the four-floor walk-up. The street was very still.

Suddenly a woman came to one of the open windows on the ground floor, looked out, and in Yiddish said, "Hershel, there's a man in a white uniform standing in front of the house. What's he doing there?"

"How should I know," Hershel asked. "I can't see him."

"So come an' look," she said, switching to English.

Jacob didn't recognize the woman. Even before his family had moved in, the Schwartz family had lived there. Mr. Schwartz was a trolley-car motorman on the Church Avenue line. There were three children in the family: all girls. The oldest, Mildred, graduated from Tilden High School when he did. The middle one was a year older than Miriam, and the youngest was in her senior year at Tilden. He felt that the Schwartzes and his parents hoped he and Mildred would someday get together.

"Never saw him before," Hershel said.

Jacob picked up his suitcase and walked toward the building. These were new people.

"Ask him what he wants," the woman pressed, lapsing back into Yiddish.

Hershel was a big, barrel-chested man with a bullet-shaped head. "Hey you, what are you doing here?" he called out.

"I live upstairs," Jacob answered.

"I never saw him before," the woman said. "Hershel, call the police!"

Jacob reached the top of the stoop, opened the front door, entered the building, and started to climb the steps.

A door on the ground floor opened,

"He's going up the steps," Hershel said. "He must live here, Frieda."

"I know everybody who lives here," she answered. "I never saw anyone in a white suit like that before."

Jacob reached the second landing. The hallway still smelled of the previous night's cooking. Its metal walls were still covered with grime.

Finally, when he was at the door of his family's apartment, he realized that Hershel had followed him up the steps. "This is where I live," he said.

"You must be the one everybody on the street is talking about," Hershel said. "You're the hero."

Jacob flushed.

"You're the Miller boy, aren't you?"

"I'm Jacob."

"Frieda, it's the Miller boy, the hero!" Hershel shouted. "He's home. Frieda, it's our hero." And he offered his beefy hand. "Hey, you're really here."

Doors opened and people came out on the landings to look at him. Those who knew him called his name, and some of the men came up and shook his hand.

Then suddenly the door to his apartment opened. His father started to speak, saw him, and began to tremble.

"Papa," Jacob said, enfolding the man in his arms. "Papa."

"What's going on out there, Sam?" his mother asked, even as she came to the door.

"Mom," Jacob said, letting go of his father with one arm and embracing his mother with it.

All the neighbors clapped.

His mother kissed his face. "Thank God you're safe," she whispered; then to the neighbors she said, "There'll be a party in my house on Saturday night. Everyone is invited. Everyone!"

Miriam came to the door.

Jacob let go of his parents and swept his sister into his arms. "Tony is all right," he told her.

"You saw him?" she asked.

"There's something about him in today's *Times*," he said, and realizing it had fallen to the floor, he started to reach for it, but Hershel picked it up and handed it to him; he gave it to his sister.

"It's good to be home," he said, looking at all of the people he knew.

"Those medals?" one of the teenaged boys asked, pointing to Jacob's chest.

"Sure, they're medals," Jacob's father answered.

"I'm just making breakfast," his mother said, looking at him. "Come inside." Then she turned to her neighbors. "I know he belongs to you also, but let me have him for a little while."

"Thank you for welcoming me home," Jacob said, picked up his suitcase, and linked his free arm with his mother's.

"I'll carry that," his father said.

Jacob was about to object, when he suddenly realized it was important for his father to carry it.

Miriam brought up the rear and closed the door, as soon as all of them were inside the apartment.

"Now, let me look at you," his mother said, stopping and taking a few steps backward. "You've got a nice tan ... maybe a little thinner and —"

He realized she was looking into his eyes. She always put great stock in what she said she could see in people's eyes.

She came close to him, taking hold of his face between her two hands, and whispered, though everyone else in the room could hear, "There's nothing there I understand... Nothing!"

"Hanna, he's tired. Don't bother him with your nonsense now!" his father told her.

"Your papa is right," she said. "I have coffee already in the percolator, and I can make you toast and a couple of eggs."

"That will be fine," Jacob said. "Mostly I want to sleep."

Suddenly Miriam began to shout. "Papa, Mom, Tony saved his boat. He's getting a medal for it and he's going to be a lieutenant. That's what you are, aren't you, Jacob?"

"No, I'm one grade above that," Jacob said.

"I'm so proud of him!" Miriam exclaimed. "And I'm so proud of you, Jacob. All my friends ask me about you all the time."

The family moved to the kitchen.

"You should have let us know that you were coming home," his father said.

"I wanted to surprise you," Jacob said.

"I couldn't believe my eyes."

"It was one of the few times I've ever seen you speechless," Jacob laughed.

"That I'd like to have seen," his mother said.

The time at the breakfast table passed quickly. Miriam went off to work and, as his father got ready to leave, he asked, "Will you come with me to the shul on the Shabbos?"

Jacob hadn't been to Friday night services for years. "Yes, Papa, I'll go."

His father smiled broadly. "Tonight, I'll be home early," he announced.

"Well," his mother said, "do whatever you want to do."

"Shower and then sleep," Jacob answered.

His mother reached across the table and took hold of his hand. "You just made your father very happy," she said.

"And what can I do to make you happy, Mom?" he asked.

She smiled. "Be happy yourself."

"I'm serious," Jacob said. "Tell me and I'll do it."

She nodded and said, "I just did, Jacob."

"Sometimes, Mom, it's not so easy to be happy."

"Not so easy at all," his mother answered.

Jacob managed a smile and, kissing the back of his mother's hand, he said, "I'll be happy, Mom, I really will."

CHAPTER 39

Without disturbing Irene, Warren left the bed, found a pack of cigarettes and a lighter on the dresser in the darkness of the room, and went to the open window to smoke. In 10 days' time, he was going to be finished with the training course and reassigned to an operational area. The six weeks passed much more quickly than he had imagined they would. Much of the reason for this was his relationship to Irene. Whenever he was not involved with the training course, he was involved with her. He looked back at the bed. She was naked. When they were together, that was the way they slept. He liked her that way. He was in love with her, but wasn't sure whether he should be, or whether she loved him. Though she wasn't in the least inhibited sexually, she was always guarded about her feelings.

Making the cigarette tip glow red, Warren took a long drag on it and savored the smoke before letting it pour out of his mouth and nostrils. Then suddenly he felt the soft, warm press of Irene's breasts on his back.

She reached around for the cigarette, took a drag, and almost immediately freeing the smoke, asked, "How long have you been standing here?"

"Not long," he answered.

She returned the cigarette to him. "You're thinking about when you leave?" she asked.

"I guess, in a way."

She put her arms around him and pressed her face to his back. "Frightened?"

"Yes. I'd be a fool not to be."

"Word is around that we're going to be making some sort of big push," she said, kissing his back.

"I heard the same thing," Warren answered.

"Your father should know. Did he drop any hints when you saw him?"

"Nothing. We spoke about the family and —"

"And what?" Irene asked.

"He made not so oblique references to the woman with whom he's having an affair."

"You never mentioned that before," she said, taking the cigarette from him again.

Warren shrugged. "Not much reason to," he said. "He's entitled to be happy and, from what I can see, he is."

"What about your mother?" she asked, before she put the cigarette in her mouth. "What about her feelings?"

"I think she almost prefers it," he answered. "It gives her another excuse to feel sorry for herself and drink."

She took a drag on the cigarette, held the smoke for a moment before she freed it, and handing the cigarette back to him, said, "You don't seem to have much pity for her."

"Strange, but I really do," Warren responded. "I also know she doesn't need my pity, or anyone else's, for that matter." He was aware that their conversation was going in an unexpected direction.

"I've been thinking about us," she said, still close to him. "Have you?"

"Yes," he admitted.

"You'll be leaving soon," Irene said matter-of-factly.

"My training ends in 10 days," he told her, pinching out the head of the cigarette and dropping it in the nearby wastepaper basket.

"What conclusion did you come to about us?" she asked.

He took hold of her hands and pulled her even more tightly against him. "I think I'm in love with you," he said.

"You make it sound as if you've reached the edge of doom," she commented.

"I didn't mean to. But I'm not sure whether that makes much sense now," he said.

"Hardly any at all," she whispered, just loud enough for him to hear.

"And —"

"And what?" she asked quickly.

"I don't really know your feelings about me," he told her, instantly aware of how foolishly juvenile the words sounded.

Irene gently freed her hands from his and stepped back. "I think I love you too," she said. "I know I enjoy being with you in or out of bed."

Warren faced her.

"I don't want to risk being your widow," she said. "I don't think I could bear that. The time that I've spent with you during these few weeks means more to me than I could ever tell you."

He took her in his arms.

"I can't run that risk," she said softly. "I can't. And I know that if I marry you, I will have to accept that risk as part of the marriage, just as if it were the color of your eyes or hair. You come with the risk."

Warren was very still. She was telling him that she wasn't going to marry him.

"But I do love you," she said in a low, passionate voice, putting her hand over his mouth. "Both of us know it's going to be a long war," she said, "and by the time it's over, we won't be the same and the things we want then won't be the things we want now."

He kissed her gently on the ear. "I want you now," he said.

Jacob wore his uniform when he accompanied his father to shul on Friday night. The shul was several blocks up the street from where they lived and in the long, gathering twilight of a June day they walked side by side. His mother and Miriam were several paces behind them.

Word of Jacob's homecoming spread through the neighborhood, and almost everyone along the way was out in the street to see them.

Now and then a man would greet his father and his father would respond with a nod.

To Jacob, the houses along the way were even more shabby than he remembered. The flood of money that the war was supposed to have brought to the civilian population didn't seem to affect the people he saw.

The shul that his father belonged to was a big rambling building, with a huge stained-glass window in the shape of a Jewish star. Jacob knew every corner, every dark space in the building. He started Hebrew school there when he was five and continued for another two years after he was bar mitzvahed. There was a time when he hated it and often dreamt that it would burn to the ground, though he never dared tell anyone about his feelings or his dreams.

"Your name was even in the *Forward*," his father said, referring to the Yiddish newspaper he read. "Your name, the family name, even your mother's and Miriam's. Reporters came to see me in the exchange. Such a commotion!"

From the sound of his father's voice, Jacob could tell he was proud of him.

"In today's *Forward*, it says that you're going to help the government sell war bonds," his father said.

"Yes, before I left Pearl, I was told that I would be doing that," Jacob answered.

"For the rest of the war?" his father asked, looking at him.

"No, Papa," Jacob answered. "I'll be doing that for a while; then I'll probably teach new pilots. But after a while, I'll be sent back."

"You want to go back?"

"Papa, I'm a fighter pilot," Jacob said, hoping that his father wouldn't start an argument.

"I know. I know you're one of the best, but you don't talk about it, and when I ask you a question, you change the subject."

"Papa, the things I want to talk about, I can't," Jacob said.

"And why not? I'm your papa."

Jacob's step faltered.

His father grabbed his arm. "You all right?" he asked.

"Sam, is anything wrong?" his mother called, hurrying to them.

"Nothing," Jacob lied. "I just missed my footing."

"I thought you were going to fall," she said.

"Let him be, Hanna," his father said. "Happens a man can lose his footing. Just look at these sidewalks; they're made of pieces of slate. Now let us walk without anyone bothering us." And taking Jacob by the arm, he led him away.

"I have to unscramble a few things," Jacob said, when they were some distance from his mother and sister.

"What things?"

Jacob bit his lower lip and shook his head.

"Whatever you did, God understands and will forgive you," his father said.

"It has nothing to do with what I did, at least not the way you think."

"So tell me how do I think?"

"Papa, you can't help me... I have to find the answer in myself."

"Are you afraid?"

"No more than anyone else," Jacob answered; then he said, "Papa, my friend died in my arms. I held him and I couldn't do anything to help him."

"The one you wrote me about, Yancy?" his father asked.

Jacob nodded, took out a handkerchief, and wiped the tears from his eyes. He felt his father's hand on his shoulder.

"But you saved a life. That surely should be worth something to you, shouldn't it?"

"It is," Jacob answered. "But I can't seem to get Yancy out of mind."

"You never will," his father said. "In the first war, I was in the trenches on the German side —"

"I never knew that!"

"No need for you to until now," his father said. "My friend was killed during a British attack on our front. I didn't know he was dead. I carried him to the hospital on my back. That was in 1916. Now it's 1942 and I never forgot a single detail. His name was Moishe Grunfeldt. He was 19 years old..." His father sighed. "Maybe the good Lord has a reason for wanting us to remember things like that."

"Maybe," Jacob answered. "Maybe He does."

CHAPTER 40

Troost sat at his desk in CinPacFleet Headquarters. It was nine o'clock at night. He leaned back, rubbed his eyes, and then bent over the thick sheaf of papers and began to read again. The operation's code name was Watchdog. Its purpose was to seize control of the islands of Guadalcanal and Tulagi for a later assault on the Japanese stronghold of Rabaul, on the northern coast of the island of New Britain.

Before Troost became involved in the planning of the operation, he had some notion where the Solomon Islands were and he even remembered reading about the islands in a very old issue of the *National Geographic* that featured the animal collecting adventures of Martin and Osa Johnson. But when word came from the Joint Chiefs of Staff in Washington that the Solomons were to be the first target of the American westward push in the Pacific, he was as surprised as anyone else in CinPacFleet.

Because his destroyers and cruisers would be involved in gunfire support of the amphibious landing forces, Troost studied the charts of the area and found that there were enormous stretches of coastline and open water that were completely uncharted. His ships would have to depend on their Fathometers to find safe water. But there was an even more serious situation: the navy wasn't ready to undertake an operation that would undoubtedly bring it into a confrontation with numerically superior Japanese surface forces and land-based aircraft. He and others senior to him voiced this objection. But nothing they said had any effect. The operation was scheduled for Friday, August 14th. "H" hour was 6:14 local time.

Troost stacked the sheets neatly, summoned his aide, Commander Ritten, and handing him the stack of papers, said, "Have this delivered to Admiral Floyde's office now."

"Aye, aye sir," Ritten answered; then he said, "You had two calls, Admiral. One from your son and the other from Mrs. Hasse. Your son asked if your dinner appointment with him tomorrow night was still a go situation. I took the liberty of telling him it was."

Troost nodded. "Did Mrs. Hasse leave a message?" he asked.

"No sir," Ritten replied.

"As soon as you get rid of that OPS plan, take off," Troost said, and lifting the phone, he asked the operator to connect him with Kate's number. "Did I wake you?" he asked, when she came on the line.

"No, I was reading Louis Bromfield's latest novel, *Wild is the River*," she answered.

"Do you like it?"

"Yes," she said.

"I have a few things to finish before I leave," he said.

"Have you had any dinner?"

He laughed. "I don't even remember if I had lunch."

"I'll have something ready for you," she said.

"Thanks. I'll see you in a little while," he said, and put the phone down.

"We're shipping out soon," Glen said, looking across a small round table at Lillian. He had called her the previous evening, and at the end of a stormy conversation she agreed to meet him the following afternoon in the cocktail lounge where they'd first met.

"That's what you do in the navy," she answered, pushing the side of her blonde hair back into place.

"Listen, I wanted to see you because I had to see you," he said. "I've spent a lot of time thinking about us."

She looked particularly beautiful. She wore a white linen skirt and a white silk blouse, open at the neck.

"*Us*? What do you mean by *us*?" she practically shrieked. "There isn't any us."

Glen lifted the shot glass in front of him and downed half the scotch he ordered. "I wanted to set things straight between us," he said.

"It's a little late for that," she answered bitterly.

"Have something to drink," he said.

Lillian shook her head. "I don't want anything from you, not even a drink."

"Then why did you come?" Glen asked.

"Because —" she faltered.

"Listen," he said, taking hold of her hands, "I didn't want to hurt you."

"For someone who didn't want to hurt me, you sure did a good job," she responded in a thin voice.

"I'm sorry. I really am."

"All right, you're sorry."

"Marry me," he said.

She pulled her hands away. "What?"

"I never loved Lucy," he said, taking a cigarette and lighting it.

"She's going to have your baby."

"When I get back to Pearl," he said, "I'll ask her for a divorce."

"But —"

251

He took hold of her hands again. "I love you," he said. "After I met your brother —"

"When did you meet him?"

"A few weeks back," he said. "Listen, I don't want to talk about him or anything else. I want to talk about us."

"What do you want me to say?" she asked.

"Yes. I want you to say yes."

"I can't say yes just like that. Not when I know that your wife is going to have a baby."

"I love you," Glen said.

"I just don't know."

Glen finished the scotch and looked straight at her. "I haven't been able to get you out of my mind. I tried. I even tried a couple of other women, but it wasn't the same as it was with you."

"I'd like a drink now," Lillian told him. "A very dry martini."

"I'll get it for you from the bar," Glen said. "Want anything else?"

She shook her head.

Glen left the table and walked to the bar. "One very dry martini," he ordered.

"One very dry martini," the barkeep repeated.

"How much?" Glen asked.

"Six bits."

Glen put three quarters down on the bar, left a 15-cent tip, and returning to the table, said, "When you finish your drink, let's get out of here."

"Where do you want to go?"

"Someplace where we can be alone," Glen answered, devouring her with his eyes.

Lillian picked up her drink, sipped at it, and then, looking at him over the rim of the glass, said, "My mother won't be back until sometime late this evening."

"I love you," Glen told her.

Warren arrived at the Sing Bo restaurant a few minutes early and gave his name to the maître d', a small Chinese man.

"Yes, there's a reservation for three under that name," the man said.

"For three?" Warren questioned.

"It was made by your aide."

Warren smiled. "My father's aide," he said. "Lieutenant commanders don't have aides."

The man nodded and asked, "May I show you to the table, Commander?"

"I think I'll wait at the bar," Warren said, knowing he'd feel very uncomfortable sitting alone at the table.

The man gestured toward the bar. There were several couples there.

"On second thought," Warren said, "I'll go to the table."

"Please follow me," the maître d' said.

Warren sat facing the center of the room. The restaurant was crowded, but the noise level was tolerable. The food, from what he could tell as the waiters passed him, looked and smelled delicious.

He lit a cigarette. Certain the third person would be the woman with whom his father was having an affair, he wondered how he'd react. He stubbed out the cigarette in a brass ashtray and checked his watch. His father was already five minutes late. He looked at the nearby tables. Several were occupied by officers his own age and their wives or sweethearts. He was sorry Irene wasn't with him, but she was on duty and wouldn't be off until the next morning. He pursed his lips. Despite the fact they were still lovers, they were becoming more distant from each other in anticipation of the day he'd leave and —

His father and the woman were being escorted to the table by the maître d'.

Warren stood up.

"My son Warren," Troost said. "Mrs. Hasse."

Warren shook her hand.

"It's a pleasure," she said.

The three of them sat down and Troost said, "I'm sorry I'm late but the traffic is very heavy."

"Have you been waiting long, Commander?" she asked.

"Please, call me Warren," he said, before he added, "A few minutes."

"Then you must call me Kate," she said. "Everyone does."

"Would you care for something to drink?" Troost asked.

"Only if the two of you have something," Kate responded.

"I'll —" he was going to say *I'll pass*, but he caught the look in his father's eyes and said, "Yes, I'll have a scotch and water."

"Kate?" his father asked again.

"Gin and tonic," she said.

"And I'll have a vodka martini," Troost announced.

As soon as the waiter took the bar order, Kate said, "Andrew tells me that you'll be finishing your training soon."

"Wednesday of next week," Warren answered.

"From what your father has told me," she said, 'the training consists of a lot more than learning to handle a PT boat."

"I'm told it's similar to the training given the British commandos," Warren said.

Their drinks came and Troost raised his glass, "To peace."

"To peace," Warren and Kate echoed together.

The three of them touched glasses and then drank.

Warren could see that his father was very much in love with Kate. His voice even sounded different when he used her name. Softer. And there wasn't any doubt in Warren's mind that she was in love with him.

When it came time to order, his father summoned the maître d' to the table and said, "I'd very much appreciate it if you would do the ordering for us."

"I would be pleased to," the man said and left the table.

"Admiral Sprat told me it's the best way to order here," Troost explained.

"I was wondering how you found this place," Warren said. "Ordinarily, I know you don't like Chinese food."

"Andrew, you never said a word about that," Kate chided. "And I've been making you various Chinese dishes."

Troost smiled. "They're fine," he said, patting her hand. "If they weren't, I would have told you."

The dinner started with fried dumplings, followed by a spicy soup with bits of shrimp and other seafood. After the soup came four large casseroles: one was a chicken dish, another was mixed seafood with Chinese vegetables, the third was pieces of spicy steak, and the fourth was pork fried rice.

The three of them used chopsticks, and as they ate, Warren found himself talking more to Kate than to his father. He was surprised to learn that she was going to the university and that she wanted to write.

"She's very good," his father said, when she mentioned her desire to write. "I read some of her stories and they held my interest."

Kate squeezed his hand and laughed. "Of course, he's not prejudiced, is he?"

"Purely an objective viewpoint," Troost responded.

Before any of them realized it, they had finished eating and it was almost curfew time.

"If you'll excuse me," Kate said, "I'll visit the powder room before we leave."

Warren and his father started to stand.

"Please," Kate said. "There's no need to do that."

Warren waited until his father sat down before he did.

"I'm glad you're here," his father said.

"I like her," Warren told him. "She's good for you."

"Very good for me," Troost said.

"You look happier than I ever remember."

"I am. I really am. What about you?" his father asked. "I mean, is there anyone special in your life?"

"I've been seeing an army nurse," Warren said. "But neither of us is sure."

"Sure?"

"Dad, if you don't mind, I'd rather not talk about it."

Troost shrugged; then he leaned toward Warren. "You know there's a big operation in the making," he said.

"I heard rumors about it."

"It's true," his father said. "I'll be there, and I know several PT squadrons will be used in the operation."

"Then maybe I'll see you wherever *there* is?" Warren responded.

"Maybe," Troost said; then he asked, "Do you love the woman?"

"Yes."

"And I take it she loves you?"

Warren nodded.

"Then don't waste the time you have," his father advised. "Don't waste it!"

"Waste what?" Kate asked, returning to the table.

Neither Warren nor his father realized she was close by until they heard her voice.

"Just some fatherly advice," Warren said, trying to sound nonchalant.

Kate put her hand over Troost's. "Your father is a very wise man," she said.

Warren looked at her, then at his father. That was something his mother never would have said, much less believed. "Yes," Warren answered, "I've always thought he was." Then he added, "I'm happy he has you."

"Thank you," Kate said, and she leaned over to kiss him on the cheek.

Named the City Desk, the bar was practically alongside the *New York Post* building on Front Street. This was the third time Jacob had gone there to meet Connie and it was also the third time she was late, though this time he expected her to be.

Jacob sat at the bar and tried not to feel out of place. But it was almost impossible. Everyone else there had some connection with the newspaper. He was the only one in uniform. Despite the fans, the place was hot and filled with cigarette smoke, which made it seem as if a gray cloud had settled in the center of the room.

Two men on Jacob's left were arguing loudly about the Brooklyn Dodgers' chances of winning the National League Pennant race, while a group of four on the other side of him were talking about going to the races the following day.

Jacob was on his second bourbon and soda when Connie came up behind him and said, "Sorry I'm late, love, but something big seems to be brewing."

He turned around. "Where?" he asked.

She kissed him on the cheek. "Somewhere out in your old stomping grounds," she said, then called out to the barkeep, "Willy, give me the usual."

"You must know a little more," Jacob said.

She shrugged. "Just rumors for now," she responded. "But we do know that a number of ships have left Pearl and other ports. Your old ship, the Big E, appears to be involved."

Jacob finished his drink. Suddenly he felt trapped. He looked around. What the hell was he doing there?

"Is anything wrong?" Connie asked.

He shook his head. "I just need some fresh air," he lied.

"Can you wait until I finish my drink?"

"Yes," he answered. "But —"

"Ah, Connie, there you are!" a man called out. "I was hoping to see you."

Jacob turned around. The man was tall, somewhere in his 30s. He had a drink in his right hand, a cigarette dangled out of his mouth. The top button on his shirt was open and his tie pulled down.

He came straight up to Connie and put his left arm around her and his hand over her breast. "My God, I've missed you," he said, kissing her on the lips.

Connie pushed his hand away.

"Come on, Connie," he said. "I was hoping we'd make some beautiful music together again."

She flushed.

"You know I've still got the hots for you," he said; then suddenly he looked at Jacob.

"Why don't you leave Miss Burke alone," Jacob said.

The man looked at him. "Who the hell is that?" he asked, pointing at Jacob.

"Lieutenant Commander Jacob Miller," she said. "Mr. Niles Drumb."

Jacob made no effort to shake Drumb's hand.

"Ain't you the guy who killed all those Japs?" he asked, and before Jacob could answer, he turned around and shouted, "Hey, guys, we got a 100-percent gold-plated hero here!"

"It's all right," Connie yelled. "Niles has had a few too many."

"Let's get out of here," Jacob said, dropping three singles on the bar and reaching over to help Connie off the stool.

Drumb grabbed hold of Jacob's wrist. "I got first dibs," he growled.

Jacob backhanded him across the face.

Connie gasped.

Drumb's head went to one side. Blood spurted from his nose. His cigarette fell to the floor. He dropped his drink. "Son-of-a-mother-fucking-bitch!" he roared and flung himself on Jacob.

"Don't," Connie screamed. "Oh don't!"

"Fight," a man yelled. "Fight!"

"I'll kill you," Drumb growled, getting his hand around Jacob's throat. "I'll kill you."

"Someone do something!" Connie cried.

Jacob felt Drumb's fingers press in on his windpipe. He struggled to free himself; then suddenly he thrust his arms upward, breaking Drumb's hold.

"Enough," Connie yelled. "For God's sake, enough!"

Drumb panted, launching himself again at Jacob.

Jacob threw a right cross. Drumb staggered. Jacob jabbed a left at his chin and loosed another right cross. Drumb crouched and tried to rush him. Jacob caught him with an upper cut. Drumb dropped to his knees. Blood was pouring out of his nose and mouth. He looked at Connie, then tried to get to his feet.

Still breathing hard, Jacob grabbed hold of him.

Drumb tried to shake him off. "Don't need your fucking help, Admiral."

"Looks to me like you need all the help you can get," Jacob answered, pulling him up to his feet and sitting him down on a bar stool. "Take care of him, Connie," he said.

"Wait, I'll go with you."

"No," Jacob answered quietly.

Drumb's head slumped down on the bar.

"I want to go with you," she cried.

Jacob put on his white beaked hat. "He loves you," he said. "He just proved that the hard way."

"Oh God, I didn't want this to happen," Connie wept.

Jacob squared his shoulders and walked slowly to the door.

CHAPTER 41

Troost was on his bridge on the *Appalachia*. He was in command of the ships that would provide fire support to the First Marine Division, which later that day would storm ashore and take the airfield that the Japanese had hacked out of the jungle. His ships moved steadily through the morning twilight around the western end of Guadalcanal Cape Esperance to Lunga Point, where the amphibious assault would begin.

One by one the ships of the bombardment force signaled "Ready to commence firing," and at 0600 the *Appalachia*'s main battery of eight-inch guns and her secondary five-inch battery opened fire. The sudden fire from the big guns sent a heavy shock through the ship.

The other ships commenced firing.

Smoke arcs marked the path of the shells from ship to the shoreline at Lunga Point.

Troost watched the shelling through powerful glasses. Huge chunks of the beach and the jungle beyond suddenly leapt up and became enveloped in smoke. That must be what Hell is like, he thought.

"No return fire, so far," Troost commented with a note of relief in his voice, as he lowered his glasses.

"None, sir," the watch officer answered.

"We'll continue firing for another 10 minutes," Troost said. "Then we will lift our gunfire to allow the Airdales in their SBDs to attack their targets. Let's hope they are on time."

"Aye, aye, sir," the WO said.

Troost raised the glasses to his eyes again. In minutes the beach was turned into a moonscape, and the jungle behind it shattered. Huge trees were reduced to stumps. It was an awesome sight!

Suddenly, radar reported, "Bogey aircraft... Bearing, one eight seven degrees... Range, 15 miles... Angles, 18,000 feet..."

The captain's voice came over the squawk box: "Admiral, my antiaircraft guns are ready if the bogies aren't ours." Almost immediately, he followed with, "Admiral, IFF shows aircraft to be the friendlies we expected."

"Very well, thank you," Troost responded.

On schedule at 0610 all shore bombardment ceased, and a flight of 12 SBDs, in two separate lines of attack, swooped down over the beach and dropped their 500-pound bombs with devastating effectiveness. Enemy antiaircraft fire was very light. The SBDs zigzagged away from their targets at a low altitude and then climbing rapidly over the water, turned and in long lines, dived again to deliver their remaining bombs.

"Landing craft are moving in, sir," the WO reported.

The marines landed without any opposition and immediately began moving inland toward the airfield.

At 0100 Troost was unable to sleep and went out to his bridge. The night was sultry, with low, dark rain clouds. A rainstorm to the west obscured Savo Island. Intermittent flashes of lightning in the distance momentarily silhouetted other ships of the force. The night was calm. But oddly it was the calmness that was making him edgy. Earlier, one of his picket ships reported that a plane was over Savo. But nothing came of it. They were now steaming in a column of darkened ships down "the Slot" for another amphibious assault in two days.

Troost returned to his sea cabin and, sitting down at the desk, he began to write to Kate. There really wasn't very much he could tell her about what was happening. He did mention that Warren's PT squadron was nearby and then wrote, "I think you should take the plunge and send one or two of your stories to magazines on the mainland. Why not? You really have nothing to lose —"

The klaxon screamed.

Troost raced back to the bridge. The ship was illuminated by two magnesium flares; then suddenly a lookout on the starboard side shouted, "Enemy gunfire!"

An instant later the lookout on the portside yelled, "Gunfire to port!"

Seconds later the starboard side exploded and the first Japanese shells smashed into her. There were flames along the length of the ship.

Troost's force had steamed into a trap: Japanese warships were waiting for them on either side of the slot.

A shell smashed into the bridge.

Troost was thrown against the bulkhead. His left arm was slashed open. When he managed to get to his feet, he saw that the watch officer's chest was torn open, and another member of the bridge watch lay crumpled in the doorway. Troost raced down to the ship's navigation bridge.

"The skipper and the EXO are dead," the officer of the deck reported, with a note of panic in his voice. "Damage control says there's serious flooding amidships below the waterline."

"I have lost rudder control, sir," the helmsman reported.

One of the ship's five-inch guns began firing, and somehow the torpedo crew fired two torpedoes.

A star shell exploded above the ship, starkly illuminating her. Then four more rounds slammed into her. The five-inch gun mount exploded.

An engine room phone rang. The OOD answered it. "All engineering space has been abandoned, sir. Damage Control reports many fires are out of control. Recommends abandon ship! She cannot be saved."

Without hesitation, Troost switched on the 1MC. "Now hear this… All hands, now hear this… This is Admiral Troost… I have taken command of the ship —" Three explosions rocked the *Appalachia*. "Abandon ship," Troost ordered. "Abandon ship… All hands abandon ship."

"Jesus, we're already listing more than 10 degrees to the starboard side," the quartermaster of the watch exclaimed.

"You men get out now," Troost told the OOD, the helmsman, and the quartermaster.

"If it's just the same to you," the sailor said, "I'll stay with you, sir."

Their eyes locked.

"You've got a bad arm," the younger man told him. "You might need some help."

"All right, stay," Troost answered. "But let's get down to the main deck and make sure the men get off."

There were hundreds of men already in the water.

A destroyer was standing toward the burning cruiser, now dead in the water.

Men from below decks were scrambling topside and jumping over the side into the oil-covered waters.

Troost glanced at his watch: unbelievably only 11 minutes had elapsed from the time he heard the klaxon.

Deep inside the ship the ammunition stored in the magazines exploded.

"I don't think there's anyone else on board," the quartermaster said.

Troost nodded. "I'll follow," he told him, suddenly remembering the *Broadwater*. An eerie déjà vu sensation overwhelmed him.

"Good luck, sir," his helper said.

Troost shook his hand. "Good luck."

The young sailor kicked off his shoes and dived into the water.

Then suddenly the destroyer trying to assist came under fire and a huge fire erupted from her bow.

Troost was just about to jump when the *Appalachia* abruptly rolled over on her starboard side and capsized. In a terrifying instant, he realized he would not be able to get clear of her before she went down. An enormous roar filled his ears. "Kate!" he shouted, "I'll love you forever! God help us!" And he gave himself up to the sea.

CHAPTER 42

With his legs braced, Warren was standing behind the helmsman of his boat, the *PT 116*. The five-boat squadron hurriedly left their base on Tulagi as soon as word of the shooting at Savo was received. With the throttles wide open, the three 1200-horsepower Packard engines were driving each of the boats through the water at 40 knots.

From the radio reports, Warren knew the *Appalachia* was dead in the water and on fire and that four other U.S. ships were in the same condition.

"There are ships on fire everywhere!" Mike Frass, the yeoman at the helm exclaimed.

Warren peered into the night. A heavy rain squall was off to the starboard, but in front of him were five huge pyres. Then suddenly toward the west there was the rumble of gunfire.

"Skipper, the destroyer *Karl* and cruiser *Perry* are under attack," the radio man reported.

"Christ," Warren swore, "the Japs just came through here and shot the shit out of us!"

"Squadron Commander is on the horn," the radio man said.

"Put him through." Warren switched on the bridge radio and put on a set of earphones. "Troost here," he said.

"Stand by," a voice said.

Frass suddenly pointed to the starboard, where the rain squall was.

Warren looked. A ship was moving rapidly out of it. "Target," he said into the mike, "bearing, zero eight zero." Then to Frass he said, "Come to zero eight zero."

The boat, at full throttle, heeled over to the starboard.

Warren held the left earphone to his ear. "Ready torpedo tubes," he yelled down to Phil Harris, the boat's chief quartermaster.

"The other boats are turning," Frass said.

"Troost?" the squadron leader, Commander George Hopkins, called.

"Standing by," Warren answered.

"Take him from the port side with boats one one five and one one seven. The rest of us will go in on his starboard."

"Aye, aye, sir," Troost answered.

"There's another ship behind him!" Frass exclaimed.

"Troost," Hopkins said, "you and one one five and one one seven attack as ordered; the rest of us will go for the second target."

"Aye, aye, sir," Warren responded.

"Torpedoes armed and ready," Harris reported. "All gun stations ready."

Warren watched the Japanese destroyer loom larger and larger. They would hear his and the other boats before they saw them. He picked up the mike. "One one five and one one seven. They'll be sighting us any moment now. We're going to do a lot of zigging and zagging. Keep a sharp lookout before you change course."

The other skippers acknowledged his transmission.

Suddenly the Japanese searchlights came on. Their long thin beams cut through the darkness and turned the black water into a yellow circle.

"Go for the lights," he yelled to Harris.

A half dozen powerful beams on both ships began to slide over the water.

Warren watched one of the yellow circles. "Hard left," he ordered.

The boat swung away from the light.

"Bring her back as you were," he said.

Frass spun the wheel over. "Coming to zero eight zero," he said.

The yellow circles crisscrossed over the water. Then one of them captured and steadied on PT 115. The destroyer's number one mount began firing.

Plumes of water rose alongside the boat.

She swung to the starboard.

The light followed her; then suddenly PT 115 exploded into a mass of debris and flame.

"Closing fast," Frass said.

"Going in," Warren said. "Stand by to launch torpedoes."

"She's starting to turn!" Frass yelled.

"Fire one and two," Warren ordered. "Shoot out that fucking searchlight!"

"Torpedoes in the water," Harris responded.

The dual .50 mounts behind Warren chattered.

One of the destroyer's searchlights went out.

"Full left rudder," Warren ordered, watching the luminescent wakes of his torpedoes as they ran toward the target.

The boat heeled to port and began a tight turn. "Come all the way around and head directly for him," Warren yelled above the noise of the engine.

A searchlight suddenly poured over them.

"Hard right," Warren yelled.

The light followed.

Two geysers erupted directly in front of the boat and lifted its bow out of the water.

The boat's .40mm aft gun spewed round after round at the insistent light.

Then suddenly there was an enormous explosion.

Warren looked back over his shoulder and saw his torpedoes smash into the destroyer. The ship staggered. A burst of flames engulfed her forward.

"We got the bastard!" Frass shouted. "We got her!"

The next instant a light steadied on PT 117 and she was blown out of the water.

The second destroyer hove into view. She was going to assist the wounded ship.

"Damn good shooting, Troost," Hopkins said over the radio. "I can't get close enough for a torpedo attack."

The very next instant two of the other three boats were hit. One burst into flames and the other disintegrated.

"One one six," a voice said on the radio, "this is one one eight... Hopkins is dead... One two zero is on fire."

"Is that you, Lieutenant Greely?" Warren asked.

"Yes, sir."

"Break off and return to base," Warren said, knowing he was now the squadron's ranking officer. "We'll pick up any survivors and head back."

"Aye, aye, sir," Greely answered.

"You think you can find your way back to the base?" Warren asked Frass.

"Sure thing, skipper," the man answered.

Warren ordered the helmsman to ease the throttle back and the boat slowed. A cold, hard rain began to fall. He called down to the galley. "Do you have any coffee?" he asked.

"In a minute, skipper," a voice replied. "I'll bring it to the bridge."

"Thanks," Warren said; then he put one of the earphones next to his ear. Radio traffic indicated the destroyer Blue was standing by the *Appalachia*, taking survivors aboard. He hoped his father would be among them.

CHAPTER 43

The following day Warren was summoned to a meeting with Admiral Tyson, the commander of the amphibious forces, aboard the heavy cruiser *Washington*.

Tyson, a man in his late 50s, looked very tired. He invited Warren to sit down and said, "I regret to say that your father's body has not been recovered. From what we were told by some of the survivors who saw him just before the *Appalachia* turned over on her starboard side, he lost his footing on the deck and went down with her." He spoke in a slow monotone and his coal black eyes never left Warren's face. "There was a chief with him, who said that he would not leave the ship until he was sure no one was left on board."

Warren nodded. "He would do that," he responded.

"Your mother will be officially notified by the War Department that he was killed in action," Tyson said.

Warren understood that it was Tyson's way of telling him that there wasn't any hope that he was alive.

"Your father was a fine officer and a fine man," Tyson said. "But I don't have to tell you that, do I?"

"No, sir," Warren responded.

"I wish there was something else I could say," Tyson said. "But there isn't anything that wouldn't be superfluous. I am going to recommend that your father be given the Navy Cross posthumously for valor and dedication to duty."

"Thank you, sir," Warren answered, and wondered how his mother would react to her husband's death.

"There is one other thing I want to mention to you, now that you're here," Tyson said. "Under the circumstance, I think I could have you transferred back to Pearl for a few months."

"No, thank you, sir," Warren answered. "My boat and my crew are here. I'll wait my turn to be rotated back."

Tyson smiled; then he said, "I heard you put two fish into a Japanese destroyer last night."

"She was down at the bow when we left her," Tyson said.

"I'm also recommending to CinPacFleet that you be given command of PT Squadron Ten."

"Admiral, there's only my boat and the 108 left," Warren said.

"Six new boats and their crews are coming in within a week to 10 days," Tyson said, standing up. He shook Warren's hand. "You're a credit to the memory of your father."

"Thank you, sir," Warren responded, and he left the admiral's sea office.

CHAPTER 44

On a hot humid Tuesday in the second week of August at 3:30 in the afternoon, Jacob found himself on a bus entering Thornton, Mississippi. The bus rolled down Main Street, turned into an alleyway between Bert's Feed & Hardware Store and Miss Lee's Luncheonette and Ice cream Parlor; then it made a U-turn and came to a stop alongside a rickety wooden platform stained gray by the weather.

"You folks goin' on to Chardin got 10 minutes," the driver announced, opening the front door.

Jacob pulled down his suitcase from the overhead rack and left the bus. There were at least a dozen people on the platform. Most of the men wore overalls and cowboy hats made of straw. Dressed in whites, he was the center of everyone's attention. He walked into the waiting room. There were signs designating which part of the room was to be used by whites and which part by negros. It took him a few minutes to realize that even the ticket windows were similarly marked. The same thing existed in Pensacola, but as soon as he'd left there, he'd put it out of his mind.

Coming straight up to Jacob, a young man asked, "You for the Yancys?"

"Yes," Jacob answered.

"I was sent by Mr. Yancy to fetch you," he said. "I got a truck outside." He wore a pair of overalls that were hooked over his right shoulder. No shirt. But a large straw hat with a torn brim shaded his eyes.

Jacob followed him outside.

The truck was parked in front of Lee's. It was an old Ford, with thin rubber tires and four posts on each corner of the flatbed that supported a wooden frame to which a dirty canvas tarpaulin was secured by pieces of rope.

"Soon as I'm old enough," the young man said, "I'm goin' ta join up."

Jacob nodded. He was interested in the countryside, which began just outside of the town. "What do you grow down here?" he asked, looking at the cultivated fields on either side of the macadam road.

"Mostly cotton, but some plant sugar beet, especially now with the war goin'," the young man answered.

"What's on either side of the road?" Jacob asked.

"Sugar beet," he answered.

Jacob took out a pack of cigarettes and held it out to the young man.

"Don't mind if I do," he said, taking one from the pack.

Jacob held the lighter for him and then lit his own.

"My pap does sharecroppin' for Mr. Yancy," the young man said. "But come next year, he says he's goin' ta buy a few acres of bottom land, near the river. He says he'll put in sugar beet and some cotton, but mostly he wants to raise hogs."

Jacob nodded.

"You knew John Yancy?" the young man asked.

"I knew him," Jacob answered. "I was his wingman."

They turned off the blacktop and onto a dirt road. A cloud of red dust rose up behind the truck.

The young man looked at him. "What's a wingman?"

"We —" Jacob wasn't quite sure how to explain it and settled for telling him that they were in the same squadron.

"John was a wild one," the young man said. "There wasn't a gal safe, married or not, with him around. All the mommas cautioned their daughters about him."

Jacob almost smiled. But the sudden memory of his friend's antics was sufficient to drive the smile from his lips.

"That be the Yancy place over yonder," the young man said, pointing off to the left.

The road made a gentle turn, and in a matter of minutes they rolled to a halt in front of a large white house with an enormous porch in front of it.

Jacob got out of the truck and the young man came around to where he was standing and said, "Somebody'll be out directly." Then he stuck out his hand. "Name's Paul Snapp."

"Jacob Miller," Jacob answered, shaking his hand.

Suddenly a screen door banged shut.

"Mr. Yancy," Paul said, letting go of Jacob's hand.

Jacob turned and looked at someone who resembled John, but who was shorter, barrel-chested, bald and sunburned.

He came down the steps and said, "I'm pleased ta meet you Mr —" He stopped and looked at Jacob's sleeve. "I don't know your rank, sir."

"Please, Jacob will be fine."

"Charley," Mr. Yancy said.

They shook hands.

"Paul," Mr. Yancy said, "you take Jacob's grip up to the guest room on the north side of the house — and Jacob you follow me. My wife and my mother want to meet you. The rest of the family will be here for dinner."

Inside the house was somewhat cooler than it was outside, and the parlor where Jacob met John's mother and grandmother had two large fans blowing air into the room.

John's grandmother was a thin, tissue-skinned woman somewhere in her late 70s, and his mother was a woman in her early 50s with faded blonde hair and dull blue eyes. Both women sat on a settee, and after the introductions, the two of them looked at him for several moments without speaking; then Mrs. Yancy said, "The only comfort I have is that John is with Christ, our Lord."

Jacob stood very still and avoided looking at her.

"Well that's no comfort to me, Laura-May," the elder Mrs. Yancy said. "I wanted gran'chil'rin from that boy. No comfort at all that he's with Christ."

"Were you with him when he died?" his mother asked.

"Yes, I was," Jacob answered, and knowing that they'd want something to hold onto for the rest of their lives, he said, though it was a lie, "He was shot down while protecting the ship."

"Yes, I knew he died doing something for someone else," Mrs. Yancy said.

"Do you think he suffered?" John's grandmother asked.

Jacob shook his head. "No. He probably didn't know it was happening."

"Will you tell us how it happened?" Mrs. Yancy asked.

"I'm sorry I can't," Jacob lied. "I was in a dogfight myself. When it was over, John was already down."

"Did you shoot down any Japs, Jacob?" she asked.

Charley, who was quiet up to that moment, said, "I told you before Jacob came that he's a hero."

Jacob's cheeks became hot.

"All he ever wrote about was being a hero," Mrs. Yancy commented. "That's what he wanted to be. Lots of folks here about didn't think he'd ever amount to much because he was one for sowin' his wild oats, if you know what I mean?" Her dull blue eyes searched his face.

"John was my best friend," Jacob said quietly; then looking at Mr. Yancy, he said, "He tried to be what you wanted him to be."

"That's mighty good of you to tell my son that," John's grandmother said. "Mighty good!"

"Jacob, could you see your way clear to come to church with us on Sunday morning an' tell the people what you just told us?" Mrs. Yancy asked. "I'd much appreciate it. They'd believe you, and my son's name would shine a little brighter in death than it did in life."

"I'd be honored," Jacob answered.

Mr. Yancy took a step forward. "Ladies, this man has been travelin' for many, many hours. He needs a few hours to rest before dinner, so if you'll excuse the two of us, I'll show him to his room and then I'll go back to work."

The two women nodded.

"Anything you want, Jacob," Mr. Yancy said as they mounted the steps to the second floor, "you just ask for it. I'll have a pitcher of cold lemonade sent to your room directly an' if you're hungry —"

"The lemonade will be fine."

Mr. Yancy led Jacob into a room with a large bed, a dresser, a night table, a rocking chair, and white curtains on the window. "The bathroom is just down the hall from here," he said.

"I saw it on the way up," Jacob answered.

"You're a good man, Jacob," Mr. Yancy said, "but you're not a good liar. Now tell me how my son died."

Jacob was about to object; then he nodded and said, "He died in my arms. His last words were, 'Tell my daddy I tried.'"

Mr. Yancy swallowed hard; then in a quiet voice, he said, "I never did think he'd amount to much. He didn't have to. He'd have the farm when I died. I really wanted him to do something, something that would make me proud of him."

"He knew that," Jacob responded.

"He was right in one thing he did," Mr. Yancy said. "He had you for a friend. You can always tell a man by his friends and you're a good man, Jacob."

"So was John, a good man."

"I'd like very much to believe that."

"Believe it, Mr. Yancy," Jacob said earnestly. "Believe it!"

CHAPTER 45

Glen's ship, the destroyer *Adams*, was at general quarters. He was at his new station in the main battery, the director above the ship's navigation bridge.

The *Adams* and the other ships of the battle group, which consisted of the cruiser *Joplin* and four other destroyers, were steaming off Cape Esperance looking for the "Tokyo Express," as the men dubbed the nightly forays that Japanese warships made down the slot, the strait between Rabaul and Guadalcanal, where the Japanese were putting up fierce resistance.

Ordinarily, Glen's position, because he was assistant gunnery officer, was in the CIC. But Lieutenant Frank Pollet, the gunnery officer, was in sick bay now, with what appeared to be acute appendicitis. Glen was, after eight engagements, confident of his ability to direct the ship's gunfire.

At 2330 the phone rang. Higgins, one of the director crew said, "Radar reports target, bearing zero two zero degrees, range 5000 yards."

Glen gave the order to Higgin's crew to set the target bearing and distance into the director. All guns swung to these bearings.

"Target —"

Suddenly two large caliber shells exploded in geysers of water close aboard the *Adam's* stern. She shuddered and her stern heaved out of the water. A third shell crashed into her bow with terrifying force.

"Give me a range and bearing of the son-of-a-bitch!" Glen screamed.

"Target bearing zero two five... Range 4000 yards," Higgins said.

The data was relayed to the CIC. Seconds later all guns reported "Ready."

"Bridge, all mounts ready to commence fire," Glen reported.

"For Christ's sake, commence firing," a voice tinged with panic responded.

"Commence firing," Glen ordered.

All guns opened up. Their shells crashed into a Japanese destroyer, setting it on fire.

Then suddenly the *Adams* recoiled from three more enemy rounds. The bridge took a direct hit and the explosion below tore a huge hole in Glen's director. Two of his crew were killed instantly. But the rest of the men miraculously were not wounded. Number three mount was knocked out of action and the ship's forward stack went down, instantly igniting powder in the number two handling room.

"Jesus, the whole ship seems to be on fire," a crew member named Jones sobbed.

"Try the bridge," Glen said.

"No answer," Higgins answered.

"CIC?" Glen questioned.

Higgins shook his head.

"Okay, let's get out of here... Follow me," Glen told his men.

When they reached the bridge, Glen found it deserted, but the ship was still moving at 15 knots. It was obvious the skipper abandoned ship without realizing there were still men aboard. "We'll work our way to the secondary conn," he said, "and see if we can raise the engine room. There must be people down there."

"Lieutenant," Higgins shouted, "there is no rudder control… Goddamn… It looks like secondary conn is out too."

Even before they could leave the bridge, the ammunition began to explode, sending huge plumes of fire into the air.

"Over the side, men," Glen ordered. "Abandon ship."

The men raced through the debris and fire to the main deck.

"All right," Glen said, "call out your name before you go over the side."

"Higgins."

"Faust."

"Jones."

"Wilson."

Glen looked along the length of the ship. There were patches where the deck plates were red hot. His four men dived into the water. He took a deep breath and jumped into the sea. The water was warm and pitch black. Glen's life jacket brought him to the surface immediately. In the glow of the burning ship, he saw his men and swam to them. He called each of them by name.

Faust didn't answer.

"Faust," he shouted. "Faust."

"I went in after him," Jones said. "I didn't see him come up."

"Goddamn!" Glen exclaimed.

"What happens now?" Jones asked.

"Now, we stay close to each other," Glen answered. "Somebody will pick us up soon."

"Let's hope it's not the Japs," Wilson sputtered. "I hear they don't treat prisoners so good."

"Cut the gab and save your strength," Glen said. That a Japanese ship might find them before one of their own had not occurred to him. But it certainly was a possibility. There seemed to be as many of their ships around as U.S. vessels.

Glen looked toward the burning *Adams*. She slowed and was listing heavily to her port side. The glare from flames cast a lurid yellowish red glow over the water that extended out to where he and his men were.

"Sharks!" Jones exclaimed, pointing to his left.

Glen looked. Jones was facing away from him, but he could see two dorsal fins. They were on the very edge of the light coming from the *Adams*. His stomach knotted with fear and his brain suddenly emptied.

"They're goin' to come for us," Jones said. "Holy Mother of God, they're goin' to come for us!" And he started to swim away.

"Stay where you are," Glen shouted. "Stay! That's a fucking order!"

Jones stopped.

"Ease your way back here," Glen said. Despite his own fear, he clearly recognized his responsibility. "Okay, now stay together and don't make any unnecessary movements."

"Mister Lascomb," Higgins said, "I read somewhere that sharks don't like loud noises."

"I see a couple of cans floating on my right side," Glen said. "Maybe if I can get to them we could bang on them whenever the bastards come close."

"It's worth a try," Higgins responded.

"Slowly, let's make for the cans," Glen said, already beginning to paddle.

"They're following us!" Wilson exclaimed.

"Okay, stop," Glen said, turning to look at the dorsal fins. There were four of them now. "Everyone, stay still... Don't move."

"One of them is comin' at us!" Jones shouted.

A single dorsal fin knifed through the water. Glen suddenly realized the shark was arrowing toward him. He saw its tapered snout. It was turning on its side, mouth wide open with hideous rows of teeth bared.

Just as it came in, Glen kicked out with both feet and struck its white belly.

The shark veered away.

"For a while that bastard isn't going to try it again!" Glen exclaimed. If he were not in the water, his pants would be sopping wet anyway.

Another dorsal fin streaked in.

"He's coming for me!" Wilson shouted. "He's coming for me."

Glen swam for the nearest powder can, reached it, and began to beat it with his fist.

"The cocksucker is turnin'," Jones yelled. "You turned him."

Pushing the can in front of him, Glen re-joined his men. "It might hold them off for a while," he said.

"I'm beginning to feel cold," Higgins complained.

Glen looked up. The sky was now overcast and a breeze sprang up out of the northwest. If they got caught in a sudden squall, there would be no way for them to stay together.

"There's a ship heading this way!" Wilson said, pointing to its dark form coming toward them. "Dear God, let it be one of ours!"

"It's too far away to hear us," Glen told them.

"What if it's a Jap ship?" Higgins asked.

"If it's a choice between a Jap ship and sharks," Jones answered, "I'd go with the Japs."

The ship was slowly on them.

"She's one of ours," Glen shouted with joy, recognizing her lines. "She's looking for survivors."

Suddenly the ship's searchlights came on and they began to sweep the water.

"Here we are," Glen shouted. "Here we are!"

The men began to shout and waved their arms.

A circle of light suddenly touched them.

"Hurry," Glen shouted, "there are sharks down here. For God's sake, hurry!" There were tears in his eyes.

CHAPTER 46

It was the day after Christmas 1943; Warren had arrived back at Pearl three days before. He was ordered to report to Admiral Harly, chief of special operations, on December 26.

Warren had hoped to surprise Irene, but when he phoned her, he was the one who was surprised. Her roommate told him she had been transferred the week before to an army hospital in Brisbane, Australia.

"Do you know if she requested the transfer?" he asked.

"She never told me," her roommate said. "But my guess is that she did."

Warren thanked her and hung up. For several moments, he remained seated in the phone booth. He was hurt and disappointed. But there wasn't a damn thing he could do about it, except not answer her letter of explanation, which he was sure would come. He shook his head. He couldn't do that to her or himself.

Warren spent Christmas with Lillian and his mother. Lillian seemed to be more beautiful than he remembered, and his mother didn't have one drink during or after dinner.

The day after Christmas at 0900, Warren was in Admiral Harly's office. Harly, an owlish-looking man with a bald pate and metal-frame eyeglasses, looked more like a college professor than a Naval officer.

After an informal greeting, Harly said, "I hope you've enjoyed your Christmas." He spoke with a broad New England accent.

"Yes, sir, I did," Warren answered.

Harly nodded. "I need a man like you to work for me," he said, without any introduction. "I know your record. I even know why you were booted out of flight training."

Warren felt his cheeks color.

Harly smiled. "But I won't embarrass you by mentioning it."

"Thank you, sir."

"I need someone with the professional qualities and seamanship capabilities that you possess," Harly said.

"Sir, with all due respect, I'd be miserable tied to a desk," Warren said.

"Who said anything about being tied to a desk?" Harly answered. "Troost, you're too good to waste behind one of these," he said, slapping the top of the desk with the palm of his hand.

Confused, Warren leaned slightly forward in his chair.

"Interested now, eh?"

"Enough to be a little nervous," Warren said.

Harly guffawed. "I don't believe you have the capacity to be nervous, at least not in the normal sense — afraid, yes, but not nervous."

Warren wasn't going to contradict him. If he was happy believing that, then why should he make him unhappy?

"In about a year," Harly said, "we're going to invade the Philippines. That's no real secret. The enemy know it, but of course that's all they know. We need people there before the invasion takes place. A small army of guerrillas are operating there now, but Washington and Admiral Nimitz believe that something more is needed, something that would make life for the Japanese commander thoroughly miserable."

"PT boats," Warren said, guessing.

Harly nodded. "Several secret bases scattered through the islands could wreak havoc with Jap shipping."

"I met one of the guerrilla leaders when I was on the *Dee*," Warren said.

"Rudy Luis," Harly responded.

Warren tried not to show his surprise.

"Your mission would be to operate in the waters around the Philippines. Your squadron's mission would be to harass enemy shipping, to take part in guerrilla raids whenever feasible, and, of course, as we begin to evolve air strikes, to rescue downed pilots."

"Thank you, sir," Warren said. "I'd appreciate the opportunity to work for you."

Harly smiled. "I thought you would," he said. "You'll be getting 12 new boats," he said. "That means 12 new crews. They'll be here in Pearl by the end of February. You should be in the Philippines by the latest — say, the end of June. That should give you enough time to plan where you want to set up your base."

"I'd much prefer it if there were three or even four different bases. All close enough to support one another, but far enough away from each other to make it more difficult for the Japs to find us," Warren said.

"The show is yours, Commander," Harly said; then he added, "and I do mean commander. I've already requested that you be spot promoted a grade. And I'm sure it will go through."

"Thank you, sir," Warren replied.

"By the way, your new boats will be equipped with radar equipment that works," Harly said. "That should give you a tremendous edge."

"We'll need it."

"Report back to me after New Year's," Harly said, "and you and my staff will get some basic planning done."

The two men stood up.

"I was sorry to hear about your father," Harly said. "I served under him for a while when he was Chief of Staff of Destroyer Division Four."

"Thank you for remembering him," Warren responded, as they shook hands across the desk.

Later that day, Warren went to see Kate.

She had brewed tea and made a tray of small sandwiches that she set out on a Carrara marble-topped table.

They sat across from each other, avoiding eye contact, and after cautiously exchanging comments about the weather, neither one seemed to have anything else to say.

Warren was very uncomfortable. It wasn't a good idea to — dredge up…

"My God," Kate exclaimed, "this is positively ridiculous! I want to hug you and tell you how happy I am to see you."

"Then do it," he said, standing up and crossing the distance between them.

She kissed him on the forehead. "I am so happy to see you and so pleased that you came here." Letting go of him, she took a step backward. "And so very grateful that you wrote to me after Andrew was killed."

"He would have wanted me to," Warren answered.

She nodded and they sat down again.

"Your father was very proud of you," Kate said.

Warren nodded.

"Are your mother and sister well?" she asked.

"Yes… I think my mother has stopped drinking…"

"Oh, how really wonderful!" Kate exclaimed.

Warren nodded. He felt he was in the presence of a rare and unique woman and understood why his father had fallen in love with her.

"Since I saw you last," Kate said, "two of my stories have been published — one in the *Atlantic* and the other in *The New Yorker*."

"My father would have been very pleased," Warren replied. "He was an avid reader. I was always surprised when he would suddenly quote something from one of Shakespeare's plays that happened to fit the situation at the time."

"Would you like to read the stories?" she asked.

"Very much."

She stood up, went out of the room for a few moments, and returned with the two magazines. "One of the stories is something of a love story," she said, handing them to him. "It was my final love letter to your father."

Warren developed a sudden tightness in his throat.

Kate sat down again. "There's something I want to tell you," she said. "Something that until now I never told anyone."

Warren nodded.

"I loved two men in my life: my husband and your father. Your father and I came together at a time in both our lives when there was a need in each of us for the other. The physical attraction between us was strong and exciting. Your father was a considerate lover," she said, looking straight at Warren.

Warren shifted his position. He'd never heard anyone speak about his father that way.

"There is no need for you to be embarrassed," Kate told him. "I'm telling you these things because it will help you understand him. He was also considerate in hundreds of other ways. He believed in me, in my ability to write, even when I had doubts about it. Without his encouragement, I never would have believed that anyone would publish my stories." She paused again, took a sip of tea, and then continued. "He often told me what I gave him," she said. "Much of it had to do with my giving him the love he did not get from your mother. I was the woman with whom he could be a man, with whom he could share his thoughts, with whom he was comfortable."

"I know he loved you," Warren commented.

"He was another part of me, a part that no other man ever knew," Kate said. "That way, I came to him a virgin."

"I'm sure he sensed that," Warren answered softly.

"Yes," Kate said. "I'm sure he did too. He was a very perceptive man. Even when I didn't think he was aware of something, I'd find out later that he was." A few moments of silence passed before Kate asked, "Will you be in Honolulu for a while?"

"For a while," Warren answered.

Kate smiled. "From the pictures your father showed me of himself when he was younger, I'd say you look very much like he did."

"Some people thought he was good-looking," Warren said, teasingly.

"So are you."

"That's because you're being totally objective, aren't you?"

"Of course," she countered. "Of course!"

Warren reached for a sandwich, bit into it, nodded, and said, "Absolutely delicious. What is it?"

"Cucumbers!" she laughed.

"Who would have thought anyone could make cucumbers taste like, like —"

Kate threw up her hands. "You made your point," she laughed. "But allow me my biased objectivity."

Warren picked up another small sandwich, examined it critically, and then flourishing it in front of him, said, "Certainly, the epitome of cucumber sandwiches."

By the time Warren was ready to leave, the sun was setting.

"Come again," Kate said, standing in the half-opened doorway. "You're always welcome here."

"I will," he said. "But you must promise to come to dinner with me soon."

"I'd like that," she answered, her cheeks wet with tears.

Warren leaned forward and gently kissed her on the lips.

"Vaya con Dios," she whispered.

"Vaya con Dios," Warren answered, then turned and walked down the pathway to the rapidly darkening street. He was very glad he had visited Kate. She gave him something to hold on to about his father that he'd never before known.

CHAPTER 47

It was the *Tarpon*'s sixth patrol. She was out of Brisbane 35 days and had managed to sink an enemy Japanese transport on the 16th of January and damage a freighter on the 30th. On the night of February 4, the *Tarpon* was on the surface recharging her batteries south of the Steffen Strait, along the route used by Japanese ships involved in the evacuation of the remaining enemy troops on Guadalcanal.

The night was clear and moonlit and Tony was relaxing on the bridge with Chris, the X.O., enjoying the feel of the light breeze and thinking of Miriam.

In his last letter to her before leaving Brisbane, he had asked her to marry him. He was certain her answer would be "yes." But there was always the possibility of a —

"Conning tower to bridge, radar contact... Targets, bearing zero eight five... Range 15,000 yards."

"Targets on radar bearing zero eight five," Tony said, alerting the forward, starboard lookout.

"Got him!" the lookout said, peering through his glasses. "Looks like two freighters and a patrol boat."

Chris picked up the sound powered phone and pressed the buzzer to Brisson's cabin. "Bridge to skipper, three targets, bearing zero eight five... Range 15,000 yards."

Tony and Chris waited until Brisson was at the periscope in the Conning Tower below the bridge before they dropped through the hatch. Tony positioned himself behind the radar officer. Chris descended into the control room immediately below.

The three green blips were clearly visible every time the rotating sweep touched them.

Brisson ordered the boat to General Quarters and the alarm sounded.

Tony went to the TDC and turned it out Brisson's voice came over 1MC. "We've got ourselves three good targets," he said. "Looks like they're on their way into Rabaul and we'll take them on an end run." He paused before he said, "Helmsman, come to new courses zero nine five."

"Zero nine five," the helmsman answered.

"All full ahead," Brisson ordered.

"All ahead full, answered," the engine room signal man responded.

The sound of the diesels became louder, almost, it seemed to Tony, with a sense of urgency.

The flow of cool air through the open bridge hatch into the conning tower increased.

"Captain," the radar officer reported, "radar contact very intermittent... I'm trying to hold on them."

For the next hour, the *Tarpon* sped through the smooth surface of the water.

"Targets, bearing zero two zero," Radar suddenly reported. "Range, 6000 yards and closing."

"He put us right on them," the RO commented in a loud whisper.

"All ahead two thirds," Brisson ordered.

"All ahead two thirds answered," the engine room signal man said.

"Radar, I'm having trouble getting periscope contact... You feed bearing and distance to the TDC... We'll go for a surface shot."

"Aye, aye, sir," the RO answered.

Brisson reduced the *Tarpon*'s speed to "All ahead, one third."

"Targets, bearing zero two nine... Range, 5000 yards... Speed, one five knots."

"Load forward torpedo tubes," Brisson ordered.

The phone, talker passed the word.

Then suddenly two enemy rounds exploded close aboard on the *Tarpon*'s starboard side.

The klaxon screamed.

"Dive!" Brisson shouted. "Dive."

The diesels were cut out and the electric motors began to hum. The lookouts came through the bridge hatch; then the quartermaster came down and pulled the hatch shut and dogged it down.

"XO," Brisson, ordered, "take her down to 100 feet."

Chris ordered the diving planes rigged out and set for the dive. The *Tarpon*'s bow pitched forward.

"Two five feet," Chris called out from the control room.

Tony's eyes went to the depth gage. And saw it unwind rapidly.

"Target, bearing zero three zero... Range 3000 yards, closing fast... Twin screws, skipper," sonar called out.

"Rig for depth charges," Brisson ordered.

The hull was filled with the sounds of watertight doors being shut.

"Zero one zero on the bow planes," Chris ordered, his eyes on the depth gage.

The churning sound of the Japanese screws became louder and louder.

The *Tarpon*'s bow dipped.

"Two cans," the sonar officer reported.

Tony sucked in his breath.

The explosions hammered down on the *Tarpon* with a mighty force.

"Conn, we're taking water," the forward torpedo officer reported. "Damage control party one is already here."

"Report damage and repair progress," Brisson said.

"Aye, aye, sir," the FTO answered.

"100 feet and coming to level," Chris reported.

"Another can coming down off our bow," the SO called out.

"Right, full rudder," Brisson ordered.

There was a strange note in the sound of Brisson's voice that made Tony turn sharply to look at him.

"Right, full rudder," the helmsman answered.

Brisson's face contorted with pain. He staggered and clutched his chest.

"The skipper!" Tony shouted, crossing the few steps separating them to grab Brisson, even as he started to fall. "Get the medic."

"Medic to the conn," Chris shouted over the 1MC. "Medic to the Conning Tower, on the double."

The concussion from the exploding depth charge rolled the *Tarpon* to her port side.

Tony fought to hold his footing and did. He stretched Brisson out on the deck and felt for a pulse in his left hand.

The pharmacist mate and the Executive Officer scrambled up through the control room hatch.

"No pulse, doc," Tony said.

The doc hunkered down next to Brisson and putting his hand inside the skipper's shirt, he held it there for several moments. "I'm afraid, sir, he's gone," he said, slowly standing.

"Conn, the forward ballast tank's manhole gasket ruptured," the DCO reported. "Bilge flooding is being controlled by the bilge pumps and we've put a temporary rubber sheet cover over the manhole cover. The deck plates are being held by shores and jacks. The gasket can't be replaced until we're on the surface."

Tony looked at Chris. "It's yours now," he said.

"Roger that," Chris answered.

"Screws fading," the SO reported.

Chris switched on the 1MC. "All hands, now hear this... All hands... This is Mr. Bond... The skipper —" He stopped, took a deep breath, and said, "The skipper apparently suffered a heart attack. He's dead. I have assumed command, Mr. Trapasso will be acting XO!"

"Contacts lost," the SO reported.

"Doc, get the skipper ready for burial at sea," Chris said. "We'll hold services for him at dusk."

"Aye, aye, sir," the doc answered.

Two of the men volunteered to carry the skipper to his cabin.

"Helmsman," Chris said, his voice unsteady, "come to two seven zero. Tony, secure from general quarters."

"Two seven zero," the helmsman answered.

"All ahead full," Chris ordered.

"All ahead full," answered the engine room signal man.

The *Tarpon*'s crew was subdued; even those who were jokers were not their usual selves, and though the men liked and respected Chris, Tony noticed, they were more formal with him than they ever were with Brisson. But the routine continued without any change.

Three days after Brisson was buried at sea, Chris asked Tony to join him in the tiny wardroom and shut the door. "We have to talk," he said, pouring himself a cup of coffee.

Tony sat down at the table and glanced at the wardroom clock. It was just 0110. The *Tarpon* was running on the surface to recharge her batteries.

Mug in hand, Chris joined him. "I have two choices," he began. "As I see it, I can abort the patrol and return to Brisbane, or —" He lifted the mug, but didn't put it to his lips. "Or I could turn the command over to you."

Tony started to stand.

"Sit down, Tony," Chris said. "This isn't easy for me. There are 75 men aboard who depend on the skipper. Well, I know I'm not that good ... not as a skipper." He put the mug to his lips and drank.

"You've got years of service," Tony said, completely taken aback.

"The men sense —"

"Give them time, Chris," Tony said, "they just lost someone they loved and trusted."

"Trusted is the key word," Chris said. "If I don't trust myself, how could I expect them to trust me."

"Give yourself time —"

Suddenly the wardroom phone rang. Tony answered it.

"Target, bearing zero one zero relative... Range, 2000 yards, moving on a one eight five true course," the RO reported.

Tony repeated the RO's report and added, "She's moving on an opposite course to ours and crossing."

"Sound general quarters," Chris ordered and rushed from the wardroom to the bridge.

Tony followed.

Topside, the visibility was reduced by rain showers.

Chris peered into the murky darkness. "I can't see a damn thing," he said, wiping the rain from his face.

"Target holding course... Range 1800 and closing."

"One third ahead," Chris ordered.

"One third ahead, answered," the engine room signal man responded.

"Load forward torpedo tubes," Chris ordered. "Open outer doors."

"Target changing course," the RO reported. "Bearing zero one zero... Range, 400 yards."

"She's crossing close ahead!" Tony shouted.

"Right full rudder," Chris ordered.

"Right full —"

Tony hit the collision alarm button.

An instant later the Japanese gunboat's searchlights swept the *Tarpon*'s deck.

The *Tarpon*'s bow crashed into the gunboat's port side.

All hands on the bridge were thrown down by the terrible impact.

The *Tarpon* heeled over, and as she righted, Japanese heavy caliber automatic weapon fire whipped across the *Tarpon*'s deck and into the bridge.

The OOD and the Chief Quartermaster of the watch were killed instantly. Two of the four lookouts were hit by fragments. A section of the bridge coaming peeled back and a jagged spear of metal impaled Chris's right leg literally stapling him in agony to the bridge.

"Clear the bridge," Chris shouted above the continuing sound of gunfire. "Clear the bridge."

Bullets continued to ricochet around the bridge.

The two remaining lookouts scrambled through the hatch into the conning tower.

"Dive. Dive," Chris screamed. "Take her down. Don't wait for me! Save the boat!"

Tony hesitated, then dropped through the hatch.

One of the lookouts pulled it closed and dogged it shut.

"Take her down!" Tony shouted through the open hatch to the control room.

A dozen machine-gun bullets pierced the conning tower's thin skin.

Dazed, Tony held himself against the periscope tube. "Make 80 feet," he ordered.

High-pressure streams of water shot into the conning tower through the machine gun bullet holes.

The control room and the pump room were flooding. The gyros were out of commission. The intercommunication system failed, and heater circuits badly damaged.

"We must surface!" the DCO reported. "Otherwise we are goners!"

"Coming level at 80 feet," the DO reported; then he said, "Forward diving planes are inoperative."

"Anything on the sonar?" Tony asked.

"Damaged," the SO reported.

"Periscope depth," Tony ordered.

"Periscope depth," the DO answered.

Tony watched the depth gage with fearful fascination. Miraculously it showed the boat to be rising. When it reached 58 feet, he bent down, snapped out the handles, and rode the periscope up. He made a quick 360° sweep... Nothing... He made a second sweep... Nothing. "Down periscope," he ordered, snapping the handles closed. "Surface," he ordered.

Minutes later, he cracked the bridge hatch, flung it open, and pulled himself onto the bridge. Chris's body was gone. He looked toward the bow — at least 20 feet of it was bent at a 90° angle away from the rest of the hull. But thank God, the *Tarpon* still had power and her steering gear was intact. "We'll take her home," he said, patting the side of the crumpled bridge coaming. "We'll take her home."

CHAPTER 48

Glen was home on a 30-day leave and was driving a tractor with a harrow behind it to help his father and brother put in the corn crop. He'd much rather work than be in the house and around Lucy.

Now a Lieutenant (JG), Glen was secretly looking forward to going back to sea. He had seven days left before he reported to his new ship, the destroyer James Polk. He was also looking forward to the time he'd see Lillian again.

His son, named Jessy after Lucy's grandfather, cried a lot, especially when he picked him up and held him. And as far as he could see, the boy didn't look anything like him. He had Lucy's green eyes and her upturned nose.

Though they slept in the same bed, Glen scarcely touched Lucy during the time he was home. Several times, he was on the verge of asking her for a divorce. But somehow, he could never bring himself to even hint that he wanted one.

Then that evening, after dinner, his mother asked, "Are you going back out to the war?" she asked.

"I don't really know," he answered. "But I would guess I am."

"You sound as if you want to go!" Lucy cried, throwing her napkin on the table and bolting from the room.

Glen looked questioningly at his mother.

"You best go after her and find out what's wrong," she said.

Glen nodded, and leaving the table, he followed Lucy out of the house. She went down to creek. "Now what was all that about?" he asked, coming up behind her.

She faced him. "You have another woman, don't you?"

Glen took a deep breath and slowly exhaled. Now was the time to tell her. "I want a divorce," he said.

She gasped.

"I met someone —"

Lucy looked straight at him. "Is that why you haven't made love to me?"

"I want —"

"You want," she sneered. "You don't think about what other people want, or need, do you? You have a wife and a son. What about them?"

"Things like this happen," he said defensively, "I don't blame you for being angry and hurt, and I'm sorry —"

"You're not sorry!" she suddenly shouted. "You're not in the least bit sorry. When I saw you in San Diego, I knew that you didn't love me. But as God is my judge, I love you, and Jessy is your son. No other man has ever touched me."

Glen remained silent.

"All right," she wept, "I don't want to make three people unhappy for the rest of their lives. I'll give you the divorce." And she started to run along the length of the creek.

Too stunned to move, Glen suddenly realized she was running away from him and went after her.

"I don't want you near me," she shouted at him.

He grabbed hold of her. "Stop running!" he told her, panting hard.

"You got what you wanted," she yelled. "You got what you wanted."

Glen looked hard at her. This was a side of Lucy he'd never seen, never knew existed. She was a lot stronger than he'd ever thought.

"You tell me what you want," she said.

"Where are you going?" he asked. "Come back to the house."

Lucy shrugged and shook her head. "I don't want to —"

Glen put his arm around her shoulders.

"Don't touch me!"

"We'll work it out," he said gently.

"Are you sure, Glen Lascomb? Are you really sure?"

Glen nodded. "I'm sure," he said. "I'm very sure. I don't want you to go."

CHAPTER 49

"All right," Warren said, listening to Rudy being briefed by a guerrilla scout at Warren's makeshift headquarters in Tulagi, "what the hell is the man saying?" He was seated behind a crude desk made of two wooden horses and four one-by-12-inch planks laid across them and nailed down. He was tired and hot, had a three-day growth, and was generally in a pissed-off mood.

"He says the Japs are building a radar station on Bansiki Island," Rudy said.

"Bansiki?" Warren asked. The name wasn't in the least bit familiar and he was sure he knew all of them within a 200-mile radius of the base.

"It's more just a nipple of land sticking out of the water," Rudy said. "Here, I'll show you." He went to the chart table at the back of the room and looked at a chart of the area. "Not here," he announced, shaking his head.

Warren lit a cigarette, stood up, shifted the .45 he wore on his hip, and joined him.

"Should be about here," Rudy said, putting the ball of his right forefinger on the chart, near the southern tip of Palawan, which was only a few hundred miles away from the north coast of Borneo. "He says about 50 troops and maybe 300 workers."

Warren ran his hand over his beard. The cigarette dangled out from between his lips. He studied the man; then he said, "Ask him if he has seen the place himself, or has just heard about it?"

"He already told me he saw it himself," Rudy answered.

"What's his name?"

"Silvano."

"Thank him, give him a few packs of cigarettes, and tell him he can stay here a few days and rest," Warren said.

Rudy spoke to Silvano.

The man brought himself to attention and saluted.

Warren returned the courtesy, went back to his desk, put his feet up on it, and when Rudy returned, said, "Keep a sharp lookout on the man."

"You think his information is no good?" Rudy asked.

"It's too good," Warren answered. "For a place that's as isolated as that is, he knows a lot about it."

"His village is on another nearby island," Rudy explained. "His cousin was taken by the Japs to work on the island."

"How come the Japs didn't get him too?"

"They did, but he ran away into the jungle and joined up with one of the guerrilla bands. You know there are lots of them in the islands."

Warren nodded. "Just the same, keep a sharp lookout on him. If he does anything in the least bit suspicious, shoot him."

Rudy's eyes opened wide.

"I wouldn't want to wake up one morning with a couple of Jap destroyers standing offshore and shooting the hell out of this place," Warren said.

Rudy shook his head. "I'll have him watched."

Warren stubbed out the cigarette in half a clam shell, swung his feet to the floor, and stood up. "If we do hit that radar station," he said, "we'll have to leapfrog it down there and back. That means we have to have fuel dumps along the way and maybe even a temporary base midway between here and there."

"That would be bigger than any raid we've made yet," Rudy commented.

304

"And a lot more dangerous," Warren said, going to the map and looking at the area where the island was located. "Two nights down and two nights back if we have good weather. Okay, we'll do it, but first I want to recon the place myself. We'll leave tonight and take our friend with us. I want you and five of your men — better take those who were in the army. I'll have two other boats carry fuel down to a halfway point and guard it until we return."

"Two BAR men?" Rudy asked.

"Yes," Warren answered. "But let's hope we don't need them. We'll leave at sunset."

Rudy went to the door. "You know," he said, "I don't even feel as if it's Christmas."

"Christmas?" Warren questioned. He completely forgot that Christmas was so close.

"In two days... Check your calendar," Rudy told him, walking out of the palm-thatched house.

Warren turned his attention back to the chart and began to plan the recon operation.

"Ease her in close to the shore," Warren ordered the machinist mate at the helm, who also controlled the engine throttle. The engines were just putting out sufficient RPMs for him to have steerageway. He watched the shoreline. "Full stop," he ordered. "Full stop," the machinist mate answered.

The boat lost headway, then lay dead in the water about five yards from the shore.

"Tie up to that big tree there," Warren said to Ensign Bates, the boat's third officer.

"Aye, aye, skipper," Bates answered.

Warren turned to the XO, Donald Greer. "If I'm not back by nightfall tomorrow, you get the hell out of here as fast as you can. Nightfall is at 1830. By 1831, you're on your way."

Greer nodded. He was tall and thin, with a pockmarked face and prominent cheekbones that gave him an Indian-like look, which was accentuated by his straight black hair and black eyes. But he was born and raised in Philadelphia, where his father was a physician. "I'd much rather go with you," Greer said. "Bates can run the boat back just as well as I can."

"You're right," Warren answered. "But I need someone to bother the next skipper if I don't make it back."

Greer made a face; then offering his hand, he said, "Good luck, skipper."

"Thanks," Warren said and, with a wave of his hand, he signaled Rudy, who was waiting on the afterdeck, to move his men over the side and into the jungle. He picked up his carbine and nimbly dropped into the warm, waist-high water.

Within a few moments, Warren and the others were in the jungle, heading for Silvano's village. He, Rudy, and Silvano were up front. A BAR man was point, about thirty yards in front of them, another BAR man held the center, and the third brought up the rear.

Warren's plan was to use a fishing boat to reconnoiter the island, return to the village in the late afternoon, and be back aboard the boat by no later than 1700.

"Silvano says the village is up ahead, about a mile," Rudy whispered.

Warren looked up through the tangled growth. The sky was much lighter than it was when they left the boat and the birds were beginning to make a racket.

"Silvano says there're monkeys up in the trees," Rudy commented, still whispering, "and snakes on the ground."

"Happy combination," Warren answered in a low voice. The trail they were following appeared to be well used and he didn't like that at all; then suddenly he realized it wasn't the usual narrow jungle trail. In the last four months he'd used enough of them to know that this one was at least twice as wide as it should be. He held up his hand and said to Rudy, "Take your .45, cock it, and put it against Silvano's head."

Silvano pushed Rudy out of the way and crashed into the jungle.

"Get him!" Warren ordered.

The second BAR man fired a short burst.

Silvano screamed, stumbled, and fell face forward.

The next instant they were taking fire from all sides. The three BAR men were cut down.

"Hit the deck!" Warren shouted, diving into the jungle. Even as he dropped, a searing pain slashed through his left arm.

The Japanese were systematically subjecting every inch of jungle alongside the trail to heavy small-arms fire.

"Three left and us," Rudy said, bellying up to where Warren lay. "Jesus, you're hit." And he pulled a dirty bandanna off his neck and tied it tightly around Warren's arm.

"They can't see us and we can't see them," Warren said. "But we can hear them. You better have a good throwing arm, Rudy, or we're dead. Take a grenade, release the plunger, count five, and throw it. I'll do the same."

"Five more and we're dead."

Warren nodded. "You throw first."

Rudy pulled the pin and released the plunger. "One ... two ... three, four, and five." He hurled the grenade toward the Japanese.

Warren threw his.

The explosions tore up the trail and brought screams from the Japanese.

"Okay, now," Warren said, crashing through the jungle with Rudy and the other men after him.

Three booms of thunder came from up the trail.

Warren stopped. "The boat!" he exclaimed.

Rudy pointed to the column of black smoke already climbing above trees.

"I fell into this one," Warren said bitterly. "This was a fucking disaster waiting for me to take the bait, and I took it *hook, line, and sinker*." He turned around and motioned to the man to continue chopping through the jungle with his machete.

Almost as soon as the sun was above the horizon, the heat, humidity, and insects became intolerable. "We've got to rest," Rudy said, "or we'll drop."

Warren nodded, sat down on the ground, and leaned against the trunk of a huge tree. "We've got to get some kind of a boat, or we'll never get out of here alive."

"Where and how are we going to get a boat?" Rudy asked.

"The where and how are easy to answer," Warren said. "But doing it may be impossible. We'll get a boat from the village."

"You think they'll just give us one?"

"No. We'll steal it."

Rudy snapped his fingers. "Just like that!"

"It's either we try, give ourselves up, or die fighting," Warren said.

"Have you any idea what the Japs will do to us, if we give ourselves up?" Rudy asked. "Before you answer, let me tell you that they will make you beg them to kill you, because death would put an end to your pain."

"I've heard," Warren said.

"We don't even know where the village is," Rudy commented.

"It has to be at the end of the trail, or close to it," Warren said. "We'll wait until nightfall, go back to the trail, and follow it to the village."

"Don't you think the Jap commander might guess we'd try something like that?"

"Yes," Warren said. "But it's our only chance of getting off this island."

Rudy remained silent for several minutes; then he said, "He might have the trail guarded, but he wouldn't expect us to come out of the water."

"Rudy," Warren exclaimed, "you're a genius. You should have been a general."

"I told MacArthur that," Rudy said, "but he didn't believe me. I also told him that his defense line on Bataan wouldn't hold, and he didn't believe that either."

Warren made a clicking sound with his tongue. "Some men are just hard-headed about things." And he added, "We'll rest here a few minutes longer, then move to a safer place and wait until dusk before we head for the water."

"No guns," Rudy said, touching the canvas sheath of his trench knife.

"No guns," Warren agreed.

Warren and his men waded and swam through the absolutely black and tepid water in front of the village, which was black too, except for the yellow glow of two lanterns outside of one of the palm-thatched houses that probably was the Japanese headquarters.

"Boats are tied up there," Rudy said, gesturing to a rickety-looking wharf that jutted ten or fifteen yards out from the beach.

"What's on the other side of it?" Warren asked, and before Rudy could answer, he said, "It's one of their PTs, a Jap motor torpedo boat."

Both men stopped swimming and did a dog paddle; the three men with them did the same.

"That would get us out of here in a hurry," Warren said.

"And probably have every Jap ship around here after us," Rudy added.

"Sure, but we could sure use something like that to bait a few traps ourselves," he said, starting to swim again.

The boat was on the far side of the wharf, with a line forward and aft securing it.

A single sentry was posted at the bow.

"Manuel," Rudy said to one of the three men, drawing his finger across his neck. "Get his gun."

The man left the group and swam under the wharf.

"You and you," Warren told the other two men, "cut the lines as soon as Manuel finishes." He turned to Rudy. "You go up on the bow; I'll take the stern."

"What if some of the crew is aboard?" Rudy asked.

"I'm gambling that all of them are ashore," Warren answered.

From where they were in the water, they watched Manuel lift himself out of the water and under the deck of the boat; then crouching, he moved swiftly to the sentry, who at the last instant started to turn, but the blade of Manuel's knife was already at his throat. The man never screamed. He almost fell into the water, but Manuel grabbed him, eased him down on the wharf's planking, and then took his gun.

"Now let's board her," Warren said, swimming toward the already drifting boat. In moments, he grabbed onto the hand of one of the men already on board.

Suddenly there was the sound of conversation below.

Warren signaled for silence. He crouched to the side of the companionway and waited.

A head emerged from the cabin.

Warren took a deep breath.

The back of the man!

Warren drove the knife into the man's back to its hilt.

The man gave a startled cry.

Someone called from below.

The man impaled on the knife tried desperately to reach it.

The same voice called out from the cabin.

Warren pushed the man to the side and overboard. "Manuel, shoot the other one," he said in a low voice.

Manuel charged down the steps and squeezed off two rounds.

"Rudy, the helm and throttle," Warren ordered.

"Aye, aye, skipper," Rudy said.

"Manuel, you and one of the other men on the deck gun," Warren said.

"Yes, sir," Manuel answered.

"Get on the machine guns," Warren told the two remaining men. "Let's hope it starts the same way as ours," he said, pressing what he thought was the button to start the engines. It was. "Okay, Manuel, you fire as soon as you see anyone on the beach. You guys on the machine guns do the same. Flank speed," Warren ordered. "Push that throttle as far forward as you can, then full right rudder, spin the wheel over as far as she'll go to the right."

The boat leaped forward.

"Nothing on the beach," Manuel called out.

"Give them a minute or two," Warren said, as the boat heeled over to her starboard in a tight turn. He reached over to the helm and eased it back. "Hold it steady," he ordered.

"There they are!" Manuel exclaimed, swinging the deck gun around to rake the beach, while the two machine guns opened up.

CHAPTER 50

The family party was for Tony. He was home on leave before taking command of his own boat, the *Manta*. For bringing the *Tarpon* and its crew safely back to Brisbane, Tony was awarded the Navy Cross and promoted to Lieutenant Commander.

Because the party was "family," not only were there members of Tony's real family there, but many of the guests belonged to his father's other family. Among them was Carlo Spilachi, the father of all of them.

"So," Spilachi asked, "you had enough of the war, Tony?" He was a dignified-looking man, with pure white hair and bottomless gray eyes. He ate very little and only occasionally sipped the wine in his glass.

"I had enough," Tony answered, "but the war is still there. It won't go away."

"I can make it go away for you," Spilachi said. "You did your share. How many times do you want to be a hero? Maybe one time you'll wind up a dead hero."

Everyone in the Trapasso dining room stopped talking and the silence, like some viscous liquid, flowed quickly into the kitchen, bringing his mother and her two sisters to the door.

Tony nodded. Everyone was waiting not only for his answer, but for how he'd answer. He was expected to phrase his answer, regardless of what it would be, in such a way that he would be subservient to Spilachi and thereby give the man the respect due to him. Tony smiled, looked straight at him, and said, "Because you are a guest in my father's house and have come to join my family in this celebration, I will not say what I want to."

The people at the table stirred uneasily.

"Certainly," Spilachi answered, "you've won the right to say what you want to say."

"No," Tony said. "I think you know what I was going to say, Mr. Spilachi."

Spilachi looked at Tony's father. "I'll say this for him, he's not afraid."

"You're wrong, Mr. Spilachi," Tony said. "Over these past three years I have been afraid more times than I ever want to remember. All of those times I had something to fear, but from you —" He let that hang in the air for a few moments; then he finished by saying, "Nothing, absolutely nothing."

Spilachi's face became red.

"All right," Tony said, in a loud voice, "I have an announcement to make. Everyone, listen. I'm going to be married."

"Holy Mother of God!" his mother cried from the kitchen doorway. "How could you do that to me. The girl isn't one of us; she isn't Catholic. Tony," she wept, "it's not a marriage unless it's in the Church."

Tony left the table and went to his mother. "I thought you'd be happy," he said.

"Oh Tony," she cried, "I wanted to see you married, but what you're going to do is wrong!"

"Come sit down," he said.

She shook her head. "The party was for you," she said, "and now you've ruined it."

Tony looked at the table. It was empty.

CHAPTER 51

Jacob sat in between Tony and Glen at the Hali Kalani bar. Tony was now his brother-in-law. Two days before, he'd returned from his first successful patrol as skipper of the *Manta*. Glen's ship, the *Edison*, was in for repairs at Pearl after being struck in the stern by a kamikaze off the island of Samar in the Philippines.

"A toast to Warren," Tony said, raising his martini. "Did you know that bastard stole a Jap torpedo boat?"

"It made the headlines when the news was released," Jacob said. "But it actually happened in '43, on Christmas day. The censors didn't want to release anything about it."

"To Warren," Glen said, raising his glass of scotch.

"Warren," Jacob echoed, touching the glasses of the other two with his.

"How long do you have here?" Tony asked, looking at Jacob.

"A month, maybe six weeks," Jacob said. "I'm now an air group commander of Air Group Twenty and skipper of the Fighting Squadron as well. I have a whole group of young, inexperienced pilots to get ready for what they're going to face." For the past year he instructed student pilots in operational tactics at the Naval Air Station, in Opalocka, Florida and was promoted to a Lieutenant Commander. Now he was back at sea and his new Air Group was assigned to the fight attack carrier, CVL-20, *Alamo*.

"Yeah," Glen commented, "the new men seem to be younger and younger."

"I have some men aboard the *Manta* that still have fuzz on their face," Trapasso said.

The three of them laughed.

"How's your son?" Jacob asked, looking at Glen.

"Wait, I'll show you his picture," Glen said, pulling out his wallet and removing the photograph. "Does he, or doesn't he look like me?" he asked proudly.

"How could he look like you?" Jacob asked. "He's good-looking."

Tony nodded, looked at Jacob, and said, "How would you like to be called Uncle Jake?"

"You're joking!"

"Not unless Miriam is," Tony answered. "In her last letter she was already four months gone."

"Bartender," Jacob said, "give us a bottle of your best —"

"Commander Jacob Miller," a bellboy called. "Is there a Commander Jacob Miller here."

"Probably the base," Glen said.

Jacob stood up, summoned the bellboy, and said, "I'm Commander Miller."

"Sir, you have a phone call. You may take it in the lobby," the bellboy said.

Jacob tipped him, went to the lobby, picked up the phone, and told the operator who he was.

"Go ahead," the operator said.

"Commander Miller," the woman said, "this is Miss Ryder from the American Red Cross. Your duty officer was kind enough to tell me where I might be able to find you. Commander, I am sorry that I have to be the one to tell you that your father has suffered a very serious heart attack and is not expected to survive…"

Jacob didn't hear the rest of what the woman said. He put the phone down and walked back to the bar.

"What's wrong?" Tony asked, getting up to meet him.

"Papa has had a heart attack and is not expected to live," Jacob said.

"Are you going to try and go home?" Glen asked.

Jacob shook his head. "I've got to train my men," he said fiercely. "I don't want to lose any of them because of something I didn't tell or show them." He looked at Tony. "Papa would understand that, wouldn't he?"

"He'd understand," Tony answered.

"Listen you guys," Jacob said, "I'm going to try and get a call through to New York."

"The Red Cross will help do it in an emergency," Glen said.

Jacob nodded. "I'll get in touch with both of you in a few days," he said, reaching for his wallet.

"It's covered," Glen told him.

"I'll try to speak to Miriam in a little while," Tony said.

"Yes, that'll be good," Jacob said and walked slowly away.

CHAPTER 52

Warren's squadron was part of the 39 PT boats ordered to take up positions in the coves of the islands off the southern entrance to the Surigao Strait. The order came from Bull Gower, now over all commander of the United States Third Fleet. The PTs were the first line of defense against the Japanese push into the strait; behind them was a line of destroyers, and to the rear of the destroyers were the cruisers and battleships.

The orders to all of the squadron commanders were terse and simple: "Your task is to intercept and sink as many of the enemy ships as possible." From the succinctness of the order, it was clear to Warren, and all of the other squadron commanders, that Gower considered them expendable.

Warren cupped his hand over the cigarette and took a long drag on it, then let the smoke pour out of his mouth and nostrils.

"Skipper," Phil, the radar operator, said, "I have three unknowns on the screen... Bearing, zero, two nine five... Range, 12,000 yards and closing fast."

Warren quickly radioed the target bearing and range to the other squadron commanders. Then he said to Sean Devlin, his EXO, "Check with the other boat skippers and make sure we don't have anyone developing engine trouble at the last minute."

"Aye, aye, skipper," Devlin answered.

"Pass the word that all boats stand by for full throttle operation."

"Yes, sir," Devlin said and left the bridge to go to the radio shack.

Warren didn't particularly like Devlin and he was sure the feeling was mutual. Sean, the same age as himself, was the only man Warren knew who could actually twist his face into a disdainful sneer, and what made it worse, the man was disdainful of just about everything. Almost as soon as Devlin joined the squadron, he let it be known that he wasn't *really navy*, and that after the war the men would be able to proudly tell their friends that they had served with him.

A radio intercept from the battleship *Kansas*, Gower's flagship, indicated that it had radar contact with a "probable enemy bearing one eight five — range 18,000 yards."

Warren turned to the radar operator. "Check your bearing and range," he ordered.

"Target bearing two nine five, range 10,000 yards and closing," the radar operator said.

Warren was just about to radio the *Kansas*, when a voice over the radio said, "Separate enemy contacts — one made up of four ships, bearing two nine five, range 15,000 yards from K; second of six ships, bearing one eight five, range 18,000 yards from K... Expect two forces to join into one."

The battle plan for the PTs was simple: attack as soon as the enemy comes into visual contact.

"Stand by," Warren announced over the 1MC.

Sean came back to the bridge. "All boats report engines idling," he said.

"We'll be underway in another minute or two," Warren said.

"I feel like I'm with the U.S. cavalry in one of those spectacular Hollywood charges," Sean commented.

"Believe me," Warren said, remembering the engagement in Iron Bottom Sound, off Savo Island, "this is going to be like nothing you've ever experienced."

That look of disdain came to Devlin's face. "Captain, I have been in combat before," he said.

Ignoring Devlin, Warren asked for a radar check.

"Bearing, two nine eight; range 5000 yards and closing," Phil answered.

Warren radioed the bearings and range to the other boats in his command. Each of them, with the exception of the one with him in the cove, would have, as a result of their positions, different readings on their radar. He touched the machinist mate, who was both throttle man and helmsman, on the shoulder. "There they are... Full throttle!" he ordered.

With a roar, the boat leaped forward; then settling stern down, it raced through the water, creating two huge fans of water at the bow and a white wake at the stern.

The night was moonless and the water was a black surface.

Warren switched on the mike. "Get in and out as quickly as you can," he told his skippers. "Have your gunners go for the searchlights. Remember, what they can't see, they can't hit." He switched off the mike. "Check torpedo tubes," he said.

"Torpedos armed and loaded," Devlin reported.

"Come to two eight five," Warren ordered.

"Two eight five," the helmsman answered.

Warren could see the Japanese ships now. There were four destroyers leading the van, and behind them were cruisers and battleships, screened port and starboard by additional destroyers. He glanced to port, then to starboard. There were PT boats on either side of his. He turned on the 1MC. "Attack... Attack!" he ordered.

Suddenly the searchlights came on and swept the water. Some boats were instantly caught in a yellow circle of light. A second later the Japanese guns opened up.

"Rudder, hard right," Warren ordered.

"Hard right," the helmsman answered.

The boat heeled over and started to make a turn.

"Rudder, hard left," Warren ordered.

The yellow circle of light skidded past them. Two geysers of water shot up on the boat's starboard side, drenching it under a torrent of water.

"Close!" Devlin exclaimed, wiping his face.

Suddenly the forward deck gunner opened up. A searchlight above the navigation bridge aboard the nearest destroyer blazed white then went out.

"Good shooting," Warren shouted.

Suddenly the boat next to his became a mass of flames.

Warren ordered the helmsman to steer directly for the target. "Stand by to launch torpedoes," he ordered.

"Christ," Devlin shouted, "we're being shot to pieces!"

There were burning and sinking boats in every direction.

Warren kept his eyes on the destroyer. He maneuvered his boat to come at her port side.

The Japanese searchlights frantically tried to find him. One finally did.

"Fire tube one!" he ordered.

The boat's starboard side rose slightly.

"Torpedo one on its way," the officer reported.

The boat's gunners were trying desperately to shoot out the destroyer's searchlights.

"Launch tube two," Warren ordered.

The boat leveled itself.

"Torpedo two on its way."

"Full left rudder," Warren ordered.

A huge explosion staggered the Japanese destroyer.

"Got the fucker," one of the men yelled.

"Full right rudder," Warren ordered.

Two shells burst over the stern of the boat. The rear deck gunner's head dropped to the deck and rolled into the sea, as the rest of the body fell to the deck.

Just as a second explosion broke the destroyer in half, an explosion lifted the U.S. boat out of the water and heaved it on its port side!

Warren found himself in the water. He was dazed and fought not to lose consciousness.

"That you, Captain?" a voice called.

He recognized Devlin's voice. "Over here," he called. "Over here!" And as he felt himself slide under the black water, he heard his father shout, "Go back Warren... Go back... Go back!"

CHAPTER 53

Warren opened his eyes. The room was in semidarkness. From the feel of the bed and the sheets, he realized he was in a hospital. There was a bed on either side of him. The one on the right was empty, but there was someone in the one on the left.

He tried to move and felt a jagged slash of pain in his right shoulder and across his chest. He remembered being in the water, but didn't remember being wounded. The pain subsided and he realized he was very hungry.

Suddenly he heard footsteps in the room and called, "Nurse... Nurse."

"Yes," the woman answered, coming up to the foot of the bed.

"Where am I?" he asked.

"In the hospital in Pearl," she answered, with a smile.

"Pearl?"

"You were flown here two days ago," she said. "Now you sleep. In a few hours the doctor will tell you everything you want to know."

"One more question, please?"

"Go ahead, ask. I'll try to answer it if I can," she said.

"I remember being in the water, but —"

"Lieutenant Devlin saved you, Commander," she said. "He held on to you all night and well into the next morning, when the two of you were picked up by the destroyer *Edison*, whose navigator, it turned out, was a friend of yours, Lieutenant Commander Glen Lascomb. I'd say you were a very lucky man."

"Lucky isn't the word for it," Warren answered.

"Since you arrived," she said, "your mother, your sister, and Mrs. Hasse have been here."

"Together?" he asked in astonishment.

"No, Mrs. Hasse comes alone and in the early morning."

Warren smiled, closed his eyes, and felt himself sliding into sleep.

"Aerology says we have some heavy weather coming in from the east," Henry Blake, the *Alamo*'s XO, said to Jacob.

"Are we still going to refuel?" Jacob asked. He and Henry were in the wardroom drinking coffee. They became friends just before the ship had left Pearl. Jacob had received another phone call; this time his sister, Miriam, was on the line. He knew what she was going to tell him, even before she said, "Papa is dead…"

When Jacob put the phone down, he left the booth and found himself standing in front of Blake, a man ten years his senior, whose family owned the New York stockbrokerage firm of Blake & Blake.

Henry was of middling height, with an impish face, dark gray eyes and close-cropped brown hair. "My father died," Jacob said and tried to sidestep Blake.

Blake grabbed hold of his arm. "Easy," he said with quiet authority. "Easy, man. We'll go somewhere we can talk."

And talk they did, or rather Jacob talked and Blake listened.

When Jacob finally ran out of words, Blake said, "I have a son and I hope that when he's a man he loves me half as much as you love your father. Now, let's get back to the ship and have a cup of coffee." From that moment on, Jacob felt he had a friend in the older man.

As soon as they were aboard the *Alamo*, they went to Blake's cabin and Blake had a steward bring them a pot of coffee and two pieces of cake. "Admiral to push hard against the Japanese is what Gower wants," Blake said, slowly sipping his coffee. "From what the skipper says, the admiral intends to move into the South China Sea for a few days and hit the Philippines hard." Jacob shrugged. It didn't matter to him where they went. "Have you thought about what you're going to do after the war?" Blake asked.

Jacob smiled. "Who hasn't," he answered.

"Well, tell me, or do I have to wait until the war is over before you reveal the secret?"

"I'm going to stay in the navy," he said.

"You?"

"Yes, me."

"That surprises me," Blake said. "I know you're Annapolis, but I figured that your going there was for different reasons. I mean, I didn't think you were the type to be a *professional*."

"I don't really know if I am, as you put it, a professional, but I love flying and the navy is one of the few places where I can continue to do it."

"You do what you have to do," Blake said, as he finished his coffee, "but if you ever change your mind, there'll be a place for you with Blake and Blake. It will always be there, Jake. Five years from the time the war ends, or 25 years."

"That's nice to know," Jacob responded, surprised by the offer. "It really is."

Blake stood up. "We'll be getting underway in a few hours," he said, looking at the bulkhead clock. "Keep the ball pumped up!"

"Thank you, sir. I appreciate your kindness," Jacob answered and left the cabin.

CHAPTER 54

Two weeks had passed since the *Alamo* left Pearl Harbor. Jacob's task group was striking at targets on Luzon in preparation for the planned invasion. The group retired to the east for a day of replenishment, but the sea became too rough to continue refueling. At 1700, on Gower's orders, it was suspended, and the task group steamed west in an attempt to get away from the growing storm. But the weather only worsened. Rain came down in torrents from low black clouds and tons of water began to crash over the flight deck as the *Alamo* rolled and plunged into the building seas.

The ship rolled constantly and heavily from one side to the other. Jacob found it almost impossible to lie in his bunk without being thrown to the deck. No one on board the *Alamo*, from the captain down, had ever experienced a storm of this magnitude. It was a major typhoon!

Just before dawn the following day, the general alarm sounded. Then a voice came over the 1MC. "General Quarters... General Quarters... All hands man your battle station."

"What the hell is going on?" one of Jacob's pilots asked, as they filed into the fighter ready room.

"Just sit tight," Jacob answered; then to a group of pilots, he said, "Lash the chairs together and stow any other loose gear. This heavy weather isn't going to stop soon."

"The fucking ship's plates are screaming," one of the pilots said.

Suddenly the ship rolled to the starboard side.

Jacob lost his footing and was thrown against the bulkhead. Each time the ship rolled, the sounds of heavy crashing came from the hangar deck below the ready room.

An instant later the 1MC blared: "Fire... Fire... Fire in the hangar deck."

The ready room phone rang.

One of the men answered it. "Skipper, it's the bridge."

Jacob pulled himself up. "Miller here," he said.

"We have a bad fire in the hangar," Blake said. "Keep your men where they are."

"Yes, sir," Jacob answered, but almost as soon as he put the phone down, heavy smoke from below began to infiltrate the ready room. In a matter of minutes, it became difficult to see for more than a few feet. All hands were having difficulty breathing. "Everyone," Jacob shouted, "topside to the flight deck on the double."

The men rushed out of the fighter ready room.

Jacob moved quickly to the torpedo squadron ready room. "Topside, to the flight deck — on the double," he ordered.

The pilots struggled to maintain their footing on their way to the flight deck as the ship continued to roll heavily. It was impossible for them to stand and Jacob, crawling on his hands and knees, led the way to the base of the Island Structure.

"I think some of our planes in the hangar have broken loose and are crashing back and forth,"

Jacob shouted to his XO. "I hope to Christ the residual fuel in the fighter belly tanks doesn't go off."

The wind was gusting to almost 100 knots, and the rain, driven by the wind, felt like machine-gun bullets. Smoke was streaming up from below decks.

"Everyone down on the deck," Jacob ordered; then to his XO, he shouted, "These guys will die of exposure if we don't do something fast. Stack them on top of one another. It'll keep some of them warm."

Suddenly there was a deafening explosion in the hangar. Then as the ship rolled, the sounds of debris crashing inside the hangar rose above the banshee scream of the wind. Smoke continued to pour from below the flight deck, and the intense heat from the fire bubbled the pitch between the wooden planks on the deck.

"There go our aircraft," Jacob shouted.

"Skipper," the XO answered, "I think the ship has gone dead in the water!"

The 1MC came on. "This is the captain speaking. We have lost fireroom one and will be lying-to so that our remaining boiler power can be used for fire and boiler pumps... All hands exercise extreme caution."

A huge wave struck the ship and she started to roll.

"Christ, she's going over!" came from several men at the base of the structure.

The wind and the rain tore at the ship and howled around its mast. A radar antenna was twisted off and crashed into the raging sea. As the ship rolled, two torpedo aircraft among those tied down on the after part of the flight deck suddenly broke free and were flung like toys into the sea. Two more went overboard on the next roll.

Wave after wave crashed over the deck.

In a matter of minutes, Jacob's men were shivering from the cold and the wind-driven rain, while in the hangar deck below, the fire, fed by the fuel in the aircraft's exploding belly tanks, raged.

"I'm scared shitless!" one of the men shouted, above the scream of the wind.

"Goddamn it! Shut up and just worry about holding on," Jacob yelled back, aware that the ship was sometimes hogging across the crests of two mountainous waves with no water supporting it amidships. He could hear the ship groaning in protest as she resisted breaking into two halves.

Suddenly the ship rolled heavily to the port side.

"I can't hold on!" a man shouted, as he broke free from the pack and slid rapidly toward the edge of the deck. He was going overboard!

The ship was lifted by the sea and she rolled to the starboard.

The man came sliding back toward Jacob. As he came close, Jacob grabbed him, and the two of them crashed against the Island's base.

The man's leg doubled under him and he screamed in pain.

As the *Alamo* hung momentarily and precariously to the starboard, Jacob shouted, "Now." And crawling, he pulled the injured man back to an arresting cable, and wrapping one arm around it, he wrapped the other around the man's chest. Exhausted, blinded by the rain, he felt as if his arms were slowly being torn out of their sockets. Nothing he'd ever done required the strength he now used to hold onto the man and the cable.

Suddenly Jacob felt a slight tremor pass through the *Alamo* as her twin screws began to turn. The bridge regained power. Slowly, she was being eased into the screaming wind. But then another muffled explosion from somewhere below rocked the ship.

Jacob closed his eyes and forced his thoughts away from what now seemed to be certain disaster. His mind was cut away by the knifelike pains in both his arms.

Then someone yelled, "She ain't rolling the way she was."

Jacob opened his eyes and looked toward the Island. The arc made by its broken mast was indeed less than before. And the clouds, though still dark, weren't black. The wind force dropped dramatically, and the seas flattened.

"Good Christ, the wind has dropped," one of the pilots said.

"I think I can let go of you," Jacob told the man he was holding.

"Just pull me up so I can grab hold of the cable. I'll be all right now, skipper," the man said.

Jacob pulled at him, while he pushed against the wet deck with his feet until he was able to grab hold of the restraining cable.

"Skipper," one of the other men said, "I think the worst is over as far as the storm is concerned."

Jacob got to his feet and found he could maintain his balance. He was cold and wet, and his body ached as though he'd been subjected to hours of torture on the rack. But he was alive and his squadron hadn't lost a man. "All right men, everyone on his feet," he ordered. "Let's find someplace where it's warm and dry."

The IMC came on. "This is the captain speaking... Fires in the hangar are out and we are underway with good control of the ship. To the last man of you, I say: well done! We are now heading for fleet anchorage at Ulithi. I expect we will then head back to Pearl Harbor for repairs."

Jacob's men began to cheer.

"New Year's Eve in Pearl, can you beat that!" a man exclaimed.

"I'm going to have one hell of a wild time," his wingman said. "What about you, skipper?"

"Me too," Jacob laughed. "Me too!"

CHAPTER 55

"There's a letter here for you, Warren," Kate said, waving the blue V-letter in front of her. "The nurse at the nurse's station asked me to bring it to you. From the looks of it, it must have followed you all over the Pacific."

Warren smiled. He looked forward to Kate's morning visits. "Read it," he said.

"Looks like a woman's handwriting," she said, sitting down on the white chair alongside the bed.

"I don't know any woman who'd take the trouble to write to me," Warren responded.

Kate deftly opened the envelope, took the letter out, and putting on her glasses, began to read: "My Dearest Warren, I am sorry that I did not say good-bye to you, but such a good-bye would have been too painful for me to bear. I did love you —" Kate paused. "Are you sure that you want me to continue?" she asked.

"Yes," he said.

"I did love you and still do," Kate read. "'But all my other doubts are the same. Perhaps our relationship is the best of all possible relationships, or to put it another way, I'll never forget you and I hope you'll never forget me. Love, Irene Hacker.'"

Kate refolded the letter, put it back in the envelope, and handing it to Warren, asked, "Is she worth what you're feeling now?"

He nodded.

"What are you going to do?"

"I have some leave time coming. Maybe I'll be able to hitch a flight to Australia."

"She might not be there," Kate said. "There was something in the newspaper just after the invasion of Luzon about army nurses landing behind the troops with field hospital units. I could do some of the legwork and find out if she's still in Australia."

Warren suddenly saw his mother and blanched.

"What's wrong?" Kate asked, alarmed.

"My mother," he said tightly.

"Oh dear!" Kate exclaimed.

Gloria slowed her pace, but when she was close to the foot of the bed, Warren forced a smile and said, "Good morning, Mother."

"Good morning," she answered.

"Mother, this is Mrs. Katherine Hasse," Warren said, hoping that she wouldn't create a scene.

"A pleasure," Kate responded.

Gloria studied her for a few moments; then she said, "Thank you for taking care of my son. When I was told about the woman who visits him every morning, I knew it had to be you." Her voice cracked.

"If you want me to leave —"

Gloria waved her hand. "Please no," she said; then with a wan smile on her lips, she added, "I know Andy would want you here."

"Thank you," Kate answered.

"I often wondered how I'd react when I met you," Gloria said. "But here I am face-to-face with you over my son's bed, and all I can feel, and I'm not sure *feel* is the correct word, is that you must have loved Andy a great deal to be here now."

"I did," Kate said honestly.

"I envy you, but not because Andy loved you, but because I never felt toward him, or, for that matter, any man, what you felt."

"I'm sorry for you," Kate said. "I'm truly sorry."

Warren realized that his mother was graciously acknowledging Kate's right to be there.

The wan smile came back to Gloria's lips, and looking at Warren, she said, "Andy would have been very proud of him."

"He certainly would have," Kate agreed.

"Do you think between the two of us, Katherine —"

"Kate, please."

"Kate, do you think between the two of us we might get him up and around soon?" Gloria asked.

"I'm sure we could," Kate said.

Warren reached out and taking hold of their hands, he gently kissed the back of each of them.

"Well, Admiral, you certainly do have a way of getting your name in the newspaper," the woman said.

Jacob didn't even have to look in the mirror behind the bar to make sure it was Connie.

"What, no answer?" she chided, sitting down on the stool next to him. "Or are you still pissed about what happened in New York? Bartender," she called without pausing for a breath, "give me something — whatever the admiral here is drinking."

"That'll be bourbon and branch water," the barkeep told her.

"God, that's awful! Give me a gin and tonic," she said.

Jacob faced her. She was still very desirable. He put his drink down on the bar. "Forget about the lady's drink," he said. "This should cover mine and hers." He put five dollars down and took hold of her wrist.

"What the hell do you think you're doing?" she asked, trying to pull her hand away from him.

He bent close to her. "I'm taking you to a hotel room!"

"What?" she questioned, her eyes opening wide.

Still close to her, he said, "I'm going to fuck the brains out of you."

She grinned. "Didn't the navy teach you that's not where you fuck?"

"I know —"

"Yes," she said quietly, "I really do know you know."

"Are you going to come?"

"I hope so," she answered, getting off the stool.

"There's a place not far from here," Jacob said, squinting in the bright sunlight.

"I have an apartment 10 minutes from here by cab," she said.

"All right, your apartment," he answered, after a moment's hesitation. He hailed a cab and Connie gave the driver her address. Neither one of them spoke until Jacob closed and locked the door to the apartment; then taking her in his arms, he said, "I never was able to get you out of my mind." And he kissed her fiercely on the lips.

She responded by opening her mouth.

His hands moved over her breasts, down her flanks, and over her buttocks.

"Undress me," she said, loosening his tie.

Leaving a trail of clothes in their wake, they moved into the bedroom and, finally naked, faced each other.

Jacob drew her to him and kissed the tip of her nose, then her lips, her chin, and the side of her neck.

She raised her head and gently moved her hands over his chest. "I thought about you often," she told him. "I was sorry about —"

He put his finger across her mouth. "It's gone, over with… The only thing that really matters is that you're here with me now."

She kissed his finger and said, "Yes, my darling."

Jacob suddenly scooped her up and put her down on the bed.

Connie raised her arms to embrace him. "I want you inside of me, deep inside of me."

Entering her, Jacob whispered, "I want to love you."

"And I want to love you," she answered, caressing his back.

Jacob reveled in the exquisite sensations that coursed through his body, and the feel of her naked body totally belonging to him drove him to a frenzy of excitement that suddenly exploded into a searing orgasmic climax.

She thrust her body against his and raking his back with her nails, she uttered a wordless cry of delight.

"Marry me," he said, kissing her closed eyelids.

"Yes," she whispered, looking up at him.

Jacob smiled and kissed the tip of her nose.

Tony was on the *Manta*'s bridge. The OOD was Lieutenant (JG) Ned Jackson, the boat's radar officer. This was Jackson's second patrol with Tony.

"Skipper, just how far away are we from the coast of China?" Ned asked.

"Shanghai is 300 miles due west of here," Tony answered, looking at the stars. The sky was absolutely cloudless and a thin crescent moon was just rising in the eastern sky. He looked at his watch: it was 0300. The *Manta* had been on the surface since 1700 the previous evening. More than enough time to get a full charge on her batteries.

"Target, two points off the port bow," the lookout called out.

"There it is," Ned said, pointing to a dark shape.

"Bridge, target, bearing two zero degrees... Range, 15,000 yards... Speed, one five... Course, one one zero," the radar operator reported.

"I have the conn," Tony said.

"Aye, aye, sir," Jackson answered.

Tony hit the klaxon button.

The XO came up through the open hatch to the bridge.

Tony switched on the 1MC. "Battle stations... All hands, battle stations," he ordered; then turning to Jackson, he said, "Go below to the radar."

"Aye, aye, sir," Jackson said and dropped through the open hatch.

"Come to course one one five," Tony ordered.

"One one five," the helmsman answered.

"Full ahead," Tony ordered.

"Full ahead answered," the engine room signalman responded.

The noise made by the *Manta*'s diesels increased, and the ship's bow created a white arc on either side of it.

"Holding course and speed," radar reported.

Tony's plan was to run ahead of the ship and position himself for a midship shot.

"Can't make out what she is yet?" the XO said.

"Another few minutes and we'll be close enough to see," Tony answered. If he sank this one, it would give him six for this patrol and leave him with only two fish left.

"If there was just a little more moon, we'd be able to see what she is by now," the XO said.

Over 1MC Tony ordered the diving officer to take her down ten feet. "Just enough to put the deck under."

"Zero one zero feet," the DO responded.

The ballast tank valves opened and water rushed into them. The sea suddenly began to swirl over the *Manta*'s decks; then the valves were closed.

"Steady at 10 feet," the DO reported.

Tony checked the level indicator. The bubble was centered.

"Bridge, target changing course," Radar reported.

"Give it to me as soon as you have it," Tony said, wondering if the *Manta* was spotted and the Japanese ship was going to start zigzagging.

"Bridge, target bearing —"

"Torpedo, off the starboard beam," the starboard lookout shouted.

"Rudder, hard left," Tony ordered.

The explosion blew Tony off the bridge, pushed the *Manta* heavily to her port and snapped her in half. Within a matter of a minute or two, both halves sank.

Tony just managed to remain conscious. His head ached, and it felt as if all of his ribs were cracked.

Suddenly he heard the swishing sound of a submarine breaking surface, then the roar of the diesels being cut in. Figures came up on her deck; a searchlight was turned on and moved over the black water until it found him. He was going to be taken prisoner and there wasn't anything he could do to stop it from happening.

CHAPTER 56

"Ease back on the throttle," Warren ordered.

"Easing back," the machinist mate answered.

"Take her in close to the beach," Warren said.

"Aye, aye, skipper," the man answered.

The field hospital, with its big red cross painted on the canvas roof of a large army tent, was back a ways from the beach, in the sheltering shade of a half dozen tall palm trees.

"Looks to me as if they recently must have had a hard time," the XO commented. "There's a dozen good-sized shell holes over to the starboard just above the beach."

Warren switched on the 1MC and ordered, "All gunners and ammo handlers, battle stations." Then to the EXO, he said, "Anything starts here, pull out and pick me up after dark. I'll be on the point we passed coming in here on our starboard side."

"How long to figure on staying?" the XO asked.

"A couple — maybe three hours," Warren answered. "I'm just going to visit an old friend."

The XO nodded and smiled knowingly.

Warren looked away. This was the first time in his professional career he was using his command for personal reasons. Kate's guess turned out to be right: Irene was sent to the Philippines and he, after he was discharged from the hospital, asked to be reassigned to a PT squadron in the same area and tracked Irene down to this particular field hospital.

"Full stop," Warren ordered.

"Full stop."

Warren stepped from the bridge to the side of the boat and then went over the side into water that was slightly more than knee-deep.

Suddenly a lieutenant in dirty jungle fatigues with a rifle slung over his right shoulder and followed by a burly sergeant came out of an empty tent and toward him.

"Commander Troost," Warren said, identifying himself and saluting at the same time.

The lieutenant and the sergeant returned the salute; then the lieutenant said, "This is a restricted area, sir."

"Restricted?" Warren repeated.

"Yes, sir, until further notice," the lieutenant said.

"Will you please tell the CO that I want to see him," Warren said.

"He's dead," the lieutenant answered.

"Then his adjutant?"

"He's dead too," the lieutenant said.

The skin on Warren's back suddenly began to crawl. He looked past the lieutenant and the sergeant to where the big tent was and men, stripped to the waist, were moving things.

"Everyone is dead, sir," the lieutenant said. "The Japs mortared it last night, then broke through our defense line, came down here, and killed everyone: doctors, nurses, and all of the wounded."

"Raped and mutilated the nurses before they killed them," the sergeant added.

Warren brought himself to attention.

"Sir?" the lieutenant questioned.

"I'd like to see the bodies of the nurses," Warren said, forcing the words out. "I was engaged to one of them," he lied.

"Sir, most of them are buried —"

"I'd like to see those that aren't," Warren insisted.

The lieutenant nodded and the sergeant said, "Follow me, sir."

They crossed the beach and went past the tent to where a dozen graves were freshly dug.

"The bodies are there," the sergeant said, pointing to a dozen canvas-covered mounds.

"Thank you, sergeant," Warren said, "but if you don't mind, I'd rather be alone."

"I'm not going anywhere," the sergeant answered.

Warren lifted the canvas off the first corpse. It lacked a nose and two ears. He dropped the canvas back over it. The second woman's face was laid open to the bone. The third's throat was slashed. And the fourth was Irene. There wasn't a mark on her face and yet her mouth was contorted into a now silent scream that would sound through eternity. Something else was done to her.

Warren hunkered down and started to pull the canvas farther down the body.

"Sir, I don't think you should do that," the sergeant said, coming up to him.

Warren squinted up at him.

"Sir —"

Warren pulled the cover down and looked. Both her breasts were missing. Warren dropped the cover, moved his head to one side, and vomited.

"I'm sorry, sir," the sergeant said, as he reached down and helped Warren to his feet.

"Thank you, sergeant."

"Some are worse than that," the sergeant said in a low voice.

Warren nodded and started back to the beach. Suddenly, he felt as if he were a very old man. Tears clouded his vision. "She was so afraid that something terrible was going to happen to me," he said, speaking his thoughts, "and something terrible happened to her."

"If I were you, Commander," the sergeant answered, "I'd find me a bottle of whiskey and drink until what you saw back there was washed out of your brain."

"It never will be washed out of my brain," Warren said.

"Maybe it won't, but it might help you to live with it."

Warren didn't answer. A few minutes later he was back aboard the boat. "Full throttle," he ordered.

"Full throttle," the machinist mate answered.

CHAPTER 57

At 0600 on May 6, 1945, Glen, the *Edison*'s navigator, passed the halfway mark of the morning watch. The sky was clear, with a few cotton-puff-like clouds over the island of Okinawa, which lay to the west. There, on the first of May, which happened to be Easter Sunday, the *Edison* was part of the bombardment group that raked the beaches before the tens of thousands of army troops landed. But now the *Edison* was some 15 miles offshore doing picket duty.

Glen's thoughts drifted to Lucy and Lillian. Whenever he was back in Pearl, he always managed to see her and wind up in the sack with her. There was something about her that drew him like a magnet, something about the way she made love.

"Three bogies... Bearing, zero two eight five... Range, 15 miles... Elevation, zero three five... Closing fast," radar reported.

Glen sounded GQ.

"Four bogies... Bearing, zero one nine six... Range, 15 miles... Elevation, zero two two... Closing fast," radar reported.

"I have the conn," the *Edison*'s skipper, Commander Robert Burns, said, coming onto the bridge.

Right behind him was Lieutenant Commander Harold Price, the ship's XO.

When the ship went to battle stations, Glen remained on the bridge and automatically became the ship's tactical officer.

"Come to zero three six zero," the helmsman answered.

"All ahead flank speed."

"All ahead flank speed answered," the engine room signalman answered.

The radar reports continued to place the bogies on a line with the ship. It soon became apparent that there were hundreds of incoming enemy planes. "Kamikazes!" Price exclaimed.

Suddenly the antiaircraft guns of the outer picket ships began firing.

The *Edison*'s five-inch guns began to blaze at two incoming targets. One blew apart 1000 yards off the stern and the second was picked up on the port side by the .40mm mounts. The plane's starboard wing bent back, then came off, and the plane cartwheeled into the sea.

Four more planes came screaming down on the *Edison*.

"Rudder, hard left," Burns ordered.

"Rudder, hard left answered," the helmsman replied.

"Lay smoke," Burns ordered.

The five-inch guns were hammering away at three different enemy planes; then suddenly a plane came in on the starboard side just over the water. The starboard .44mm mounts opened up. The plane began to smoke, rose slightly, appeared to veer off, and then turned and smashed into the number three five-inch mount.

The *Edison* heeled to the port side; then as she rolled back, ammunition exploded.

The damage control rushed to the twisted, smoking gun mount.

The *Edison*'s smoke was beginning to hide her, when another explosion in the stern rocked the ship, leaving her dead in the water.

Two more bogies came hurtling in at the *Edison* on her starboard side. But now she couldn't run; she could only stand and fight.

"Fire in the steering gear room," Price reported, answering a phone.

The .40mm mounts began firing.

The first plane slammed into the starboard side of the ship.

The *Edison* shuddered, rolled to the port, righted, and exploded into roaring flames amidships.

The second plane blew up in front of the bridge. Burns clutched his chest and fell to the deck. Everyone else was slammed against the back wall.

The bone in Glen's left arm showed through the skin.

Price had a piece of metal sticking in his left shoulder and a gash across the top of his head.

"Glen, I'm not going to make it," he said. "Order abandon ship."

"Try to —"

"Order abandon ship," Price gasped, then went limp.

Glen pulled himself up to his feet and over to the ship's broadcasting system. "All hands, now hear this... All hands, abandon ship... Abandon ship!"

Within minutes, Glen was in the water with the ship's other survivors watching the *Edison* burn and be torn apart by explosion after explosion until there was nothing left but twisted steel and a smoldering hulk that, in her last death throes, rolled over, blew apart and sank.

"Rescue boats coming," someone shouted. "Rescue boats!"

Two PT boats slowed down. One of them came to a full stop a few yards from Glen. He looked up and saw Warren peering down at him.

Jacob was in the air on combat patrol over the *Endeavor*. The threat of kamikaze attacks was always present as Japan became more desperate in her response to the victories of the United States in the Western Pacific.

Flying at 13,000 feet, Jacob spotted eight enemy planes below and to his port side. He radioed, "Bogies, nine o'clock, below." He kicked the plane over to the left to engage.

He looked over his right shoulder: his wingman turned in tight and the other planes were following him down.

The wind whistled over the Hellcat's wings.

As he closed, Jacob realized the enemy aircraft were Kates.

"Look sharp," Jacob said, over the radio, "as soon as they know we're here, they'll scatter." His eyes moved to the altimeter. He was passing through 6000 feet.

Jacob sucked in his breath. The Kate was centered in his sights. He waited until he was close enough to see the forward part of the cockpit before he pressed the stick trigger, counted to three while the guns chattered, and releasing the trigger, pulled back on the stick. The Gs pushed him back into the seat. He looked back. The Kate was spiraling down.

"Under you, Red Leader," a voice warned.

To locate the enemy aircraft, Jacob turned hard to his left.

"He's still below you, skipper," the same voice said. "I've got him in my sights... Got him!"

Jacob came out of the roll and climbed steadily. Ahead of him a Kate slammed into one of his men, shearing the plane's tail section off and its own starboard wing. Both planes tumbled into the sea.

The melee lasted three minutes and when it was over, Jacob radioed the carrier. "Bridge, four bogies coming through. Miller."

"Roger that," came the answer.

Jacob ordered his squadron to gather into formation. Two were missing. "We'll go up to 15," he said over the radio, "and head over toward the island."

By 1000, Jacob's flight engaged the determined enemy in two more dogfights. His flight was recovered to refuel and rearm. In less than an hour, Jacob and his flight were back in the air. The Kamikazes seemed to be all over the skies and some managed to smash their aircraft into the ships below, inflicting terrible damage.

The threat continued into the twilight and only came to an end at sunset.

As the last combat air patrol of the day was recovered aboard the *Endeavor*, Jacob landed. When his plane finally came to a stop in the arresting gear, he slumped slightly forward and wondered where he'd find the strength to climb out of the cockpit and make it to the ready room for the debriefing. He taxied into the parking area, and when the taxi director indicated chocks were on his wheels, he unbuckled his safety harness and chute. Then he lifted himself out of the cockpit, climbed down on the wing, and dropped to the deck.

That night, Jacob was almost too exhausted to sleep, but he did, and the next day at 0600 he and his men were back in the air in a repetition of the previous day. The dogfights swirled all over the sky. Three of his pilots were shot down, and he took several hits in the fuselage, but none of them was serious.

At 1600, he led his flight back to the carrier. The first two planes were already down, and the third was on its final approach, when suddenly the LSO waved the plane off and the carrier radioed, "Red Leader, vector one zero six... Angels two... Buster!"

"Red Base," Jacob radioed, "I have less than 10 minutes' worth of fuel and then I'm empty."

"Get on with it!"

"Roger," Jacob answered. He was 500 feet above the carrier's deck and turned to the heading ordered by the Fighter Director. His wingman joined up on him, and he climbed to 5000 feet before he leveled off.

"There they are!" his wingman radioed. "12 o'clock low!"

There were six Kates.

"Here we go!" Jacob ordered, pushing the stick forward. He dived toward the lead plane.

The plane rolled over to its port side and went down toward the water.

Jacob kept him in his gun sight and pressed the trigger button.

The plane swooped low over the water, started to climb, and then exploded.

Jacob pulled the stick back, executed a tight loop that brought him head-on with the second Kate. He fired two short bursts, and the Kate spun off to the port side and into the sea.

Two of the Kates broke away and began to close on the *Endeavor*.

The five-inch guns of the destroyer screen opened up.

"Christ, those sons-of-bitches are breaking through!" one of the pilots yelled. "They're going for the carrier."

"The hell they are," another pilot called. "I'm after 'em!"

For a moment, Jacob couldn't identify the pilot; then when he did, he shouted, "Ben, get 'em!"

"That's me skipper."

One of the Kates was hit and slammed into a destroyer, turning it into a mass of flames.

The second Kate was still heading for the *Endeavor*, with Ben closing on it.

"Shoot!" Jacob yelled. "Shoot!"

Ben suddenly overtook the Kate and dropped down on top of it. Both planes merged into one ball of fire and plunged into the sea yards off the *Endeavor*'s starboard side.

The fire fight ended as suddenly as it began, and Jacob joined his remaining flight up and prepared to land.

Late in the evening an announcement was made over the 1MC that planes from Admiral McCain's Task Force 58 had destroyed the Japanese battleship *Yamamoto* and other warships on their way to relieve Okinawa.

That night, Jacob again had difficulty sleeping. He left his stateroom and went up to the flight deck. The sky was stunningly beautiful. He walked toward the ship's fantail, and when he reached it, he stopped and mournfully intoned the Kaddish, the Hebrew prayer for the dead, mentioning the name of each of the squadron's pilots who were lost in the past two days. There were six names.

"Now hear this... Now hear this, all hands," the 1MC blared. "This is Admiral Gower speaking... Minutes ago we received from Washington news that our Commander and Chief President Franklin Delano Roosevelt has died... Let us observe a minute of silent prayer for our fallen leader..."

Jacob was too stunned to move, or even to hear what one of the other officers in the wardroom was saying. To him Roosevelt was indestructible, a Titan who worked miracles.

"Skipper," one of his men said, "my daddy must be happy as a pig in slop, now that we can get a whole man in the White House."

And another man commented, "That's where I'm headed, once this war is over. I'm goin' become a politician and run for president."

"You're going to run," a third pilot said, "but not for president."

"All right, wise ass, tell me what I'm going to run for?"

"Fuck-Master," the man answered.

All of them laughed.

"Incoming bogies… Incoming bogies," a voice over the 1MC announced. "All hands man your battle stations…"

"Come on, men," Jacob said, "let's get to the ready room… Let's go."

"Skipper, when the hell is this war goin' to be over?" one of his men asked.

"Soon, I hope," Jacob answered. "Soon."

By the time Jacob and his squadron reached the ready room, the sky was filled with screaming Japanese planes flying with maniacal determination through a curtain of steel. The kamikazes were back.

The 1MC blared. "Pilots, man your planes… Pilots, man your planes… All hands battle stations… All hands battle stations."

The war was still raging and would for a long time…

A NOTE TO THE READER

Dear Reader,

If you have enjoyed the novel enough to leave a review on **Amazon** and **Goodreads**, then we would be truly grateful.

Sapere Books is an exciting new publisher of brilliant fiction and popular history.

To find out more about our latest releases and our monthly bargain books visit our website:
saperebooks.com

Made in the USA
Las Vegas, NV
08 March 2021